HERE

lies

NARTH

AVA HARRISON

Here Lies North
Cover Design: Hang Le
Editor: Lawrence Editing, Editing4Indies
Content Editor: Royal Reads
Proofreader: Jaime Ryter, Marla Esposito

Sometimes you put walls up not to keep people out, but to
see who cares enough to break them down.
~ Socrates

To Eric:
See…those *endless* hours of binging criminal minds paid off.

Prologue

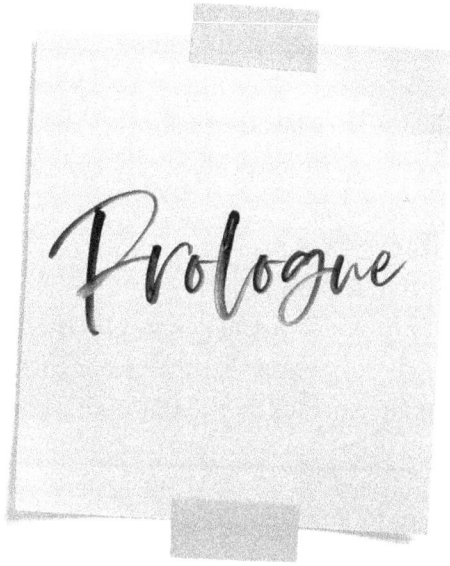

The Compass Killer—2005

Evil is real.

As real as this cabin and the dirt floor we lie on in the dead of night.

The pungent taste lingers through the air.

I breathe it in. Allow it to filter into my blood.

Pulsing. Making me want to bask in it. Feed on it.

I can feel the wicked in me begging for an outlet.

Which is why I'm here, tucked away where no one would dare search for me.

The moonlight gleams off the blade in my hand, casting a stream of light across the dark room.

A flicker of a candle is all that illuminates the space.

I enjoy the shadows it creates on the aged oak walls.

The ambience relaxes me.

But it's the body beneath me that brings me serenity. The way her chest rises and falls. Her trembles of fear that thrum through her cells.

It's a heady aphrodisiac.

I want to bask in the atmosphere her fear incites.

Drink from her perspiration.

Live in the silence that isn't truly silent.

"Please."

One word. That's all it takes for me to feel alive.

My eyes dart around the old cabin. Oh, the things this space has witnessed.

Passed down from generation to generation.

Now it's my turn to leave a mark.

Moving closer, I hover over the woman on the floor.

The knife in my hand presses firmly on her throat.

Red bubbles to the surface as the blade pricks her delicate ivory neck.

But I can't kill her yet.

I turn my head, looking around the room. When my gaze catches what I'm looking for, I smile.

It's not a real smile.

It doesn't touch my soul.

How could it?

Not when I've never had a soul for attaching such pathetic emotions.

"Please. You can't kill me."

I look back at my unwilling prey.

Spreading my lips wider.

"You should be honored." I scoff. "I don't pick just anyone."

"But—"

My free hand reaches out, silencing her before she can ruin the moment.

"Shh," I coo as I trail the blade across her throat. The pressure isn't enough to kill her. It's just a warning. "Be a good girl." She shakes beneath me, biting her lip to hold back a whimper, but she doesn't have to say it. I know she feels the pain.

Terror keeps her from speaking, and she doesn't move to answer me as I lift my hand off her mouth. Her eyes go wide at my movement. Her pupils blown out with panic.

I watch myself in her reflection for a second. Letting her emotions fuel me. Tears fill her eyes, but they don't fall.

Pity.

I would have liked to see her cry.

I lift the knife, and I'm met with a crimson line.

Red rivulets trickle out from the wound.

I follow the path as they collect in the hollow of her throat. I want to paint her skin in blood.

All in good time.

This isn't about *me* right now.

Soon, I can drain her.

This time, when I lift the knife, I dig into her skin.

Carving the intricate pattern.

Cutting through creamy, soft flesh.

This time, she can't hold back the cry.

It seeps up through her fragile throat.

Watching her bound and wriggling under my grasp, begging to be released, is the greatest thrill a man will ever experience. The pitch of her voice right before the blade takes a run across her throat.

That sound.

It alone will stand out to me for the rest of my days.

I will always remember this moment.

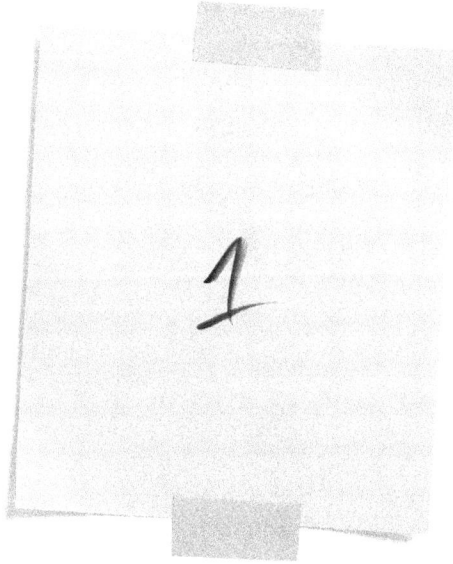

1

Layla
Seventeen years later . . .

M y fingers hit the keyboard over and over again. The sound is like nails on a chalkboard. What did I do to deserve this torture?

I freaking hate this job.

Okay. I have zero excuse to say that, but I'm bored out of my mind.

I went to journalism school to be someone. To dig into the details and find the truth.

Instead, I'm writing about which faucet to buy to make your kitchen stand out.

Really?

A kitchen is for making coffee and reheating Chinese food. Or Italian. Depends on the mood I'm in. It's most definitely my least favorite room in the apartment.

I didn't come from a family that could cook—or bake. Hell, I came from a family that couldn't communicate, let alone plan a meal and follow a recipe. No, I didn't starve. But cooking for fun was not a thing either. And now, I get to write about faucets.

Doesn't matter, though. No matter how much I bitch and moan, I still have to write this damn piece, and I shouldn't complain. The truth is, I'm damn lucky to have this job.

Even if it's not the one I actually want.

In my dreams as a child, never once did I imagine my life would revolve around faucets, light fixtures, and sconces. Writing about recessed lighting was definitely not what I had in mind when I took out a monster loan to go to school for journalism.

A loan I'm still making payments on each month.

Unfortunately, we can't always get what we want, and although I spend my time writing fluff pieces, it pays my rent.

And when you're living off ramen noodles and mac and cheese from a box like a college student while living in a tiny one-bedroom walk-up apartment . . . well, let's just say beggars can't be choosers. At least it's not a studio. This place is a palace compared to my last rental.

Back before this job, I could basically pee and cook at the same time.

I continue to stare at the document on the screen, rereading what I have typed so far, and then I hit the delete button.

Delete.

Delete.

Delete.

Now my word count is a big ole five.

Great. Just fucking great.

I pound on my keyboard in frustration. Letting out an overly dramatic groan, I bury my head in my hands.

"How's it going?" I hear the familiar voice of my coworker, Mara, who is also my best friend—the only person I talk to regularly besides my one cousin, Jordan. He's the only one who's still nice to me after the fallout with my parents.

Because really, how many lies should a person have to deal with?

Mara and I started working at the same time and instantly clicked. Both jaded and bitter. We're practically inseparable.

I let out another strangled groan.

"That good, huh?"

The thing about Mara is, despite her prickly disposition, she's got a heart of gold. Anyone would be lucky to have her in their corner.

She's the Thelma to my Louise.

Dropping my hands, I turn my head to the right to see another co-worker scurrying away.

That one isn't for me. Too cute and young. Fresh out of college and happy to be here. She's still optimistic. A glass half-filled kind of girl.

Yep, she doesn't lunch with Mara and me.

We're both seasoned members of the previously unemployed and used to struggling club. Neither of us is here because we love faucets. Mara at least has an appreciation for design, but her dream job is at a fashion magazine.

I know I'm still young and need experience, but I just want to get back to what I love. Journalism. And not just "news" but investigative reporting. Nothing gives me a better feeling of accomplishment than digging in and finding the truth at the heart of a story.

But no. I have faucets.

Mara leans over the cubicle, her wavy dark-brown hair falling forward like a curtain around her face.

At twenty-three, she shouldn't be so jaded. Hell, I shouldn't be either, but despite her being the opposite of me in the looks department—with chocolate-brown eyes and the height of a model—personality-wise, we're very similar.

I place my hands on my desk and give her a smile. I'm sure it doesn't touch my eyes, and by the way she rolls hers, she's calling me out on my fakeness.

"See. That's better. Fake it till you make it." She leans farther down until she's hanging over the divider, and now, I have a perfect view of her cleavage. *Gee, thanks, Mara.* "It will all work out. I promise."

"One, do you mind?" I gesture to her chest, and she laughs, *typical*. "Two, how?" I lift a picture of the damn sconce I wrote about yesterday. "Because this"—I swing the image around as if I'm swatting a bug—"this doesn't scream opportunity."

Her full ruby red-stained lips pull into an overly dramatic, totally fake smile. "Just hang in there. I promise you'll get out of this shithole."

"Really? That's your stance? Where is my partner in crime? Where is my Debbie Downer twin?"

"I'm maturing." She bats her eyelashes at me, and I laugh.

"If you say so."

At my words, Mara puckers her lips and blows me a kiss. "I do."

"Sure. It might include a few awful articles about paint first, though," I joke.

"Which gray is your soul mate?" she purrs, and I fake gag. "See, now you're getting it."

With a shake of my head, I place my hands back on my desk and pretend to type. The sound of my fingers hitting the surface of the wood echoes around us. "Fine, Mara. I'll rock this faucet article. Just like I rocked the piece I did on sconces."

"Don't forget the toilet in the shape of a skull article you wrote. That was solid gold."

I raise my brow. "It was solid, all right. Solid shit," I deadpan.

A laugh bubbles out of Mara's mouth. Then it bursts free. "And it was gold."

It was. The toilet was made of gold. What is wrong with some people? As we're hysterically laughing, a cough sounds from behind me.

Mara looks above my shoulder, then darts her eyes back to mine. Wide. Like a deer caught in headlights.

Damn.

Slowly, I glance over my shoulder, my swivel seat moving with me. *Busted.*

I open and shut my mouth. *Think of something to say.* "Oh. I—" Well, apparently, my brain isn't working right now. Instead, it's cataloging all the things I just said and exactly what she might have heard. This isn't good.

Unless . . .

The frown on her face doesn't give her away, but the impatient tap of her foot does.

"Janet." My lips spread into my candy-coated smile that I have perfected for this very moment. "Is there something you need?"

Her eyes narrow. "Am I interrupting something? Looks like you and Mara have more pressing things to discuss than anything I could offer." She lifts a challenging eyebrow.

"Nope. All clear here." Keeping my voice steady so as not to give myself away should be challenging, but I've mastered the art of keeping calm long ago.

"Good. Mr. Walker would like to see you immediately."

"No problem." My hand moves from where it's resting on my lap, and I quickly close out the document I'm in.

Janet pulls her gaze from me. "And you, Mara?"

"Yes," Mara responds.

"Don't you have something you need to be doing right now?" She reminds me of one of my teachers from when I was still in grade school. Her hair is pulled tightly into a bun, lines etching her forehead as she frowns.

"All over it," Mara responds as I turn my chair to face my friend. She winks at me.

"Then do that." Janet's stern voice is just as grating as my old English teacher too, completely irritating, like those nails on a chalkboard again.

I bite my lower lip to stifle my laugh at my own bad joke. Making my eyes wide, I look at Mara, who also is trying to refrain from bursting out into a fit of giggles.

Once the urge to laugh has passed, I turn back to my computer, this time closing my laptop, grabbing my notepad, and then standing from my chair.

"Ready?"

"As I'll ever be."

I have no idea what our boss, Mr. Walker, wants, but I'm not particularly looking forward to finding out.

Probably an article on the fanciest doorknobs manufactured.

Snoozefest central.

It's not that I don't like architecture or houses. I'd just prefer to be writing on a topic that fascinates me.

I want to be intrigued.

I thought I'd be a reporter. However, the only mystery in my life these days is what type of shingle is on a 1910 Cape Cod.

Still, despite my hope to teleport out of here somehow, we arrive at Mr. Walker's office. Janet swings open the door, steps inside, and I follow suit.

Behind the large, imposing desk is the editor I work under. The man who doles out all the crap work I've been writing.

Mr. Walker lifts his head from whatever he's reading and meets my stare.

I imagine, once upon a time, he was probably very popular with the ladies. With hair the color of freshly fallen snow, he still looks distinguished, just older. His face is weathered with lines that speak of years of experience. Stories I'd love to hear. I love to dig into why people are the way they are. What their story is.

However, at this moment, that's not possible, so I shake away the thoughts and give my boss all my attention.

The way he looks at me has me wanting to cross my arms over my chest, but instead, I stand perfectly still with a smile firmly planted on my face.

"You wanted to see me, sir?" I keep my tone light and pleasant. No reason for the boss to know I'm anything but.

"Yes. Let's get to it. We don't have much time if we're going to get you on the road."

"Road, sir?" I glance at Janet, who, of course, looks like she swallowed an entire lemon. God, would it hurt for her to crack a smile? She's a freaking upper-level administrative assistant. Talk about cushy job.

"What do you think?" he asks me. "This is a once-in-a-lifetime opportunity. There is nothing in the country, let alone the world, like what is being made."

I obviously zoned out a little too long because I have no clue what Mr. Walker is talking about now. Let alone why I would need to travel for something.

"Here." Mr. Walker reaches his hand out, and I look at a press sheet.

This is what he was looking at when I walked into the room. Quietly, I allow myself to read what's on the page.

Holy.

Crap.

It's perfection.

Aptly named The Elysian. Aka paradise.

That's how they're describing it. A playground for the rich and famous.

Modern. Simple. Luxurious.

Completely controlled by Artificial Intelligence to maximize efficiencies.

Set amongst the mountains in Upstate New York.

Helicopter access. A private aviation airport on the property.

I continue to read about the technology involved with this project.

This is insane. Never has a mass scale project of this magnitude existed.

"You'll be heading out to The Elysian by the end of the day," Mr. Walker says.

"What?" My mouth hangs open, and my eyes are wide. Did he just say I'm the one who's going? I shake myself out of my stupor. "Excuse me. Me?" I clear my throat. It feels dry. Like I'm choking on dust.

"Yes. We need someone to head down there for about a week, really immerse yourself in the concept. You're the only lead level journalist in the office who doesn't have kids or a family to run home to, and we can't pass this opportunity up. Mr. Archer just gave us the green light today to be on his calendar this week, and I want to jump on it."

Okay, so the no family thing hurts, seeing as I have no contact with anyone from mine, but I'm not going to let that show. I won't let it be used against me in my career. Only opportunities for this single lady.

"Who is Mr. Archer?" I ask, tentatively refocusing on the conversation. I'm still new to this design arena, and there are always names I don't know, even though I probably should.

"Here." He hands me a folder now. "Inside, there are the key points about Archer, interview questions. Everything we need for the article."

The press release talks about the team behind the project, my eyes landing on a picture.

The air in my lungs leaves my body as I stare at the most handsome man I have ever seen.

No.

"Handsome" doesn't do him justice.

He's more than that.

He's perfection. Brown, wavy hair. Dark piercing eyes. A light five o'clock shadow dusting his chiseled jaw. Wow.

"Oh. Okay. Got it." I stand from my chair. "If that's all, I have a lot of work to do to prepare for an interview and full article on this type of property."

"Layla, I don't need to tell you what an opportunity this is for you and this magazine. Don't blow it."

"Yes. Thank you. I will not disappoint you."

With nothing more to say, I step out of the office and walk down the hallway to the stairwell. Once alone, I let out the large breath I was holding, looking down at the picture again of the man who unnerved me from just a look on a paper.

Cain Archer.

2

Layla

After I calm myself, I make my way back into the hall and find Janet waiting for me.

"I can walk back to my desk on my own, Janet," I breathe out, hoping she doesn't really hear me say the words aloud.

"Too bad, Ms. Marks. I want to make sure you are back and starting your travel plans. I can assist you in getting the directions and company credit card information all settled. That way, you don't waste any more time getting distracted by your friend Mara."

I guess I didn't keep that eye roll to myself when she adds, "This is not an opportunity to be squandered. Mr. Walker doesn't give everyone travel opportunities at your level of writing."

Passive-aggressive on aisle one.

But she's not wrong.

This does have opportunity written all over it.

This is an insane chance to get out of the office, show off my investigative skills, and work on something that could transform my career. Goodbye faucets, hello travel budget.

Once Janet gets me all set up with travel in the system and goes on her ever-so-unmerry way, I pop my head over the cubicle wall to Mara.

"Pssst. You are never gonna guess what just happened."

Currently, and despite the fact that we are in the office, she's looking at her cell phone and appears to be playing a game on it. Placing it down on her desk, she cocks her head up and looks at me. "Let me guess, you're traveling to some luxury property."

"How did you know?"

"I have those things." Mara motions to her ears. "They're incredible. I can spy on anyone using them. What're they called again . . . ? Eaves? No, eels . . ."

I playfully smack her, done with her BS.

"I heard Janet helping you book the travel arrangements. And since there wasn't a hotel stay mentioned, I took a guess." Her lips are pulled into a shit-eating smile. She resembles a proud kid who just aced their math test.

"Wow, and I want to be the investigator, not the fashion correspondent."

"Okay, tell me, tell me, where are you fabulously getting to jet off to, and how long will you be living your dream job away from here? Sherlock, here, needs answers from her bestie."

I lower myself back into my chair and start to flip through the folder in front of me again with all the pertinent information. In my boss's office, I was too nervous to pay close attention.

"A place upstate that is going to be the next greatest place for the people who want to live privately but full-on tech. One week and I get to interview the architect who is dreaming the whole thing up."

Now it's Mara's turn to move from her seat and peek her head over the divider. "Who's the project lead?"

"Some guy named Cain Archer." I shrug. He might be hot, but I have no clue who he is.

"Holy shit. No way."

"Do you know anything about him?"

"Um, have you lived with your head in the sand? We work for the biggest architecture magazine in the country, and he's the most famous one of our lifetimes. I mean, for God's sake, Layla, half of the appeal alone is surrounding the secretive millionaire heartthrob behind it."

Lifting my hands, I cover my face with a groan. "So, I'm just the idiot who landed a huge story by default?"

"Pretty much. This project has been all over the news. The fact that Walker gave this to you is beyond huge. I thought you heard of the A.I. Residency project."

"Yeah, I totally know all the deets." I lower my hands and wink at her.

She, in turn, rolls her eyes at me. "You're such an ass."

Pivoting my chair, I look at her straight on. "So, what exactly do I need to know about this guy?"

I see Mara's eyes widen just a bit. "Okay, I don't know that much, but from what I've heard, not only is he an arrogant recluse, but apparently, if the rumors within the industry are true, he's a coldhearted asshole."

"No way."

"Listen. Again, I don't know him, but I can tell you what I heard, and he is supposedly dreadful to work for. Awful to the press and, quite frankly, horrendous to the women he dates."

"How so?" I ask.

"Well, the dating part is really all speculation in the tabloids. No one ever sees him with a woman outside of the standard step-and-re-peat event pictures."

"And the rest?"

"I'm not sure about everything, but I'm pretty sure the rumor that he's a coldhearted asshole comes from the fact that apparently, and again, this is just hearsay—"

I stand from my chair, placing my hand on my hip. "Just spit it out, Mara."

This is Mara; every story takes longer than the last. There is always tangent after tangent.

"Oh, yeah, okay, so the man doesn't show emotion and has never been seen to even laugh. They actually say he's some sort of a freak."

"Wait, really?"

"No, not really. Or, like, maybe. He's a ghost. He has no history from before he broke out onto the scene and then bam, he took over the architecture world."

"But why use the word freak? He's drop-dead gorgeous in this brochure picture."

"Ohhhh, someone has the hots already. No, he's a freak because, who never laughs? Never smiles? Has no relationship with anyone? And it has to be true because you can't be that rich and famous and the tabloids miss out on taking your picture with a hot woman or man hanging on your arm like candy."

"Okay, so I know nothing about the reclusive Mr. Archer. This should be fun. I gotta go get the car, run home to pack, and hit the road. I'll give you a call when I get up there and settled."

"Have fun playing with the privileged life and come back with all the words for the best article ever."

"You got it, bitch," I say before leaning forward and grabbing my purse from under my desk. Once I have my stuff, I blow Mara a kiss and head out to leave to go home so that I can prepare for my assignment.

At my apartment, I throw together a suitcase, and grab my laptop bag with notebooks, pens, and break open my laptop for a quick search on this property and Cain Archer. Google comes up practically empty. A few pictures here and there, but no drama. No scandal. For a famous person, shouldn't there be some drama?

It makes no sense.

I have never seen anyone who is as well-known as him with practically no digital footprint.

It's almost as if the Google search engine has a restriction on his name.

But that would be crazy.

There isn't much about this elusive man and nothing prior to him opening the architecture firm.

He keeps to himself. I'd expect more from a man with his looks and obvious prestige. I would expect endless pictures of him gracing the internet. A man like him would certainly be seen with a model on his arm at exclusive events surrounding his projects.

The only thing I eventually find is under information on this project. There's nothing about his personal life, though. No mention of a wife or girlfriend.

Not that it should matter to me. I'm there to interview him, not date him, but it still annoys me. I need to know what motivates and drives this man.

His résumé of world-class architecture and the accolades that have come with it suggests he is a force to be reckoned with, so why doesn't the research show that?

Four hours later and I'm lost.

As per usual, I went down a bit of a research rabbit hole on Cain. Now, it's late in the afternoon, and I swear if I knew I was going to the middle of nowhere, in Upstate New York, I would have packed a lunch and filled up the gas tank one more time.

I'm going to get stranded and die here before I even get to the property.

Goodbye, promotion. Hello, dead on the side of the road.

The GPS on my phone is telling me to turn left. But there's nothing here. Nothing but trees. A thicket of brush, to be exact. An endless row of evergreens with no clear road anywhere to be seen other than the one I'm on.

My car sputters forward, slowly creeping farther up the road as I search for the entrance to The Elysian that is clearly not here.

Today has been hell.

After a four-hour drive that should have taken only three, I've reached my destination, except like all things that can go wrong, this has, too.

According to my dumb GPS, I have found my location.

The only thing I have reached is the location of hell. That or a great field to buy my next year's Christmas tree or hide a body.

Christmas trees and dead bodies. Why does my brain work like this?

Lifting my foot off the brake, I give the car a little gas while looking for a turn.

That's when I see the road. If I wasn't looking hard, I would have missed it.

If you can even call it a road. There's nothing to mark it . . .

Just a break between one tree and the next. As I'm making the turn,

I notice the road isn't gravel like it looks, but paved. It's just painted to blend with nature.

I wonder if this is done on purpose. A way to keep trespassers out.

I continue to drive. A few feet soon turn into what must be a mile, and there's still nothing but an endless hidden road set amongst more trees. From what I can see, there are no lights here. This has to be dangerous at night.

There is no room for oncoming traffic. How is this safe? Do the trees have reflective tape on them to make sure you don't hit one? Just as I glance up at a tree in front of me to search for anything that would alert incoming traffic, everything opens up.

My mouth drops open as the picture in front of me comes into focus. Set behind large gates and amongst the foliage is a building.

Never in my life have I ever seen anything like this.

The building itself is also camouflaged. Blending seamlessly into the mixture of trees, both pine and maple, it's an extension of the plush landscape.

The gates are wrought iron, but they're not the typical gates you would find guarding an estate or mansion. These look like vines.

Like the building behind the iron, the fence is an extension of nature.

I have no idea what I was thinking when I heard about this project, but this wasn't it.

A part of me imagined that a fully artificial, intelligent building would be cold and sterile.

This, however, is anything but.

This is serene.

It's paradise.

And now the name makes sense.

I haven't even crossed over the property threshold, and I already feel calmer.

This place is amazing. I can totally see myself staying here for a week. The idea of writing this article is starting to sound better.

Despite not liking my job, this is a major perk. Sure, normally, I'm not looking forward to interviewing anyone, shadowing them, or finding out boring, mundane details about roofs, but something tells me what lies behind the walls of this façade will be fascinating.

I pull my car toward the circular drive in front of the main building, then roll to a stop.

As soon as I throw the car in park, I look around to see if anyone will tell me I can't park here.

The apartments are obviously empty as they're not finished being built, but I still expect people to be milling about.

When I step outside, I glance to see if anyone can tell me where to go.

There's no one, though.

It reminds me of an old western movie.

A ghost town.

One where a spiny, thorny tumbleweed rolls down a dusty dirt road. Followed by an outlaw with a gun.

A shiver works its way up my body, but I shake it off, looking back over at the trees.

I inhale deeply, letting the calm take over me again. I'm not sure how long I stand here. I probably look like an idiot, but eventually, I check my phone.

Damn.

I'm late.

Even if I don't love this job, I pride myself on my professionalism. Being late is one of the things that pisses me off the most, and this time, it's my fault. I didn't anticipate the traffic or the remote area with unmarked roads.

That, coupled with the fact that I have been staring at the architecture for the last few minutes, isn't boding well for me.

I step on the sidewalk, and the door to the middle building swings open.

A harried-looking woman with glasses and a clipboard strides in my direction.

"Ms. Marks?" She stops in front of me, her brow furrowed. My lips part as I nod at her.

"That's me."

"Very good. We've been expecting you. I'm Barbara Olson, Mr.

Archer's assistant. Come along now. Mr. Archer is in such a mood today, which isn't necessarily uncommon. But seeing as you're a bit late, I wanted to warn you." She grimaces, and it doesn't matter how peaceful this place is, all good feelings are gone, and I am instantly on edge again.

Barbara starts to walk into the building, and I follow suit.

I try to remain calm as the doors automatically open, but when I step inside, I'm having a tough time keeping my cool as a whispered, "Wow," escapes my lips.

If I thought the outside was special, it has nothing on the inside.

Clean lines.

All glass.

Plush vegetation everywhere.

Trees, flowers. It's as if we're on the mountain.

But it's the smell that does me in. It smells like a warm summer day. A crisp fragrance of flowers but not overwhelming. No, it's a perfect balance. Hints of jasmine and lemon. If I closed my eyes, I might almost think I'm standing outside.

It's truly like nothing I have ever seen before.

I refuse to show my awe, so I keep my head held high, back straight, and follow her through the lobby. The hallway is large, open, and all glass as well.

It's strange because, from the outside, you should be able to see inside, but the glass is reflective.

It's a mirror. The reflection of the trees bounces off it.

We continue to walk. The sound of our heels should click in the air, but there is only silence.

"Why is it so quiet?" I ask, breaking the silence.

"I'll let Mr. Archer explain the details of his vision. But it is rather remarkable, isn't it?"

Eerie is more like it.

I don't answer. There's no reason to. She knows as well as I do that there are no adequate words to describe this place.

I'm not paying attention when she suddenly turns, and we enter this beautiful, grand conference room that overlooks the atrium entrance of the building.

"Please wait here for Mr. Archer to finish his phone call, and then he'll speak with you about the property. We have a tour set up for you with one of the property managers, and then later in the week, I have time scheduled for you to interview Mr. Archer before you leave."

"Thank you, Ms. Olson. I appreciate your help."

"My pleasure. Just be calm as you speak to him and don't take any of his negative attitude personally. He most likely won't listen to what you have to say. He's a very driven man. He doesn't seem to care about anyone but himself and his beloved project."

"Okay," I draw out as she walks away, and I'm left alone.

Squaring my shoulders, I take a deep breath, and then I step toward a chair at the massive glass table. As soon as I do, my gaze shifts around the space, trying to take it all in. This room, again, is floor-to-ceiling windows. Everything is white, the floors blending into the glass. It feels like I'm standing on a cloud. As I gaze around the space, my eyes land on a man standing in the hallway.

My breath hitches when his features come into focus.

His picture didn't do him any justice.

Frozen in place, I stare at him, holding on to the chair in front of me as my knees are weak.

There, in a white Henley and blue faded jeans, is Cain Archer.

In the picture, he was wearing a suit, but now, obviously dressed casually for work, well . . . All I can say is holy hell.

I don't move to sit. Nope, I just continue to stare at him. Gawk is more like it. That is, until he notices me in the conference room. His head lifts from whatever he's looking at on the phone in his hand, and when he does, his piercing brown eyes lock on mine.

If a look could knock a person on their ass, I'd be a pile of limbs on the floor.

It feels like time stands still as we both stand there, neither of us moving, neither of us speaking.

Stop staring. You look like an idiot.

Drool is probably dripping from my mouth by how thirsty this man is making me.

Not a good look for a professional journalist.

I will myself to pull away, but I'm in a trance, and I can't.

Still staring at me, he walks into the room. "Barbara, will you please come back in here?"

There must be a speaker system set up, as within another minute, Ms. Olson has returned.

"Yes, Mr. Archer, did you want me to bring coffee or water for your meeting?" Barbara's voice cuts through the air. Mr. Archer coughs, shakes his head, and severs our connection.

Instantly, I feel lost without it.

How's that for irony? All I wanted was not to be stuck in his orbit, and now I miss it.

With the spell broken, Mr. Archer takes the few steps until he is standing in front of me. He's no longer looking at me, and I miss his gaze. Turning to Barbara and shaking his head, he says, "No, I don't think we will need anything to drink at this time. But you can cancel the tour."

I'm shocked. How did I do something wrong already to get the scheduled tour canceled?

I observe them for a second, looking for any telltale signs that he was in a bad mood, and my being late has brought on this change of plans. Despite Barbara's earlier warnings, Mr. Archer seems to be in a fine mood when he peers back over to me and smiles.

"Hi, Mr. Archer. I must apologize for being late. I got lost on the way here." I step closer, lifting my hand and extending it out toward him. "I'm Layla Marks. I work for *Concept and Space* magazine."

His hand reaches out and shakes mine. The moment our skin touches, a shiver runs down my spine. Odd reaction. I force myself to take a breath and calm the frantic beat of my heart.

It's just nerves.

It has nothing to do with the feel of his skin on mine, right?

He stares into my eyes when we shake, and the way he looks at me . . . Well, I can't put my finger on it, but it's unnerving. Persistent. He's looking for something. I'm not sure what, but for some reason, I want to help him find it.

"It's a pleasure to meet you, Ms. Marks. Please call me Cain." His voice is gruff and gravelly, but there is no malice in it. He seems genuine.

Barbara's eyes widen. She's in shock. Quickly, not to be rude, I shift my gaze back to the dazzling brown eyes belonging to Cain.

"And you can call me Layla."

I reach into my bag and pull out the itinerary Mr. Walker provided me with before I left the city. "Again, I'm sorry I'm late, but I know my magazine would really appreciate doing an article on The Elysian. It says here on the agenda Ms. Olson sent, that I'll be starting with a tour of the property with a Simon Murphy—"

"No," he says forcefully, and I'm taken aback by the change in his voice. I move a step away from him, and he must realize I'm uncomfortable because he's quick to soften his jaw, smiling again at me.

"Is there a problem with moving forward on this piece?" I ask, my voice low and cautious.

"Sorry." He starts to pace the room, and I'm not sure what happened, but when he's back to standing in front of me, he stops and speaks. "Simon won't be taking you. I will."

"But, Mr. Archer, you have—" Barbara intervenes, but Cain Archer raises his hand to stop her.

"Barbara, I said I'll be taking Layla on her tour." His voice is curt and to the point. "Cancel the rest of my day. Evening plans, too." He leaves no room for objection. "I need to be the one to take you," he tells me.

"But, Cain, if I could remind you of the plans for the fundraising event you are to review today—"

Glaring at Barbara, he mutters, "It's Mr. Archer, and you get paid very well to make my calendar work for me. Make it happen."

She nods and scurries off.

The idea of Cain Archer being my tour guide has the pulse in my neck picking up.

"Just today?" I ask. *Please say only today.* I don't think I can be in this close of proximity to him and keep my cool.

"Actually, I'll be taking you for your whole visit." From his monotone reply, I can't tell if he is pissed or just indifferent that he has to do this.

"While I appreciate that, I know you're a busy man."

"It must be me. No one else will do for you."

I incline my head at his words. He must see the concern on my face as he averts his gaze momentarily. When he looks back, his eyes are brighter, and he smiles.

"You're writing a piece on The Elysian. No one is better suited than me. The key to the project's success can only be told by me. I need to ensure the correct information is shared. Not because I don't trust you to convey it properly, but some of the other people involved in the project don't have the eye or ability to convey the uniqueness of The Elysian."

I nod. He has a point. As the architect, I'm sure this is his baby.

"Layla, will you mind if I'm your shadow for the next week?"

His voice reminds me of warm chocolate, dripping with sin. I can barely keep my head straight, and it's only been five minutes. Can I do this for a week?

Will I be able to manage being with him every day? To have him in such proximity to me?

My palms become sweaty, and my cheeks feel warm. I can barely handle him telling me this.

I only hope not to be a blubbering idiot around him.

Finally, I nod, our eyes locking.

He grins.

Shit. I'm in so much trouble.

3

Cain

The thing about me is I don't feel emotions.

But standing here, right now, in front of this stranger sent here to interview me, I can tell the very moment our gazes lock that something is different about her. I can't put my finger on what makes this different, but a sensation I can't comprehend is weaving its way through my blood, making my heart beat faster.

What is this?

Anger?

No.

This is something else entirely.

Intrigue?

I can't look away from the blond woman who stands before me. I watch as she fiddles with her fingers, and instead of being annoyed by the movement like I normally would, I have a desire to ask her what's wrong, tell her that there's no reason to be nervous, and even, dare I say, ask her why she's fidgeting.

It's a strange feeling to look at someone and want to know more.

Not something that happens to me often. *If ever.*

But when I look into her blue eyes, eyes that resemble a deep sea

24

with an abyss that never ends, I have to remind myself I don't know her, and a question like that would be presumptuous.

Still, despite this, I watch her. Enthralled by the way her chest rises and falls with each inhale of breath, I'm mesmerized by the flush of her cheeks and how the color clashes against her pale skin.

I have no idea why this woman puts me off-kilter, but she does.

And it's alarming.

Looking at her, I can see how gorgeous she is. But there are many attractive women in this world. With long hair that flows down her back in soft waves, she could be any pretty face, but something other than her appearance intrigues me.

I can appreciate beauty. To me, it reminds me of architecture. I can see the lines. The curves. But underneath, it's only a circuit of interconnected organs keeping the vessel moving.

Like my buildings. Just a *different* vessel.

But when I look at Layla Marks, it's not the same.

I drop my hands to my jeans, placing my hands in my pocket. The urge to storm out of the room, slam the door, and shut this woman out of my life rears its head. But I won't.

I can't.

My desire to understand is too great. This curiosity will be my poison. Einstein said the important thing is not to stop questioning, but I don't think he had me in mind. Fixation isn't a good thing. Objects of my affection don't always like the outcome.

Walk away.

The thing is, despite all the reasons I should allow Simon to lead this tour, I can't. Because it's been a very long time since I've felt anything like excitement. To feel the rush in my bloodstream again . . .

I'm a parched man wandering through a desert, and she's the water.

And I need to see why this time is different.

I continue to look at her and am curious about how her blue eyes widen with her own set of emotions. Conflicting emotions if I'm reading her correctly. Fear. Curiosity. Excitement.

She looks young. If I had to harbor a guess, she's in her mid-twenties. There are no lines that pepper her face. Something most would take for granted, and it makes me wonder if she knows how precious life is.

My hand reaches up, and I scrub at my eyes, trying to push these thoughts away, but instead, as I squint, I see something. *Her.* I see the similarities.

They're there. Clear as day.

Is that where my fascination stems from? That she reminds me of before. Of my youth.

Maybe she's karma sent to taunt me. To remind me. She's the Angel of Death come to claim me for my past sins.

I've lived a long enough life, so if that's her goal, I'd welcome her with open arms.

At thirty-five, I'm not old by any means, but I don't look toward the future either. I don't get weighed down by mundane details like that. Not when I know I don't deserve a happy ending.

"Follow me," I say, pulling myself away from her gaze and starting to walk.

If I don't stop watching her, I know I'll scare her with the intensity. That cannot happen. As I stride through the corridor, I watch her reflection on the hallway walls, a perk to windows everywhere.

Her pace is fast, her arms cutting through the air to keep up with me. I slow my steps. With Layla following closely now, I lead her across the room until we are standing by the glass door up ahead. I lift my wrist, and then the wall parts open to the outside.

She gasps beside me at the movement, and I find myself liking the sound of her surprise.

Stepping back, I allow her to pass, and when she does, my hand touches the small of her back.

What the actual fuck?

What am I doing?

Normally, I'm not one to seek contact. Yet I'm not backing away; I'm moving toward it.

She's a burning candle, and I want to feel the intensity of her heat.

When she steps forward, I quickly move to the side to watch her. To see her reaction. Her eyes are wide. Shock. Maybe even awe glimmering back at me.

The late afternoon sunlight casts shadows around her. It's like she has a halo. For a second, a desire to snuff out the glow rushes through my brain. Then suddenly, my mind says *move closer*, and I must.

A gravitational pull forward to bask in her light.

I do neither. Instead, I give myself a shake and point my hand toward where the Wrangler 4 x 4 sits.

She follows my line of sight. "We're going for a drive?"

"This place is bigger than you think," I tell her. Her brows lift, and I marvel at how expressive she is. I, on the other hand, have to remind myself to smile.

And I don't mean that figuratively. I actually have to make myself. Or I wouldn't.

Although . . . come to think of it, when I smirked at her before, there was no mental prompting.

Interesting.

I lead her to the vehicle, but the moment I do, I realize it will be impossible for her to get in without help. This has a raised chassis without running boards.

She's trying to step in but can't really reach the handle.

I knew she was smaller than me, but I'd have to clock her at no taller than five foot two.

"Can I help you?" I ask.

She snarls at me. A look that should piss me off. The truth is, I would be pissed off with anyone else, but instead, I find my lips parting again. She's cute in a fiery way.

"Suit yourself," I respond, still watching her. Every moment I do, I find it becomes harder and harder to look away.

Finally, she jumps up, grabs the handle, and gets in.

I'm impressed. She didn't give up. Tenacious little thing. With her now settled, I walk to my side of the car, slide in, and throw it in reverse.

Then I start to drive.

We pull around the front of the building five minutes later.

"At this location, we only have a few buildings," I tell her.

"It's really quite unique. I didn't even realize they were buildings. The reflective glass mirrors pick up the surroundings."

I slow the car down to look at her face and gauge her voice's sincerity. It's odd. I don't understand why, but I'm drawn to her expression. The way her eyes widen, the way I feel when I see it. I want to see this place through her eyes. I want to experience her awe. The way she takes it all in.

I nod. "Yes. Exactly. That's the point. For there to be no difference between building and nature. This was my vision, to preserve its integrity and beauty."

"It's seamless."

"Thank you."

"And fully AI," she states.

"Yes. As you must have noticed, all the doors open as you step toward them, but that's only the beginning. The computer will know who is walking in and when and change its response to the person approaching."

"Are you serious?" she asks, craning her head to look.

"As a heart attack."

I pull farther down the road, then turn us onto a dirt road. The car jerks and she grabs the *oh-shit* bar. "Sorry."

"It's fine."

Pulling through the road, I hear her exquisite gasps as what I'm showing her comes into focus. I like that I keep surprising her to get those delicious sounds.

"These are the private residences. Each house will blend in with the trees. Since the glass is reflective, you can't see in, and the wood is synthetic to blend with the branches."

"It feels like it's set in the tree."

"As close as I could possibly design it to be."

We continue driving, and I point out the men and trucks building another home.

"We aren't complete yet, but we should be soon. The main buildings are finished, but the private residences are still being constructed, yet because of the way it branches out within the mountain, homeowners will never be disturbed by their neighbors or ongoing development."

Layla is practically hanging out of the car. With each house we pass, she seems truly fascinated with what she sees. "And the homes, are they also controlled by the same artificial intelligence system as the main building?"

"They are. Each homeowner will have a choice of how they want to use it, but the option is defaulted for fully functional."

"So, what you've *really* set out to do is make The Elysian take over the world, starting right here in Upstate New York. Someone has been reading too much Vonnegut."

That makes me smile.

Again, with the damn smile.

An expression I don't do often. *Try never.* Normally, I have to prep myself to smile so I don't appear strange to others. But today, since I met this woman, it has come naturally.

And I don't understand why.

It's fascinating, and I need to investigate this further.

All my life, I have been told these emotions won't come naturally to me. That I am not wired normally. *He* said I would never be right.

I come from damaged stock. No matter how much money I make, nothing can overcome my cold, dead heart.

I don't feel at all. Yet . . .

"How do you control it?" Her question cuts through my inner rambling.

Pulling my attention back to her, I park in front of a smaller home. One that's not equipped yet.

"This is where you'll be staying."

"Is it fully online?"

"No. Not yet. I think it would be better and less confusing for you to stay in this unit before it's networked."

"Aren't I here to see the AI systems function as part of the design, though?"

"You'll see everything, I promise you. But each home is cus-tom-made for the owner."

"Okay. That makes sense. I'm not moving in here, so this is going to be functional for someone else." She laughs through the question.

"Think of it like a custom blueprint. The only person the house will work for is the creator."

"So this house is still normal."

"Yes."

"Got it, but you will show me one that's not . . ." she presses.

"Of course. There's a lot to do during your stay. A lot to see."

I don't bother to pull the car over since we're the only ones on this street. Instead, I throw it into park. "This is where you'll stay. Get settled. I'll pick you up at eight for dinner."

"What about getting started? The itinerary?"

"I think we've seen enough for one day. It was a long drive. I'm sure you could use the rest before I overwhelm you. We can jump in tomorrow with the full property viewing."

She narrows her eyes. A different look on her. This is the first time she looks at me like that. Normally, if someone looked at me like this, I wouldn't even care. Nor would I humor them with a comment. But I find that with her, I do.

"If you're busy right now, I'm sure—"

I shake my head. "Here's the thing. I've already shifted stuff because of a delay in the project. I need my crews to focus on something else this week, not this tour."

It's not true. I just don't want any of the others around her yet. I want her to myself, and it's bizarre for me to be thinking this way.

The problem is, I have a feeling this obsession won't end well for her.

I'll break her spirit without trying, and maybe I should back off and allow others to take the reins for her benefit.

Yeah. Fuck that.

That's never going to happen.

She's mine for the duration of her stay.

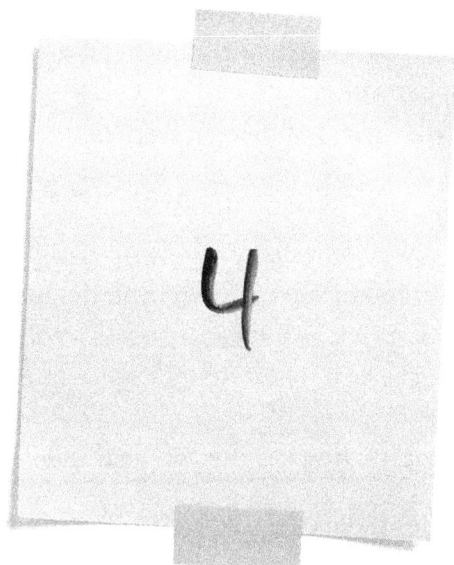

4

Layla

I wait for him to pull away, but it's obvious he doesn't plan to. Not until I go inside. Turning away from him, I head to the door.

A part of me expects it to open automatically, but he did say this house hasn't been fitted yet with the program to make it work.

I turn the knob the old-fashioned way, and once I step inside, I can hear the gravel kicking up as the Wrangler pulls away.

Once I know he's gone, I allow myself to take in the house, and as soon as I do, the breath in my lungs leaves my body.

This place is phenomenal.

It feels like I'm staying in a glamorous tree house. But instead of it being for children, this was built with adults in mind. Of course, this is designed with all the luxuries your heart can desire.

Marble floors.

Clean lines.

Contemporary furnishings.

Impressive light fixtures.

Yep, I see the irony.

The same girl who was bored with faucets is marveling at the chandelier hanging from the ceiling.

But in all due respect, it's something else.

Small glass balls reflect light out, allowing it to bounce off the room with a kaleidoscope of color.

In my twenty-five years of being alive, I have never seen anything like this.

The truth is, I guess, why would I?

It's not like I'm well-traveled or grew up with this luxury, but regardless, I watch TV, and never, not even in all the Netflix movies I have watched, have I ever seen anything that comes remotely close to being as spectacular as this.

Jeez.

I can't even imagine it when the artificial intelligence program is up and running.

Making a path inside the small home, I realize it's much bigger than I originally thought. My apartment in the city could fit in the living room. Oh, who am I kidding, this living room is even bigger.

But it's not the size that's so remarkable. No, it's that it blends so seamlessly. I can barely tell where the room ends and nature begins. The funny thing is, despite how immense it is in here, I assume this is one of the smaller units.

Walking through the open floor plan, I see this is a one-bedroom house. My initial assessment of the size isn't exactly correct. The hallways alone make this home double, if not triple, the size of my apartment in the city.

The decoration is serene, although not over the top. You can tell each piece has been selected for a calming element. Grays, whites, and light blue accent pieces. The blue reminds me of the ocean.

Who do they intend to have live in this unit? Regardless of the architecture spin my boss wants for the magazine, this is a perfect opportunity to ask hard-hitting questions. I want details on why Cain thinks the uber-rich need another playground when there are so many other people that need homes in this country. Isn't artificial intelligence becoming too powerful to take over our home spaces?

However, all the litany of questions on my itinerary has now been pushed back by Cain. I'll dig back in tomorrow when I have his attention again.

When I first arrived, or hell, on the ride up, I couldn't even fathom why I would be needed to stay so long here. But after seeing the immense size of this small home alone plus the three buildings in the center, I almost don't think a week will be enough.

The bedroom is beautiful. The wall to the left of the bed is floor-to-ceiling windows. The bed is high and fluffy with big white pillows and blankets. It looks like a cloud. And the view gives the feeling of floating above the tree line.

I place my laptop bag down and spot my suitcase in the corner of the room. I also notice it's empty; someone unpacked it for me. I stand speechless for a moment. That's kind of creepy. It feels like I'm being watched. Am I?

No.

If I get freaked out now, I'll never write an unbiased article. Inhaling deeply, I decide to embrace the luxuries this place has to offer, despite my initial reaction.

Walking over to the closet, I step inside and find that my clothes are already hanging.

Since I don't have to unpack, I can now make my way into the bathroom. Upon entering, I let out a long-drawn-out sigh.

Scratch out my previous comment. My whole apartment could fit into this room, and I'll be here for almost a whole week. This is crazy.

I might not love my job, but this . . .

Yep. This has turned into a real perk.

When I first heard about the project today, I wasn't all that excited, but ever since I stepped onto the property, an overwhelming urge to do well despite not originally caring ran through me. I'm eager to do a good job on this project, which baffles me because I do hate the bland topics I write about currently.

It's not about the article. It's about The Elysian.

Something completely new and original, and I'd be lying if I didn't admit that Cain Archer makes it all the better.

Something about Cain and this place demands my best work.

Taking a deep breath, I can see him in my mind, standing by the window. He isn't supposed to be this charming. I wasn't prepared.

But he is.

His grin.

That damn smirk.

Hell, when his lips part, I swear it makes my legs give out. His looks are dangerous, and his charm is downright lethal. I can't make the mistake of lusting after the head architect of this project.

Pulling the glass shower door open, I turn on the water, then strip down and get inside.

The hot water works its way down my body, instantly relaxing me from a hard day of travel.

I'm not sure how much time I stand there. How long I allow my muscles to uncoil, but eventually, when my fingers begin to prune, I shut the water off and step out of the shower, grabbing the fluffy white towel hanging from the hook on the wall.

Then I pull it around my body and take care to wipe off the water, all while slipping my feet into the slippers and robe that I also find hanging.

I can get used to this place.

Well, I can't. Not really.

This is only temporary.

It won't be long before I go back to my normal life, writing about mundane topics.

But, for the time being, I'm going to enjoy every minute this impromptu story has given me.

It doesn't take me very long to get ready. Instead of blow-drying my hair, I let it air dry. I have plenty of time, and as I do, I put on a light dusting of makeup.

He won't be here for an hour.

I wonder what dinner will be like.

What will we talk about?

Will we jump right into the interview?

He did say we would start tomorrow. But still, that doesn't mean he meant the questions.

Do I prepare them? Bring a recorder, just in case? I'm not sure. I don't want to insult him if tonight is just casual, but I don't want to be ill-prepared either. I could use my phone if he allows my questions.

Once my makeup is done, I get dressed in a flowery pink dress that comes to my upper thighs with flats and a jean jacket. An outfit that can easily be dressed up or down. If it's fancy, I'll forgo the jean jacket.

Before he arrives, I decide I should investigate Cain and The Elysian project some more.

When was this property purchased? There should be something in the county records online. Is this his money or a conglomerate of businesspeople that made this area a possibility for building? I wonder what the surrounding community incentives are for allowing this type of development.

There's gotta be some juicy info to track down.

As I'm lost in thought, a knock on the door has me slamming the laptop screen shut.

I move across the room and swing the door open.

My cheeks heat with embarrassment for almost getting caught looking into his business. But how would he even know what I was doing? There is no way, so I need to keep cool and not make a complete ass of myself.

Too late.

When I lift my head to meet his eyes, I see they're narrowed, and then he smirks.

"Did I interrupt something?" he asks, which only serves to make me more mortified. He probably thinks I was masturbating or something.

I shake my head. "Nope. Let's go."

He steps back, and I move through the open space he has vacated and make my way outside. The cooler evening air dances across my exposed skin, making goose bumps rise.

It's a beautiful night out. An endless array of stars acts as a canopy, illuminating the night sky.

"Where are we going?" I ask as I place my key in my bag.

"To dinner."

Lifting my head, I look at Cain and catch him staring at me. My heart races so fast, I fear it might burst, or at least that's what it feels like as I take in the way he watches me. His perusal feels intense. As if I'm standing naked before him, and he's scrutinizing my flaws. It's almost as if he's dissecting me, and the warm fuzzy feeling I just had starts to evaporate.

Cain must see my change of emotions because the next thing I know, he beams at me. Did I imagine the scrutiny?

Quickly, I turn in the direction of the parking space in front of the house. "Are any of the restaurants on-site already open?"

"No, not tonight. Which is why I wanted to take you out. There's a town nearby, and I'm sure you'd try to head out there on your own, but it's tricky at night."

"Got it."

I start to walk, and when I am by his car, I notice it isn't the same as before.

"New ride?" I cock my head at the fancy Land Rover.

"Over the next week, you'll notice there are a lot of options. Each has their own purpose."

"Good to know. I'll find out more when you're on the record." I smirk.

He nods, steps forward, and swings open the passenger door to the SUV he's chosen for tonight.

I give him space to allow the car door to be opened, and I step up, lifting myself with both hands on the handrail so I don't fall. Behind me, I can feel the heat of his body. He's standing close. Probably close enough to spot me if, for some reason, I do trip. I'm not the tallest girl, and although this is not nearly as high as the Wrangler, I still have to pull myself up pretty far.

The good news is he doesn't make a comment about it. He just acts like a complete gentleman, as if he's waiting for me. But this isn't my first rodeo, and I know exactly what he's doing. Either waiting for me to fall or checking out my ass perched high in front of him. And he's so handsome I don't mind if he looks.

Once I'm seated, he closes the door behind me, and then a few seconds later, the driver's side door swings open, and he settles in the seat before turning the car on. A soft melody plays through the speakers.

It's not the type of music I would expect from him. I would expect Mr. Artificial Intelligence to play modern music. Instead, classical music plays in the background. An interesting choice for an interesting man.

His presence in the car feels all-encompassing. He's too big for the space, even if it is a luxury SUV. At least earlier today, when driving in the Wrangler, the sides were off, with the open air all around us, but now with the doors closed, it feels like he draws in all the oxygen in the car.

I stare out the window. For the first time in my life, I don't know what to talk about. It's not that it's awkward, but I'm not supposed to discuss the article, so I'm not sure what I can talk about.

Finally, after a few minutes, I turn to face him. He looks stern, like he's concentrating. We're still on an abandoned road, one that I'm sure in the next couple of years will become busy and prosperous, but right now, it's just dirt.

"How far are we going?" I ask him.

"In a rush? Someplace to be?" His voice is level, not giving away anything about how he's feeling.

"Just dinner with some man," I tease, trying to lighten the mood.

"Lucky guy." Now his voice drops low, giving it a husky quality that makes my heart race.

"He is. And I'm quite lucky, too."

I turn my head to look at him. He hasn't said anything. He hasn't remarked on my comment. The car has gone silent, but I see his lips twitch up.

He can't help but smile, but his smile looks different. Kind of clay-like? Does he not smile often? It almost feels unnatural.

I don't know Cain Archer, but from what his assistant said and the small glimpses I saw of him, I don't think he's emotional often. I don't think he teases anyone around him. However, for some reason, he's playful with me. *For some reason, he smiles for me.*

My belly shouldn't go warm at that thought.

I'm here for a little less than a week, and I shouldn't care what he thinks of me. He's merely a story for my job. But despite that fact and the part where I keep telling myself not to care, I can't help the flutter in my stomach at the thought that the guy might break his façade for me.

For the rest of the ride to town, we are both quiet.

It's pitch-black out as he weaves through the endless streets.

How does he see anything? I bet he could drive with his eyes closed. He's probably made this drive more often than one should, seeing as it's likely a death trap for someone like me.

Then again, I live in the city, and I don't drive very often.

It takes about fifteen minutes, give or take, before we're making a left-hand turn, and then, like walking out of a foggy mist, lights are present for the first time on our drive.

A town.

Finally, as we pull into the small village, I see things aren't as isolated here. This place is darling. It reminds me of a small country town. One with money but down-to-earth at the same time.

What came first?

The town or the concept?

I lean closer to my window to get a better view. "This is adorable."

"It's got a charm about it."

Understatement of the year. But I imagine this man has seen the world.

"It really does. I feel like I'm in Aspen, but a more relaxed version of it. Not that I've ever been." I laugh. "But I imagine this is what it's like."

"That's the feeling the developers had when they built it. During the winter, the skiing is rather popular."

The sound of the blinker echoes through the car, and then Cain maneuvers us into the space. I look out the window and notice a stone building with a red awning hanging over the window. *The Chalet.*

It even sounds like a restaurant that belongs on the slopes.

Now parked, I take a deep breath, mentally preparing myself for an evening with this enigmatic man. Once I'm ready, I swing the heavy door open. I'm taken by surprise as I step out because Cain is striding at a fast clip to be by my side.

Together, we walk into the restaurant on Main Street. As soon as we step inside, I smile. The restaurant looks like a ski lodge. A large, roaring fireplace is the focal point of the spacious dining space.

Surprisingly, despite it being the beginning of summer, the fire fails to warm up the place sufficiently. Maybe it's because we are in the mountains, and the temperature outside has dipped tremendously since this afternoon.

Cain places his hand on my back, and I have to refrain from allowing myself to shiver beneath his touch as he leads us to the hostess stand, where a pretty redhead greets us.

"Mr. Archer, I didn't expect you tonight. Would you like your normal table in the back room?"

"Yes, that would be nice and quiet. Thank you."

When we are at the table, he drops his hand, and I miss the warmth right away. I take a seat, and when he's across from me, a different look is on his face. It's almost like there is a different Cain here now. A colder one. He looks at me intently. "Please, tell me about your trip up here and your thoughts after being at The Elysian for the last few hours."

Okay. All business.

Now I feel dumb for allowing myself to linger against his touch a few seconds ago. I straighten my spine, pulling back my shoulders to appear taller.

I can do professional. "Easy drive. Longer than I anticipated but still doable. It would have helped me if the roads were marked a little better."

He nods. "Well, there's a reason for not pointing out the property too far in advance. And your first impression of the buildings?"

Cocking my head to the left, I lift a brow. "I thought I was the one interviewing you."

"Humor me." His lip tips up into a smirk, and I swear my tongue feels heavy. Dammit, I thought I could be all business, but then he has to look at me like this.

Dear God, this man is deadly.

I open my mouth, and it feels dry. "I didn't even see the road. It was flawless. The transition. And then the building. The residences are all breathtaking. But . . ."

"But what?"

"No." I nibble on my lower lip. "It's nothing. Forget it."

"Layla."

"The faucets." *Dear God, am I doing this?* Just because I wrote a few articles on faucets does not make me an expert.

"The faucets?" he presses.

"The spread of the faucet is all wrong. I'm not sure if it was an oversight, but they are only four inches, it's not comfortable. Eight inches is standard now. Easier to use and clean."

His lips part wider. No longer a smirk, now a full-fledged smile. "You're right. That will be fixed." I think I might combust. The look. Yep.

It should be illegal. This man should come with a warning label: May cause idiot journalists, who are supposed to be professional, to pass out. "Anything else?"

"How long do you have?" I wink. "But in all seriousness, the way I see it, architecture is supposed to be art that we live in. But being at The Elysian, it's more than that"—I take a deep breath, trying to gather my words— "The Elysian feels alive. I can't even imagine how spectacular this place is going to be once it's open. Especially since you've already done such an incredible job."

He nods to himself and then turns to look at the menu. I wish I could read his mind. Better yet, I wish I could see the expression now on his face. I think I've pleased him with my answer, and for some reason, it makes butterflies take flight in my stomach.

A big swarm of them, too. Wings flapping and all the flutters.

This is a strange turn of events. It's not often anyone gets to me like this. Normally, I also don't make an idiot of myself by gawking at the hot subject of an article, but I guess there is a first for everything.

The thing is, I want his approval. I want him to see me as the journalist I know I can be.

This man is a genius, and I want him to think I'm worthy of his time. That thought alone has me straightening my spine and getting back into work mode.

"Enough about my thoughts on the property. Let's talk about you."

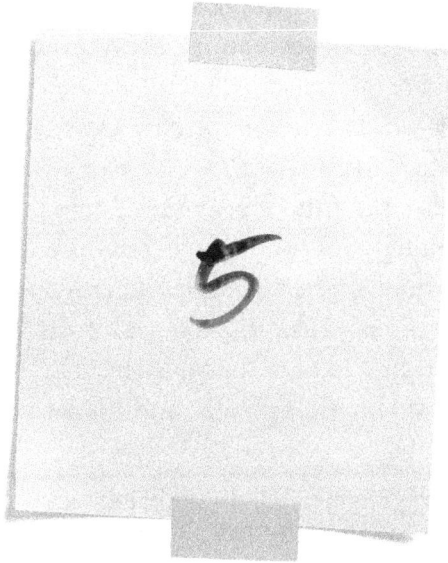

5

Cain

"**A**bout me?" I ask. This beautiful woman has me captivated. For the first time, I want to spend time with someone. I want my grand design appreciated and to hear what she has to say. But I also will not forget what I have done, even if, for a moment, her presence enthralls me. A couple of unforced smiles don't make me normal.

Clearing my throat, I say, "There isn't much to talk about besides The Elysian. I've worked hard and cultivated the right connections. I have finally brought this project to life. It's people like you, who see what this will be when complete, that I hope will be the residents here."

Layla stares at me as I speak, but this feels different than when I speak to financial backers and real estate brokers. It looks like she cares.

What is going on in my head? My thoughts are everywhere but where they should be.

From across the table, Layla leans forward, placing her elbows on the table. "And Barbara? Have you known her for long?"

"Yes, she was the first hire the temp agency sent when I started my own architectural firm. She's stayed with me ever since."

"Oh, so I should get in good with her for my interview," she says with a laugh to her tone. "I'm young, but I've been told the admin assistants are gold mines of information. They know where all the bodies are hidden."

I blench at her words. *Oh, you have no idea, sweetheart.*

"Everything okay, Mr. Archer?"

Shaking myself out of the fog, I nod. "I told you to call me Cain . . ." I give her a pointed look, and her cheeks flush that pretty shade of pink I like. It looks good on her. I wonder if her whole body flushes that color when she's nervous. "How did you get into architectural journalism, Layla?" I ask, trying to turn the tables back on her.

"Well, that's easy. It pays the bills, and I have a lot after majoring in journalism at NYU."

"Didn't your parents help pay for college?"

"No way," she huffs out. Her demeanor changes in that instant. From sitting back looking at me with kind eyes to now facing her water glass, twirling it, shoulders slumped. "When I left home after high school on graduation night, I started off at a local community college. One of the professors there was a neighbor, and she got me fast-tracked into the near-campus apartment. From there, I got my associates and transferred to NYU."

"Sounds like you were quite driven. But you said you left the night of graduation? You didn't live at home after that?"

"Um, no. I had a falling-out with my parents, and it all came to a head that night. I was not wanted, so I packed my belongings in my car and left. And yes, I'm driven. Driven by finding out the truth of situations. That's why I love being a journalist. I want to discover the facts and bring them to light so people are not stuck in the darkness."

I'm stunned.

This woman is too much.

After listening to her, can I keep her far enough away? She wants to learn the truth so badly. But I never want her to learn my realities.

I cannot help myself. I want to know everything about her.

Leaning forward across the table, I tentatively touch her hand. "You know, it's funny. We're actually very much alike. My upbringing wasn't anything special either." That's the most I can give her, but as her pupils dilate and she gives me a sad smile, I know it was the right move. I give her a little squeeze, one that tells her I understand. One I hope brings her comfort. Which is another first for me. Since when do I want to comfort anyone?

A blush creeps down her neckline as I trail my finger over her knuckle. She's not pulling away, so I don't stop. There is a pull between us, and I know she can feel it, too.

The moment is lost when the server steps up to the table.

I remove my hand, and she gives herself a little shake. Then we both proceed to order as if that moment never happened.

An hour passes, and we keep the conversation light. I tell her about the town we are eating in. Nothing earth-shattering, but I still enjoy her company.

Once the bill comes and I pay, we both stand. I know she's going to ask what's next. She probably assumes I'm going to take her home, but I'm not.

Enchanted by her and this night, I decide we need to take a walk instead. I'm not ready to leave her yet. I like the feelings she awakens inside me too much. With this new excitement, and the fact that she isn't here for long, I will take every minute I can get. Who knows if I'll ever find someone to engage me so thoroughly again?

"Come on, let me show you the park across the street." I step back so she can move ahead of me, and then, when we are out the door, I reach my hand out to guide her in the direction I want her to walk.

"At night, you want us to walk through a playground? What if you're a creepy axe murder?"

"That's a risk you'll have to take." Chuckling, I assure her, "No, it is not that kind of park. Just a walking path around a lagoon, so it's got some light to it. Plus, I promise not to kill you . . . *today*."

"Oh. That makes me feel so much better." She laughs as her body relaxes. I put my hand on the small of her back as we walk down the sidewalk and then head across the empty road to the recreation area. As we start around the trail, my hand is still on her. Layla will never know the frenetic chaos going on in my head at this moment and my inner conflict of wanting to keep it there or just move it away.

"What a beautiful space you have created. All of this open area highlights the space, yet there are woods and trails to make the outdoor activities really shine. This will be great for the article."

"We don't have to talk business, Layla," I say as we come to the curved walking bridge over the lagoon. She smiles up at me with a crooked smile. I can tell she's not certain that walking in the shadows with me and not discussing business is a good idea.

"However, this is what I wanted to show you. From the arc of the bridge, you see not only the lagoon but also down the hill where the forest takes over." I bend down so my head is practically on her shoulder. "Look," I whisper next to her ear, pointing into the darkness. "You can see the ridgeline of The Elysian main building. The only time you can tell the buildings are even there is at night when these park lights reflect off it." Breathing in her perfume, I'm a little stunned that I feel *relaxed and safe*. It reminds me of something . . . a memory.

"I can see the faint line of the roof, and it's breathtaking. What you . . . " She trails off as she turns her head. Her mouth is just a whisper away from touching mine. Lips shimmering in the darkness. Plump. Beautiful. Ripe for capturing.

We both suck in a breath, and I'm the first to move away.

Our moment broken.

Broken like I am.

I have no business being this close to a woman who shouldn't trust me.

Because if she's not careful, she will be another causality of getting close to me.

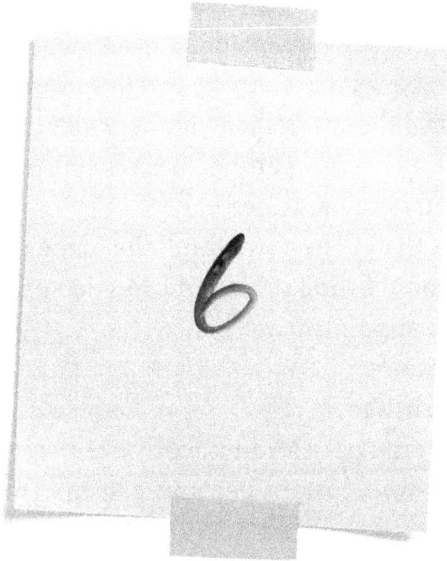

_6_

Layla

"What's on tap for tomorrow?" I ask as the car rolls down the last bit of the driveway. Tonight, has been unexpected, and I'm not sure what the next day will bring. There are equal measures of excitement and nerves churning inside me right now. Cain seemed relaxed with me. A concept that makes him even more enchanting.

But there's something beyond the surface that seems off, and I want to find out more about those traits.

Why does he seem closed off to people?

Why is there no history before his architecture firm opened? I know I can find answers; I only need to figure out which direction to look.

"Still working on it, but I'd like to show you the community center. And if we have time, the spa."

"Spa?" The thought of getting a massage has my hand lifting to my shoulder blades. That would be nice right now. My back aches from the drive up here.

"Yes."

Turning to face him, I mutter, "I didn't know there was a spa on-site." I try to remember the brochure about this place, and I don't remember seeing anything about a spa. Granted, I've been going nonstop since my boss told me about this assignment, but a spa is something I'd remember.

"You will find, Layla, that there is very little we don't offer our residents here." His voice sounds deeper, and I wonder if he means to sound so damn sexy or if it's just him and he has no control over it.

"This place truly is a paradise."

He chuckles at that. "Then you think the name is fitting," he teases.

"It would be more fitting if I could use said spa, but alas, I'm sure it's not yet open for appointments."

"Unfortunately, not."

"Next time." I shrug.

"You plan to come back? You haven't even seen the whole place yet." The tone of his voice lowers, becoming deeper, making him sound more serious.

"Maybe not, but sometimes you have a feeling. You know?"

"I do." I find myself turning to watch Cain, and we both are quiet in thought.

Tonight, has been perfect. It didn't go as I expected, but he is nothing at all like I thought he would be.

He is charming. Polite. And despite everything I heard or read about him, caring.

It's strange.

The man who took me to dinner and asked so much about me truly cared what I had to say. From what his assistant said, he didn't listen or care about anyone but himself and his project, but that is not at all what I saw. Or felt.

No. Instead, all night long, I had to stop myself from swooning.

I'm not some ditzy wallflower or historical maiden who gets attention from a cold duke, then falls to the ground.

Yet . . .

When he smiles at me, when he smirks, when he stares into my eyes, that's exactly how I feel.

The air in the car feels stiff as he parks at the house I'm staying in this week. Neither of us moves at first, and then he turns to fully face me.

There is a look in his eyes I have never seen before. It's almost like desire. There's no way this man could want me.

Sure, he was friendly at dinner, but never did it feel like he wanted more, yet as his gaze takes me in, it's exactly how it feels.

If this were any other man, I would swear he was going to kiss me. No, that can't be right. This man doesn't want me. But then his eyes drop to my lips, so I could be wrong. He might. After the way he touched me at the park, anything is possible.

Time drags as I wait. I continue to look at him, never stopping the rhythmic begging in my mind for him to close the distance.

Highly unprofessional, but I can't help that I want him to kiss me at this minute.

Later, I might come to my senses, but at this moment, this man is like a planet with his own gravitational pull. I can't help but want to be in his orbit.

He reaches an arm out and cups my cheek. Just the warmth from his skin incites a riot in my body. Cain trails a finger down my jaw to my neck, and then he traces a line across from one side to the other . . . *a strange pressure building in his touch.*

With a shake and turn of his head, he breaks the spell. Severing our connection, he drops his hand and leaves me staring at his profile.

"I'll see you tomorrow at eight o'clock. I'll be here to pick you up." His words are like a bucket of ice-cold water being poured over my head, leaving me a little irate for a second.

Here I am imagining him kissing me, and to him, I'm probably just an annoying little reporter he can't wait to part ways with.

I'm pathetic and obviously hard up, too, because a rational woman who's getting laid on a regular basis would have never fallen into the line of thinking I just did.

With nothing to say and my pride hurt, I nod and swing the door open. Stepping out, I can't help but feel off-kilter.

Moving away from the car, I head to the entrance. Once I unlock the door, I step inside and slam it closed, then begin the short slide down to the floor. Shaking my head in disbelief, I place my head in my hands and try to take a deep breath.

I am the biggest idiot ever. Who is dumb enough to think the source of her next article would want her?

Me. That's who.

And even worse, I showed him I'm nothing but a girl with a school-girl crush on the millionaire.

Dumb.

Dumb.

Dumb.

I sit on the floor for a few more minutes and berate myself.

With a huff of annoyance, I reach into my bag and dial Mara's number.

She always makes me feel better.

"You get killed by a mountain lion yet?" she answers.

That makes me laugh right off the bat, instantly making me forget my earlier self-loathing.

"Nope. Still alive. But if you ask me, I have died and gone to heaven in these houses."

"That amazing?" Mara asks.

I give a dramatic, content sigh. "There are no words."

"Well, that sucks." She laughs, and I have no idea what she's talking about.

"What do you mean?" My foot taps on the floor, waiting for her to fill me in. This is what Mara does. She likes to dangle fruit in front of me, but she doesn't give in right away. She likes to make me work for it.

A few seconds pass before she giggles. "Without words, how will you write the article? From what I heard, you'll need thousands of them. This is going to be a major spread."

"I think I'll figure it out. This place, though, Mara. It's insane. It will take me weeks and then probably years to sort it out and make sure it's perfect."

"Too bad boss man will only give you one week to research and maybe another two weeks once you're back in the office to write it up."

I groan loudly. "Pain in my ass."

"Don't I know it."

"How are things without me today? Everything good?" I ask.

"It's quiet. Annoyingly so, to be honest." She's overdramatic, but I love her for it.

"Good to know I'm missed for my witty commentary," I deadpan.

"Among other things . . ." Mara trails off for emphasis.

I jerk up to my feet and make my way into the bathroom. "What other things?"

"Aw. Are you needing a confidence boost?" Her mocking laugh should piss me off, but it's the main reason she's my best friend.

"Never met a compliment I didn't like." A laugh escapes my mouth. Now standing in front of the sink, I turn the lever. Water pours out of the spout.

"Everything okay over there, other than being speechless? Are you showering?"

"It's heaven. If heaven on earth had a zip code, this would be it. I almost never want to leave." I look around the room. *Yep, never going.* "And nope. Just about to brush my teeth and wash my face."

"And the people?"

"I haven't met anyone really but Mr. Archer and his assistant." I try to keep my voice neutral because Mara knows me better than anyone.

"And?"

"He's so different. I didn't expect him to be like . . . this." My cheeks feel warm as I think about his smile. "He's brilliant, and I have barely even touched the surface, and so kind and—"

"Damn, someone sounds giddy." Just as I suspected, she busted me.

"I'm just excited." Good excuse, but she will read through it.

"Excited about the location or Mr. Archer . . . ?" she draws out.

"I knew nothing about him or this place, and now I'm in love." Pressing the button to put the phone on speaker, I then place it on the counter and splash some water on my face. All while she continues to talk.

"Yet who was the lady who didn't like her job? Let me guess, you got the coolest gig, but I bet you bitched, moaned, and complained the whole drive up."

Reaching out, I grab the towel hanging beside the sink and blot at my face, then set it back down. "Not the whole drive . . ."

"Half of it," she adds.

"Ninety-two percent of it," I admit.

"Figured. So . . . tell me, are all the rumors true? The man who never laughs. Smiles. Has a relationship with anyone. Is he the asshole you expected to find?"

"A man dedicated to his work. And the rest of that is not true," I defend.

"What's not true?"

"He does smile. And he laughs," I add as I look at my reflection in the mirror. The flush of my cheeks is even more prominent now. It's from the warm water. *Sure, it is.* Who am I kidding? It looks like I spent the day at the beach and forgot to put on lotion. Cain Archer is the sun, and his proximity the burn.

"How do you know?" Her question has me shaking my head and pulling my attention back down to the phone that has been forgotten about on the counter. Too lost in the memory of the night and the feel of his hand on mine.

Damn, there I go again. "He did both with me," I admit, knowing this is opening a can of worms that I will never be able to close.

"What do you mean, Layla? Are you holding out on me?"

"I've been here for less than a day. How much could I be holding out?"

"Enough that you saw him smile and laugh." The line goes silent, but then I hear her let out a long, drawn-out breath. "Layla." Scolding parent mode activated.

"He took me to dinner." If she could see me, she would see that I have buried my face in my hands, but thankfully, we are not on FaceTime, so now, I just wait.

One . . .

Two . . .

"Details, woman!"

I give them to her. Grabbing my phone, I plop down once again on the floor with my back against the bathroom door this time and tell her everything.

How he listened. How he knows my story. My parents' awful truth. The truth I wasn't wanted.

I tell her how he smiled at me after.

And the worst part of the story spills out, too. I even tell her, despite my better judgment and the fact that I only just met him, I felt a connection. A part of me wanted to throw caution to the wind and be kissed by Cain. When all the words finish pouring out of my mouth, I let out a large sigh.

It feels good to confess my stupidity.

The line is silent when I finish speaking, and for a second, I think the call dropped, but then I hear Mara groan. Shit, now what?

"Just be careful."

"Be careful? No reason to be careful. Didn't you hear my story? He didn't want me. It was just a friendly dinner."

"Oh, no, it wasn't. That was no casual dinner, Layla. The man who doesn't let anyone get close, let you. That's why you need to be careful. Because from everything I have heard, he's not a good guy. He doesn't do emotions or have connections. Cain's the type of man a woman could lose her heart to, and he wouldn't blink an eye when he shatters it in the palm of his hands."

I don't speak for a second, trying to come up with some defense, but I'm left empty-handed.

"Listen, I have to go, but please think about what I said."

"I will."

I hang up and think back on my dinner as I get ready for bed.

Mara's words rattle in my head all night long as I try to chase sleep.

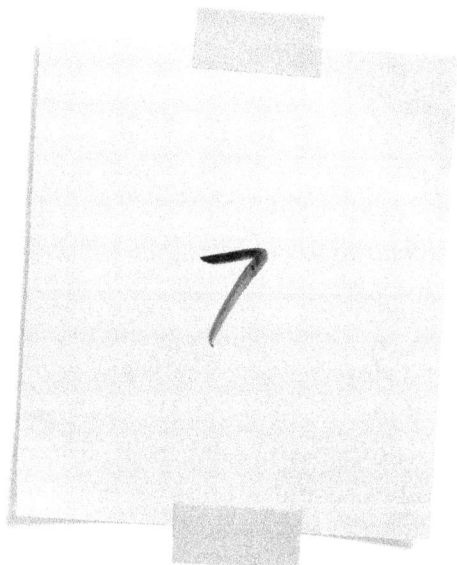

7

Cain

start my day, as always, with a sunrise walk around the property. It usually clears my head and gets my priorities in focus.

I don't know what it is about this woman.

What transpired last night has never happened to me before. Sure, I've smiled in the past. But the smiles were forced. I taught myself how to appear normal. It's a pain in the fucking ass, if I'm being totally honest. But also, a necessity.

I found it easier, though, to just fall into the stereotype. Successful antisocial architect.

When I read the first article describing my cold nature, I ran with it because the truth is, that's how I've always been. Pretending to smile didn't seem necessary any longer as a successful adult.

People were drawn to me because of my talent, despite my lack of social graces.

Life is easier when I don't have to pretend. But that's the thing about Layla; there's no need to pretend. I often find myself smiling. Which is something I don't understand.

The first time it happened, it took me off guard completely.

It's hard to remember the last time I smiled unprovoked. Come to think of it, in the past . . . even with *her*, I think I made myself. Scrubbing my hands over my face, I will myself to push out the memories.

This makes no sense at all. Why now? Why Layla?

There is something about her.

I find myself rearranging my whole schedule this week to spend more time with her.

This is a crazy thing I'm doing. There's too much work to be done, but like a moth to a flame, I need to see this out. Need to understand this feeling, to know why this is happening.

Is it because of my past?

Is this some sick misplaced emotion because she looks like . . .

Stop. Enough.

I turn the corner of the path I'm walking.

The foliage is thick in these parts, and I have to push back branches as I walk. I like to take this trail past the empty property that will soon accommodate new independent housing complexes. Seeing the sun rise over the land has my brain unlocking with possibilities.

This is the route I take every day, and here, when I do, it's like a jigsaw puzzle. The pieces come together the same way the number of a math equation does. And I see exactly what I have to do to the space.

Right now, however, all I see is her.

Figuratively, of course.

She's not here at present. Still fast asleep and tucked inside the small home I placed her in when I first recognized I saw her differently.

The home Layla is in doesn't have state-of-the-art surveillance systems inside it yet. Nor has the AI program my computer team created been installed.

How I wish it were, though. But I knew that if I could, I'd be drawn to watch her every move.

The thing that has my feet halting on this path and my legs locking is hearing *my mom's* voice in my ear when she yelled at me years ago.

When I was a kid and she screamed words saying I wasn't normal. That I would never be normal.

She told me I was wrong in the head.

Then he told me I was a sociopath.

He was the sociopath. And now, I did follow in his footsteps with my emotional detachments.

As a kid, I never loved. I never had connections. Never cared for anything or anyone.

As a teenager, the darkness inside me expanded. Like a dark mass taking over and spreading its poison throughout every crevice of my body. As a man, it's still there, but I pretend it's not. I pretend I'm normal.

I never thought anyone would get through.

Layla does.

I tilt my head up to the sky, looking at the clouds. It's going to be a nice day, but if you came out here right now, you would think it would rain.

I know better.

That's the case with everything but her.

Confusion washes over me.

There is no arguing that she is beautiful. It's more than just her looks, though. I've been with many women, but with her, I was instantly captivated. It's the way she holds herself. The way she speaks, but still, there's more.

When she looked into my eyes, I felt it deep in my gut. Like I was punched.

God, I sound like a weak asshole.

This isn't about love. Fuck. It isn't even about sex. This is about the fact that when I look at her, I don't imagine her not breathing.

I don't wonder if I'll ever let go of the hard-fought control. I don't want to be the reason she's no longer conscious.

Stop.

With a shake of my head, I lower my gaze back down to the trail I had taken. This trail runs closer to the main road. I'm trying to see what sort of access I should have from this vantage point. Should I close off the trail because it's too close to the real world, or should I let it go, let it take its own path?

Knowing I don't have that much time, I decide to head in the direction of the most recent addition to the compound.

Turning from the road, I head to where the brush is thicker.

This area hasn't been trimmed back yet, so I grab a stick and push it as I force my way through the overgrown thicket. My lack of decision about what I'm doing with this side of the property makes way for overgrown bushes, grass, and hardy vines. As I get closer to the street, I hear a noise. It makes my footsteps stop.

I stand still, making sure I don't make a sound, then listen.

At first, I don't hear anything. My ears are not yet accustomed to the silence, but as the minutes stretch, I do.

It sounds like a crunch of leaves.

I hold my breath to make sure. When I do, I hear it again, and I'm one hundred percent sure that it's the sound of leaves crushing underneath feet.

The question is, is it an animal?

I take a step, moving toward the sound, then I stop, quiet myself, and strain my ears again.

This time, I hear it, and I know it's a person. The sound is heavier. The pace and the cadence of them are definitely human.

A bear doesn't move like this. A bear doesn't halt to be quiet.

Nope, this is no bear.

At that, like a predator stalking his prey, I move around the thickness of the trees, eyes assessing for a threat.

When I turn the corner, I find what I am looking for. A camera pointed at my face.

The hand lowers, and there's a woman. From where I'm standing, I can't see much of her. I certainly can't see her face.

She's got her hair pulled back into a ponytail under a hat, and she has large sunglasses on her face. How can she even take pictures with those on?

The desire to grab the camera from her hand and smash it to the ground flows through me, but I push it back down. Smashing a camera won't bode well for me.

I take a deep breath and face her head-on.

"You're trespassing." I hiss.

"I'm n—"

"No excuses. No lies. You're trespassing." I look her up and down. It's not just her face that she's trying to hide. Her clothes are also dark as if she were trying to blend. "And by the way you're dressed, you knew that." My jaw clenches.

"There must be a mistake."

"A mistake," I grit out as I step forward. She steps back, her hands shaking. "How did you gain access to this section of the property?" There are places people can visit, but here . . . *Nope.*

"I-I came in behind a work truck," she mumbles under her breath.

"You need to leave now." My loud voice echoes through the woods. It leaves no room for misinterpretation.

Her head turns to me. I imagine she's looking at me, but I can't tell behind the sunglasses. Then her chin tips down toward her camera, and her lips split into a small smile. A smirk maybe?

Is she happy about the turn of events? Her response makes no sense.

"Leave," I say more forcefully, but she doesn't go. Instead, she steps closer.

"Do I really have to?" Something about her voice makes my brain scramble to place it. I've heard it before, but I can't place where. If only I could see her face. Then I can figure out why it sounds familiar.

Now, she cocks her head and puckers her lips; she's flirting.

Or, at least, trying to.

"Yes. You do. And if you don't get the fuck off my property, I'll make you wish you never even tried to wake up this morning. Do you understand me?" I snap before I can stop myself, and then I see my mistake.

The fate of the project rests on good publicity.

I inhale deeply, willing a calm presence over me.

This breathing shit doesn't work. But it gives me enough time to come up with a plan.

To think of what a normal person would do. What a person who isn't a maniac that wants to end her for disturbing my fucking walk would do.

Charm her.

Pretend not to be the man I truly am.

I force my lips to turn up.

And when her mouth and jaw soften, I know my plan will work.

"Today is not a good day," I pause, "but if you'll meet me tomorrow at the coffee shop in town, I'm sure we can talk."

I'm full of shit. I won't meet her, and in the meantime, I'll tighten up security, but I can't let her know that.

"Really?" she asks.

"Of course."

She's very close now. Close enough that her perfume penetrates my nose. She probably thinks it's alluring.

Spoiler alert, it's really not.

She's a gnat.

A nuisance.

And she needs to leave.

This is why I don't fucking talk to people.

"I look forward to seeing you again." Her hand reaches out and touches my arm. The moment it does, I hear a cough.

Looking up, I see a scowling Layla staring daggers at where this girl touches me.

I push her hand off.

"Am I interrupting something? I was under the impression we at *Concept* have the exclusive. If that's not the case—"

"It's very much the case." I say to Layla, and then turn back to the woman. "Leave." The one word comes out forceful, but I don't look at her long enough to see her reaction. No. Instead, I look at Layla.

I note her posture and how she's looking at this woman and realize that she's jealous. For some reason, I find myself smiling. And even more unlike me, *I want to see how this plays out.*

I'm amused.

Yet, despite my enjoyment, I also don't want her to think I'd ever entertain the other woman. I'm taken aback by this revelation and have a sick need to learn more about Layla. This woman who has me acting so out of character.

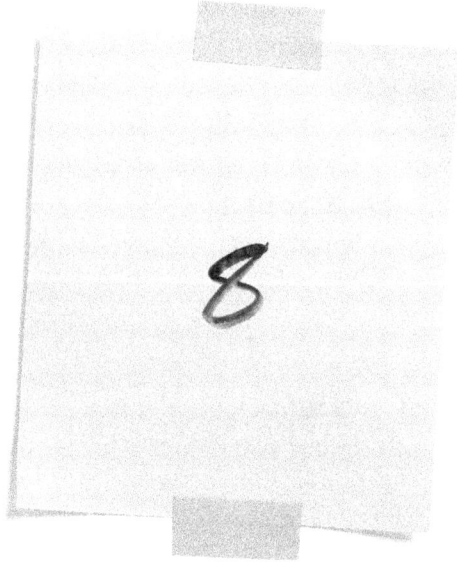

8

Layla

"Come on, let's go," he says to me. He's not smiling, and it feels unusual for him, but this is what I heard.

The way he looks at this reporter has my spine turning to steel.

Maybe there is truth to the rumors.

I don't want to believe it, but what I just witnessed . . .

This man isn't the man who went to dinner with me. This man is different. He's cold. His eyes don't even look the same.

Yes, his eyes have always been dark, but this is something entirely different.

The pupils have overtaken. It's like a light switch went off in him.

He stares at her, and she is visibly shaken now.

I'm not sure about what passes between them or what I missed before, but soon, she's scurrying away.

We both stand there, momentarily quiet, before he turns his body, no longer facing in the direction in which she went, but now facing me.

His dark eyes focus on me. This time, they look different.

Although still darker than the night sky, now they connect with mine.

Before, they didn't.

When Cain looked at me, even if it was only for a few seconds, it felt like he was looking right through me.

It takes him a beat before he moves. I watch him from where I'm standing, analyzing the way his chest rises and falls.

Eventually, his shoulders drop, and that's when he pivots away from where he's staring and meets my gaze.

The way he looks at me isn't hostile. No. The man from moments ago is long gone. Like he's shaken off the haze that had descended upon him. It's odd how differently he looks at me. Which version is the real him?

"You ready?" His voice cuts through the air, and I find myself shaking my head. The man is giving me whiplash.

"Ready?" My eyebrow arches. Did we have plans to go somewhere? Mentally, I try to remember how we left off last night. Sure, we had a meeting time, but it's not for another . . . I look down at the phone in my hand. Hour.

"Yes. For your tour. That is, unless . . ." He trails off, his gaze drifting to look in the direction of my watch. "Are you too busy?"

I have no idea what he's even talking about. I have no plans. My only plan is to write this darn article. "No. Of course not."

His brow lifts. "You sure?"

I place my hands on my hips, getting a little annoyed by this line of questioning. Can't I just have easygoing Cain again? A smile. A smirk. Something to tell me I didn't imagine the whole thing last night. Because even though he isn't currently acting hostile to me, his prior behavior still lingers in the air, like a fire that was just put out, but the remnants of burned soot won't go away. "Of course." I decide to soften my voice. Maybe if he sees I'm not annoyed by what I witnessed, he will change, too. "You're the only plans I have, obviously."

"Good. I like it that way." The line that is etched in his brow fades away. My plan worked.

"Well, then, that's good 'cause I'm here to please."

His lip tips up at that, and the moment the words leave my mouth and I realize what I said, I want to groan.

Instead, I cough. The reflex is welcome at this awkward moment. He continues to look at me, and I can't read him. But I'm happy the angry architect has vacated the premises.

Now that I know what he's capable of, I'm even more drawn to him. To the need to discover why he's different with me.

"Where are we off to today?" My fingers begin to fiddle with the hem of my shirt. I have nervous energy coursing through me, and I need an outlet.

"I'm going to show you the heart of my city," he says proudly.

"City?" That has me halting my movements and narrowing my eyes at him.

"Yes, this will essentially be a self-contained city, a paradise or a utopia, to be exact."

"Interesting. Where did you come up with this idea?" I ask, taking a step closer.

He pivots his body, but I still have a perfect view of his face. He looks up at the sky as if he's thinking or maybe remembering. "To be honest, I used to read a lot as a child, and one of the books I read inspired me."

"What book was that?"

"*Brave New World*." Cain walks back toward the path, the fallen leaves on the ground crunching beneath his feet.

My feet move faster, trying to catch up. "I've actually read it. A long time ago. I might be fuzzy on the details, but here I thought—and I could be wrong—isn't it about the dangers of technology?"

"It is. But it also inspired me to do it the right way." He looks over his shoulder and winks before he turns back and starts to walk again. "I'll lend you a copy," he says from a few steps ahead. His voice is muffled, but I still hear him. "You can tell me how I did."

His words make me halt my steps.

He must hear me stop because his movements grow slower, and he peeks back at me. His forehead furrows, and his jaw looks sharper. Maybe it's the angle, but from where I'm standing, it's like a strange look passes over his face. It resembles concern, but at the same time, it feels like bewilderment, like he's confused. But what is he confused about? The way he cocks his head and stares at me, it's almost like he's confused about his reaction to me. Not really sure. But I'm curious to find out.

"Everything okay over there?"

"Yeah, of course." I pick up my pace and fall in line next to him.

Together, in step with one another, we make our way back into the clearing, and as soon as I do, my lids blink against the harsh brightness of the early morning light. I didn't realize how dark it was on the path.

As my vision adjusts, I notice where Cain is leading me. We are headed toward the parked Wrangler.

I swear I didn't notice it before. "Was it here before?" I mutter.

"What?" He must notice my confusion because he halts his steps and looks at me with narrowed eyes.

"Was that always there?" I lift my hand and point at the car.

"Yeah. Why?"

My nose scrunches. "I didn't see it before."

"That's because you didn't enter from this path." His hand reaches out and points in the opposite direction. "That's where you entered." A dense cluster of trees stands in that location. The immense trunks and green pines stretching out into the horizon.

"Oh. I guess I didn't realize where we were going, huh?"

His response is a soft chuckle, low enough that I'm not sure I actually heard it. "Yeah, how did you find me anyway?"

His question catches me off guard. "I wasn't looking for you," I admit.

"What do you mean?"

"The path by my house. I took it for—" Now I feel dumb. I got lost, and now he knows.

"For what?"

I grimace. "Exercise."

"You have to be more careful," he snaps, and then his face softens. "It's dangerous here. The paths don't all connect."

"And? I don't understand the big deal. I got lost. So what? I have been lost before and figured it out. I just would have again, right?"

"You could have gotten lost forever."

His eyes are wide. He moves closer and reaches his hand out, but then he stops himself. Cain must think better of touching me. He stands there. Looking up at the sky as if he's willing it to open up and give him the words to say, then I see him swallow. "Come on, let's go. We have a short amount of time and a lot to see."

I follow him, feeling like a lamb walking toward the slaughter. Which makes zero sense, but I feel off-kilter.

Maybe it was the run-in with the woman.

Or maybe it's something else, but as he continues to walk and I trail behind, I don't have time to think about it.

Instead, I feel thankful that I have my backpack on me with my recorder in it. I didn't know we would be starting this early.

I also didn't know I would bump into him on my walk. A chill runs down my spine at his earlier words.

"You say you were inspired by *Brave New World*?"

"Yes, when I was younger, I read Huxley and imagined a place that was better. A place where people could thrive, and so I came up with the idea for The Elysian. When I first brainstormed the concept, I wanted to prove Huxley wrong. That technology wasn't inherently evil. That there was a way to achieve the goals without corruption. But when I began to plan, technology hadn't caught up to my ideas, but now it has. We *can* create a close to perfect place to live."

"There is no such thing as perfect," I tease, my voice soft and playful.

"That may be the case, but we can get pretty damn close." His tone is velvety, making the corner of my mouth twist up.

I rock back and forth on my heel. "How do you figure?"

"Come with me, and I'll show you." This is one of those moments. One of those turning points you read about in books and see in movies. Where the hero or heroine knows that if they take the hand and follow, their life will never be the same.

That's how I feel when Cain Archer points in the direction of the Jeep Wrangler with an outstretched hand and wants me to follow him.

And I want to.

I take his outstretched hand and let his fingers wrap around mine. When our skin touches, I swear chills actually run down my body.

I'm not sure if I'm excited, nervous, or scared.

I look up so that my gaze meets his, and he has a weird look on his face.

I've only known him for a day, so I don't know him at all. Only spent one dinner speaking to him, so I'm not surprised when I can't pinpoint the look he has.

It's almost as if he's as confused as I am. Not that it makes any sense, but that's the look he's giving me. Like he's not sure what this is between us either. Which makes me think he feels something, too.

An instant attraction?

When Cain gets in the car, we drive off. "From edge to edge, the compound is about a forty-five-minute drive." His voice is soothing. I enjoy it. I could listen to him speak for hours.

"I didn't realize it was so big."

"You came in through a separate entrance. That will be closed off eventually. The entire compound will be gated. Only those who are authorized will be allowed to enter. A city behind walls."

"It's a really interesting concept. Do you think people will leave?" I ask.

"Of course, but the idea is that once you're inside the walls, you would be safe, and you wouldn't need or want for anything. It's safe and relaxing. Everything the residence will ever need will be set within the walls. If they choose to leave, there are towns outside the compound. There is also access to planes and helicopters if you want to travel. But here inside, everything is completely monitored. When you walk into the restaurants, the staff will already know what you want because of your key.

"The coding will inform them of your likes and dislikes. It's the same for the housing. The system will keep a record of your moods, depending upon different things, and it will make sure it changes the settings of your house to try to give you the most optimal experience."

His words shock me. "Isn't that a bit controlling?"

"Some might say controlling, and others might say innovative. Why should we live lives in which we're not happy?"

"And do you think that having the right temperature will make you happy?"

"Scientifically, yes. Over time, a system can learn how to manipulate one's happiness." There is a pitch in his voice I can't put my finger on. It's almost eerie.

"But couldn't one say that's not true happiness?" I counter.

"I guess they could, but isn't an artificial happiness better than nothing?"

"I'm not sure." We're both quiet as he continues to drive. Finally, I break the silence. "Is that what you're building here, artificial happiness?"

"In a way," he says, as if this is a completely normal and mundane conversation.

"And I'm sure with the wall, this might be the safest place on earth."

His head turns to me while driving. "Not necessarily." Then he looks back at the road.

"What do you mean? These walls will keep the monsters out?"

I watch him from where I'm sitting, his hands gripping the wheel. "And what if the monsters are already inside?" The grip he has tightens as he maneuvers down the road.

"I'm sure we would see them coming," I joke because this whole topic is starting to make my skin form goose bumps.

"Monsters wear different faces." This time when I shiver, it is from fear. He's right. The walls might keep out bad influences, but what if they're already inside? "They walk among you every day and you never know it. Don't be fooled by a false sense of security. It will be your downfall."

I don't necessarily agree with what he is saying. He's probably just being overprotective, which I can respect. He cares a lot about this place, so why shouldn't he be overprotective? But something about his tone makes me wonder what horrors he's had to deal with because it feels like he's speaking from experience.

I need to learn more about him to find out where these strange actions come from.

"Which I guess brings us to a valid point. What type of security will you be implementing?" I cock my head. "For example. That reporter. She wasn't supposed to be here, right? That's what you said, so how did she get in?"

From where I sit, I can see his knuckles have now turned white from how hard he's clenching the wheel. He is getting agitated, and internally, I shrink back from him.

But then I think about it. I understand the implications of word getting out about how easy it was for one woman to sneak in. That wouldn't look good for potential buyers.

"What are you going to do about that breach of security?"

"The head of security will be fired, and we'll bring in someone capable," he grits out.

"But what about the guy? Does he have family?"

"It doesn't matter," Cain snaps. His jaw looks tight, and his shoulders are stiff. "His family is not my problem. The Elysian is only as good as its security since that's what we're selling. A secure, safe, fully immersive living experience."

"And what will this security system be . . . ?" I make my voice playful. I sense that he realizes things have gotten intense, and I'm relieved when he cracks a smile.

"Well, I really can't tell you that because then it wouldn't be secure, but I can guarantee there will be the highest level of security."

"And what about checks and balances? How are you selecting the residents? What is their say in the way the community will run?"

"The residents will have to have a full background check and answer questions. There'll be many interviews and tests to see if this is the right location for them."

"And what type of test are you looking for them to complete? What are you looking for in the ideal resident?"

"Now that's a question I'm not prepared to answer at this time." With that, Cain continues to drive me around The Elysian.

"This is the town center. When you enter, the built-in computer systems will know you have arrived from the key you carry. The key has all your information and will tell the surrounding buildings and staff how to adapt to your presence. Each light and building entrance, has built-in AI facial recognition, and this will allow the vendors that are here to cater the experience. For example, when you go into a restaurant, the staff will already know your allergies, your likes and dislikes."

Cain parks the car, then turns to face me. "Do you have everything you need?"

I tap my backpack. "I do. I'm a reporter not a photographer—"

"We already provided the approved pictures." His voice is terse, and I know he's still annoyed about earlier. I mentally chide myself for continuing to bring it up. Not a good start to my tour.

"Oh, yeah, that makes sense. But I do have my recorder. If that's okay."

"No recording devices."

I bite my lip. Maybe the damage is done. Maybe I'm getting the "other" Cain today. Mr. Hyde.

"Oh." I open my backpack and start to rummage for a notebook. "Can I jot down notes, though?"

"Yes."

I grimace at the one-word answer. "Okay, then I'll do that. Ready when you are."

"Come on." Cain gets out of the car, and I scurry to get out, as well, and fall into step with him. My chest heaves as I make my way to catch up. His legs are longer, so I have to take extra strides, but when I do finally make my way to him, together, we start walking into what is going to be the town center.

It's not fully built up yet. Stores line the streets, the structures are up, but there are no awnings yet.

The store fronts are similar to the rest of the compound. Except instead of mirrors, glass is used to give it a clean, cutting-edge look.

With each step I take in the area, from the flowers blooming in planters to the geometric statue standing tall and beautiful in the middle of the road.

Moving to stand in front of it, he proceeds to tell me of its significance. Its relevance to the *Brave New World*. Huxley's story, or a summary of his story, is the pinnacle of the design.

He then walks me to a door.

The interesting thing is there's no handle, but the moment we approach, he lifts his wrist.

I don't see anything on his wrist, but the door opens, nonetheless.

"How did you do that?" I stare—okay, gawk—at his wrist.

"There's a chip embedded in my skin." He raises it, and I take his wrist in my hand, lifting it to my face to see if I can see it.

There is nothing there.

I run my thumb over the skin, and I hear a sighing sound. Looking up, I notice his chest rising and falling as he watches me. "Is that even safe?" I whisper, still touching his skin.

"It's perfectly safe."

Realizing I have been holding him for far too long, I drop his wrist and take a step back. "That is not something I would ever do," I mumble under my breath.

"Then you wouldn't have to." His voice is nonchalant, and he starts to walk again.

"That's not something everyone has to do?" 'Cause that would suck.

"Of course not."

"Oh."

He looks over his shoulder. "We have other options."

"Such as?"

"A piece of jewelry. A credit card key in your wallet. Layla, you will find that I can be very innovative." The way he looks at me and says my name has my knees wobbling.

Why does he have to be so handsome? Head in the game, Layla. You aren't here for a romantic love affair. Just do your job and interview the man.

I let out a cough and take a step inside the building. As I suspected, the sound of my foot hitting what appears to be marble is muffled. "Am I the only one who thinks it's creepy that there are no footsteps?"

"Well, actually, now that you mention it, that is a feature that is set to the individual."

"Excuse me?"

"Yes, so the chip in my hand says I want quiet."

"But what if you're with someone like me? There's no way that can work. What if I say I don't want quiet, and you say you do? Who would win?"

Cain smiles, and when he smiles, it's like the sun has risen from beneath a cloud and has illuminated the whole sky. I want to bask in his warmth. I feel like he doesn't do this often, and when he does, it's truly special and meets his eyes.

"Has anybody ever told you that you can be a complete pain in the ass?"

"Is that comment on the record?"

Now, he chuckles, and I think I'm completely at a loss of what to say because the sound does crazy things to my insides.

Is this normal?

Can you meet someone and instantly feel a connection?

I'm not stupid enough to think it's love. Who believes in love at first sight anyway? Obviously, it's insta-lust, but it still feels like more than that.

It feels important.

Like when he looks at me, my words matter.

I matter.

This isn't a good line of thought for right now, so giving myself a little shake, I take another step.

The furniture in the foyer of whatever this building will be is sparse.

Like the outside of the building, it's floor-to-ceiling windows. And again, the dark wood blends into the mountain side. It's very tranquil, and I bet if I told the computer system that I want the sound of running water, it would happen. "What if a homeowner wanted a certain sound or ambience?"

"Well, then we'd get that for them." And the way he says it is so matter-of-fact, it's as if there's nothing he can't do. I'm not sure if it's his real personality coming out or if it's an arrogance about this place.

"Let me show you the amenities."

"Okay. Should I be scared? Is the house going to be able to change my clothes for me? Maybe read my mind. Work me out?"

"Well, now that you mention it . . ."

"Really?"

"No," he deadpans. "But speaking of working out, most of the private residences have the capabilities of having their own gym. Some homeowners prefer to go to a gym-like atmosphere, so down the hall in the clubhouse, there is a full functioning gym."

He proceeds to take me down a long hallway, and I expect the hallway to lead to a gym, but what it leads to is a room that is virtually outside.

There are no walls. There are no doors. The hallway just opens into a sun-drenched solarium.

There's still glass in this large space, but it reminds me of a room in a zoo. The room where the butterflies are. Where they are free to fly as they please and you feel like you're in the rainforest. Where the elements are fully entwined, and everything feels real.

I keep walking, and he points, then he starts telling me about each piece of equipment that will be in each section of the room.

"When will everything be finished?"

"All of the town center is complete. We're just waiting for the furnishings, which should be here within the next few days."

"And you didn't want to wait to show me?"

"I thought you would like to see the transformation. Was I wrong?"

I shake my head. "No, you weren't wrong at all. I'd love to see each step of the process."

"Something tells me that you don't want just the big reveal. You like to figure it out. You don't want things handed to you easily."

It's like he understands me in a way no one has before. He nailed my whole personality in one sentence, and we've only had one dinner together.

The idea is slightly frightening. Would he understand me better than I understand myself if he got to know me?

Stop. It's not like he's going to get to know you. You're only here for a few more days, and then you'll never see him again.

That thought makes my stomach feel hollow.

"This way." He leads, cutting off my inner ramblings.

"Where to?" I ask.

"I'm going to show you where the restaurants and markets will be."

"Food? Now you're speaking my language. Lead the way."

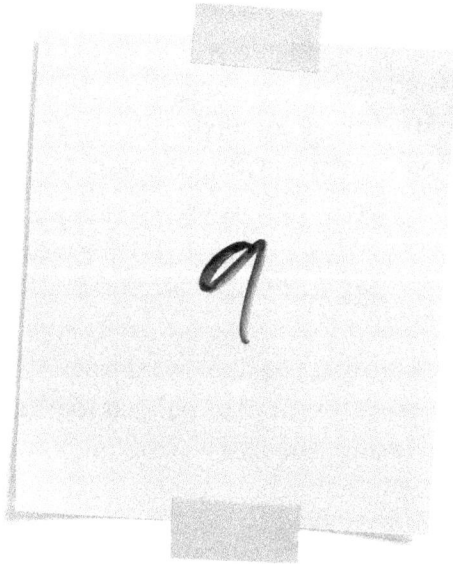

_9_

Layla

I have no idea where we are going, but the look he gives me, the little ghost of a smirk, leads me to believe I'll like it.

"Any hints?" I ask as I try my damnedest to keep pace with him as he strolls down the paved street.

I swear I'm huffing and puffing, arms cutting fast through the air to keep up, and he must notice because he slows his steps.

Now we walk on pace together. He's a little bit faster than me, but that's only because he's leading the way.

"All I can say is that you're going to enjoy it."

"Interesting. And how do you know what I enjoy?" From where he's walking, I can see his lips move, and I know he didn't miss the little undertone of flirtation in my voice.

"Will you just trust me?" he asks, and my heart beats faster in my chest.

"How can I trust you? I don't even know you. Remember what you said?"

"And what is it I said?"

"That monsters hide in plain sight," I answer.

He stops short at my words, and I regret them instantaneously. His body pivots, and then he is standing in front of me. Narrow eyes. Stiff back. Jaw locked.

He doesn't like my joke.

No, it's more than that . . .

But what?

I can't place it. Is he angry? But why?

Then Mara's words resurface.

She warned me about him.

I have seen tiny inklings of that man, but the way he looks down at me now makes me wonder if her words were accurate and the man I met at dinner was the lie.

"You're right," he says, shocking me. "You don't know me. And you shouldn't trust me."

"I didn't mean it like—" I start to say.

"No, Layla, listen to me. In life, you will think you know someone, but you can never know what lies beneath the surface."

He drills me with his stare, and I feel like, for a moment, I'm the other woman. And now I understand why she scurried away.

If I were someone else, I might flinch, but I haven't gotten where I am by backing down or showing fear, and I certainly won't become the journalist I want to be if I do.

"You don't have to worry about me, Mr. Archer."

"Cain," he corrects.

"Cain." I follow. "I might seem innocent, but I can promise you I'm not. Now, let's stop talking about this and show me this mystery location."

"You'll like it." Rays of sunlight stream down from the sky and cast a shadow over his face. It makes him look almost sinister. A handsome devil luring me. To what? I don't know, but I welcome the temptation.

"I better because you really hyped it up. I'd hate for it to be a letdown." I shrug, but I allow my lips to spread wide, letting him know that whatever just transpired is over, and I won't be holding it against him for my interview. I'm not even lying to myself. I can't imagine what it takes to build a city. Let alone one like this.

All the moving components. If I were him, I'd be frustrated, too.

"It's not," he finally answers, and I nod.

"Then show me."

Cain then turns around, breaking our connection, and I have to refrain from speeding up so I can be next to him again. We walk past a few doors, none of them open, and I assume that whatever is inside isn't ready yet.

When we reach a large, black double door that sits in the middle of the block, Cain steps up to it, lifts his wrist, and the chip in his hand must unlock it. The doors open automatically, both at the same time.

He lets me pass him, and when I go inside, my mouth drops open.

The ceilings are high, over two stories, and they're all glass. It's like an atrium. But that's not what has my mouth hanging open. This building is complete, and now I know why he brought me here.

"What is this place? Paradise?" I jest, my voice rising in pitch with amusement.

"For some." His voice is monotone.

This is not his idea of paradise, but I ask anyway. "And for you?" I want to know everything about him.

"I enjoy seeing people enjoying my vision." I can see that about him. Every second since I've met him, he's been observing me. And when I react, I've seen the way his lips tip up. He likes not only watching me, but it's almost like he feeds off my reactions.

I pucker my lips playfully. "Not much for games?"

"What gave me away?" he chides as I take a step farther into the mammoth-sized space. "This is the community center."

"Aka paradise on earth."

"If that's how you want to write it up, I won't object." This time, his voice simmers with emotion. It's deep, crisp, and clear. Not over the top, but I can tell he wants, no *needs* me to write about this.

"Hell, no, you won't. This alone will sell out your city."

He proudly nods, and I let my gaze dart across the room.

Everything is here. Bowling. Games. Pool. Air hockey. A full bar. This is like an amusement park for adults. It must have cost a fortune. No stone is unturned. They have everything, even the walls are bright with splashes of neon pink, neon yellow, and blue. It's almost sensory overload, but somehow, it works. It's elegant. All the furniture is futuristic looking. White, modern tables with clear Lucite chairs sit at one end of the space. A long, black bar with clear stools sits on the other side.

This place is fantastic.

"Do you want to try out anything?" he asks.

"Do leopards have freaking spots?" I deadpan.

"I take it that's a yes."

"It's actually a *hell yes*." My excitement must be contagious because now Cain laughs, and his smile is wide and genuine. Even his eyes look different.

He looks younger now. More at peace. And the idea of seeing him like this for a little bit longer has me feeling like a kid who just entered an arcade, ready to play all the games.

"Let's go."

I move forward, but when he doesn't follow right away, I grab his hand. His hand is still beneath mine at first, and I lift my chin to look at him. He's staring at our entwined fingers.

"Come on. Let's go." This time when I speak, his hand loosens.

"Lead the way," he commands, so I do.

I lead him straight to the bowling alley. Cain sets to work turning everything on. I grab a ball when it comes up the tunnel. "Why is this open already? I'm surprised."

"For the team working here."

"You have this whole building open so that the construction team can let off steam?"

"I do."

He is so nonchalant when he says it, as if he doesn't realize what a big deal this is. How not everyone would care about their workers.

How this proves he's not like the rumors.

Or maybe I'm grasping, but I don't think I am.

Once Cain does whatever he needs to do to get the board turned on and the pins down, I move toward where the balls are. I lift one, then another, trying to find the perfect weight for me.

Cain walks over like he doesn't have a care in the world. I wonder how accurate this portrayal is. I realize as I watch him that I could spend endless hours a day observing him.

It's for the article.

I'm so full of crap.

Sure, I want to believe that. I'm totally analyzing his every move, his every smile, his every laugh for an article.

Who am I trying to fool?

Not me.

None of that is true. I'm curious about the man for who he is, not for what he's built. He steps up to where I'm standing. "Do you need help finding a ball?"

"No. I found one."

"Good. You start."

With my ball in my hand, I walk to the line on the floor. The pins are down and ready for me to throw.

I haven't played in years, but growing up, my parents were in a league. Surprisingly, they took me with them.

I used to love to bowl, and I'm actually pretty decent at it. Or I was good at one point. I'm about to see if it's like riding a bike.

I don't tell him that I used to bowl before I'm pulling back my arm and letting my ball wisp through the air.

It rolls on the lane, then it smashes dead center in the middle of the pins.

The sound is jarring amongst the silence. Still standing at the line, I wait as they start to topple. One pin, two, and then almost all of them fall. When they are done moving, there is only one still standing in each of the corners. A 7-10 split. Shit, guess I am a little rusty.

I stretch my arms as I wait for my ball to come back to me.

When the sound starts to rumble through the tunnel and it resurfaces, I grab it, walk back to my starting location, pull back, aim, and let go.

This time, I kick it just right, knocking both remaining pins down.

"Nice."

"Beginner's luck." I shrug.

"Something tells me that statement isn't accurate at all."

I smile at his retort, lift my hand, and signal for him to go. Stepping out of the way, I take a seat on the white leather bench.

I watch as he grabs a ball, walks up, and throws. I'm not at all surprised that he's amazing at this, as well.

Strike.

74

"Are you amazing at everything you do?" I ask before I can stop myself.

"I don't know. What do you think?" He smirks.

Butterflies swarm in my belly. "I think you might be. I think you are definitely good at this, and that's why you have a bowling alley here."

"Our secret." He winks at me.

I melt.

Die.

I'm a puddle on the floor.

Trying to rein in my crazy emotions, I push them down, but I can't help but flirt with him some more the way his eyes are sparkling at me. "Hmm, I don't know. This could make an interesting turn to my story. The headline would read 'Amazing Architect, Brilliant Bowler.'"

"What do you want for your silence?" I hear the tease in his voice.

It makes me give him a smile, but mine is sly. "You can't afford it." I wink back at him, then shimmy off with a wiggle.

This time, I pay extra close attention and throw a strike, then jump up and down, cheering for myself.

When I am done throwing a mini party, I look over at Cain. I can see how amused he is. He's entertained by me. I can also see the way his brows pinch together in thought every once in a while. But I don't dwell on it. In this space, I feel great. I feel young again.

I feel like this isn't an assignment for a job to keep a roof over my head. I'm just having fun with a friend.

The whole idea is a little overwhelming.

I have been here for almost two days, and I've taken almost no notes. But I've had fun. Maybe that's the key. Maybe when I sit down to write my piece, I can remember this place as the place that had me smiling, relaxing, and feeling one with nature. Couple that with also having every amenity anyone would need.

We continue to play the whole set, and it's neck and neck. But with the final pin knocked down, I jump up, screaming, "I won!"

I have reverted back to being a child, and by the way he gleams at me, I'm sure he let me win.

I don't care, though. It's all for fun, and I had that in spades. And although he didn't really tell me anything important in the last hour, I feel like I was actually immersed in knowledge about him.

Just not the type of stuff I can use in my article, but the day is young, and I have time to find out more.

"Now what?" he asks.

I place my hand on my hip and incline my head. "You want more?"

"Well, I can't let it end like this." His voice is calm, his gaze steady, but he's challenging me.

Now it's my turn to be playful. "With you losing?"

He leans in toward me as if to tell me a secret. "Obviously. That's not good for my reputation."

"Definitely not." I nod, stepping closer to him. "You can't let anyone know you let me win."

"I didn't let you win."

I cross my hands over my chest and roll my eyes. "Sure."

"I didn't."

"I bet you tell that to all the girls."

His head inclines down, his hair falling over his eyes. "Actually, I tell that to none of the girls."

"Only me?"

"Only you." His words sound huskier now, and for a second, I forget what we are talking about.

I give myself a shake and point at the air hockey table. "Double or nothing?"

"Double or nothing."

And then we are at it again, playing to see who wins. And again, I'm either a champ of beginner's luck with this game, or it's rigged, too. I don't let on to his play at first, but then to be silly, I start to play, too. Purposely missing shots.

We both keep this up until I'm bubbling over with laughter, and he seems amused.

When the game is over, and I am the victor again, he leads me to the darts.

"Triple or nothing?" I jest.

"You know me too well."

"Yet I don't know you at all. And you don't know I have never thrown a dart."

He moves closer, standing behind me to help straighten my wrist and teach me how to throw.

He's close enough I can smell him.

Tingles rush over my body.

I feel hot all over.

His hand tightens on my wrist but in a way that only furthers my need. I like his dominating attitude. "How is this going to help me write my article?"

His mouth runs over the shell of my ear, sending chills down my spine. My eyes close and I have to hold in a moan. "You're going to sell this. Right here. How do you feel?"

"Entertained."

He bites at my ear. "Wrong word choice."

"Exhilarated." I can feel him smile against my ear.

"Better. Sell The Elysian, Layla. Make me never want to leave."

I try to string out a sentence explaining how I feel, but at the moment, it's almost impossible.

I close my eyes, open my mouth, and speak from my heart.

"This place makes me feel alive for the first time ever. The serenity of the spaces, how it's one with nature. I never feel like I'm cooped up and locked away in a home. I honestly feel more at home here than I have anywhere else. There's an integrity to the spaces you created here. I never want to leave."

By the time I'm done, I'm practically shaking from the need he elicits in me. Cain turns me around and places a sweet, gentle kiss on my cheek.

"Good girl."

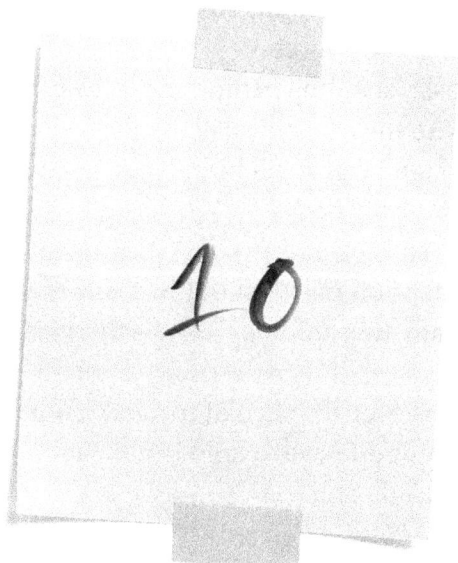

10

Layla

Yesterday was wonderful.

After the games, we spent the rest of the time eating. Cain thought of everything. Including having every type of fun bar food brought to us.

I can't remember the last time I had that much fun with someone.

Now the early morning sunlight gleams in through the floor-to-ceiling windows in my bedroom. My hand reaches up to scrub at my eyes, forcing them open to begin my day.

I only have a few days left here, and I have barely scratched the surface of this place.

Sure, I have spent time with Cain, but other than the town center and community house, I haven't seen very much.

How will I spend the remaining time here?

Maybe I need someone else to show me the grounds. When Cain Archer is around, I have a hard time concentrating on anything else.

I'm not ready, nor do I want to leave this place—or him—and that worries me.

I don't know him at all.

He might be flirtatious with me, but that doesn't mean anything. I am supposed to be listening, watching, and learning about this utopian town, and instead, I'm too busy micromanaging the fact that he might be sending me mixed signals.

One minute, I think he's attracted to me like I'm attracted to him, and the next, everything is different. He's all business.

I let out a large sigh and reach my arm out to grab my laptop that's sitting next to my bed.

I open up my notes in Word.

Nothing. There's also nothing on my recorder.

This is going to be fun when it's time to write.

Instead of jotting down notes from yesterday, I find myself opening up my browser search engine and typing in Cain Archer's name.

This time, I know not to look for anything scandalous, so instead, I type in The Elysian along with his name.

His picture comes up, and instantly I regret it. How can I be objective in the article when I'm so attracted to the man?

I pull out my phone and type in his name again.

The strange thing is, on my computer that's tied into the house's Wi-Fi, nothing but professional stories come up. But on my phone, while on the open 5G, a boatload of other stories emerge.

The details I wanted earlier are now available to me.

Despite the fact that I know I shouldn't be doing this, I still find myself clicking the buttons to dig deeper into the strange man. But unlike last time when I focused on his career, this time, I fall down the dark hole.

A path I shouldn't go down.

I start following a trail about his past relationships.

But the strange thing is, for a man of his caliber, I still don't find anything. How can a man as handsome as him have no sordid details of a relationship? I see pictures of him at events, but every time, there's a different woman on his arm.

Never the same woman, which screams commitment-phobe. Something must be wrong with him.

This is not the type of man you hang a dream on or the type of man you fantasize about marrying and having children with.

Hell, I'm not even sure if he's the type of man you fantasize about having a one-night stand with because it seems he won't even stay the hour.

If these women meant anything to him other than a quick screw, wouldn't they be photographed more than once? He's probably the type of guy to fuck you in the foyer of your apartment and never step inside.

Although for some reason, even thinking of this has my stomach fluttering and my core clenching. *No. Layla, this is not the type of man you want.*

Plus, more importantly, I cannot harbor feelings for someone I'm leaving in a few days.

Placing the phone down, I look over at the clock and realize I overslept. Cain will be here shortly, and I need to get ready still. I'm not sure what is on tap for the day, but I figure it probably will be a long day seeing as yesterday was.

I don't want to be uncomfortable, but I also don't want to look like I just rolled out of bed.

Seeing as he will be here in the next thirty minutes, I don't have time to wash my hair, so I head into the shower and only turn on the body sprays.

Then, with the speed of a race car driver, I lather up soap and wash super-fast.

My efficiency at rushing is an art.

The number of times I have almost been late to work is not something I should be proud of, but I have become very good at being low maintenance.

The fact is, normally, I don't oversleep. I'm usually late because I'm busy researching ideas for articles I want to pitch.

Today, I overslept because I spent the night tossing and turning. Why?

Because I couldn't get that damn man out of my head.

All I did the whole night was scrutinize every comment he said and the last part that kept me up all night . . .

Good girl.

Yep. One line and I'm a complete goner.

I'm that woman, the woman who goes gaga for a man who calls her a good girl.

The crazy part is, I didn't expect to go weak in the knees over this.

I had no concept that I would be affected by these words, but my knees went weak, my stomach fluttered, and my damn core clenched.

Now I know I'm screwed because if I don't kiss this man before I go, something tells me I'll regret it for the rest of my life.

Maybe a tad overdramatic, but I don't care right now. I'm too curious for my own good.

Once I'm clean, I hop out of the shower, run a brush through my hair, and throw on a light dusting of makeup.

I opt for another light summer dress, jean jacket, and my trusty flats. Professional, yet not trying too hard. I go to grab my notebook when I hear the doorbell.

I know it's him.

Taking a deep breath, I try to calm the nervous energy that has started to pump through my veins.

When I feel like I have a handle on myself, I step over to the door and throw it open.

"Hey," I say as I stand awkwardly in the foyer.

"Hey yourself."

Moving out of the way, he steps into the foyer once I give him room to pass. His presence feels all-encompassing. He's larger than life in this small space, which is ironic because this house isn't small at all. "Sleep well?"

"Like a baby." My hand lifts to the top of my head, and I push down the hair, afraid it's a mess, hence his comment. He cocks his head at me, and his lips tip up on the right side.

"Babies are actually terrible sleepers." He drills me with his stare, and I know he's trying to read me.

"Why would you say that?" I am lying. I'm not sure how he can tell, but I'm curious to find out.

"I am really good at reading people." Matter-of-fact. Arrogance dripping, but still, I find it sexy. I have some serious problems.

"What do you mean?" I ask.

"I'm not good at all things with people, but telling if someone is lying is something I'm extremely good at."

"And just what *aren't* you good at? We didn't find anything yesterday."

"Emotions." That has me cocking my head at his admittance. I didn't expect him to admit to being bad at anything.

"Care to elaborate?"

"Not particularly." His hand lifts, and he fingers a loose tendril of hair that has fallen past my ears and is now hanging over my cheek, proving his point: I have bed head. "I'd like to get back to the original question, which was you didn't sleep well."

This time he says it as a statement not a question. He knows I lied, and there's no way around it.

I let out a long, drawn-out sigh. "I tossed and turned."

"Any particular reason?"

My eyes go wider than I wanted to show when I quickly rush out a, "Nope."

He quirks an eyebrow at me. "Interesting."

"What does that mean?"

"Nothing." He points at the door. "You ready?"

"I am."

"Good, because we have a long day."

I nod, lift my bag higher on my shoulder, turn toward the door, and head outside.

It's still early. Only 9:00 a.m.

The air is still slightly damp from the early morning fog. There's a slight chill in the air, which makes me happy, but I grabbed the jean jacket because I know how it is in the mountains. In a few hours, the temperature will rise, and I'll be happy that I have on the dress.

Today, I don't need prompting to go straight to the Wrangler. Today, the doors are on. Which I'm thankful for.

I'm not surprised when he helps me get in. Instead, I just linger in the feeling of his hand touching mine.

I'm happy that he doesn't acknowledge that my cheeks are probably red from the heat crawling down my face, but luckily, Cain Archer is a gentleman, even if his reputation pictured with a different woman every night, says otherwise.

Once in the car, I fasten my seat belt, and then Cain turns the car on. We drive in the opposite direction as we did the day before and the day before that. "And where exactly are we off to today?"

"We're going to check out the completed model homes."

"Are these ones already equipped with AI?"

"They are. Of course, what you'll be seeing is the AI that's compatible with me, but once the homeowner moves in, we will customize the program for each individual resident."

My level of excitement can barely be contained as we drive into what looks like a mountain. Again, there are no homes, but that's when I see a slight glimmer.

He pulls in front of it, and the more I squint and the closer we get, the more I realize that this is a fully mirrored home. This isn't like the main building, which is half wood, half mirrors. Nor is this like the town center or the community center.

There's no frame. It's not just floor-to-ceiling windows with an illusion; this is a fully mirrored building. This is one hundred percent integrated to reflect the wilderness around it. I cannot find words to describe the feeling I get looking at this modern frame that feels like it floats in the space, part dream and part reality.

I hear a chuckle from beside me, and I pull my gaze away, realizing he is staring at me.

"This is spectacular," I say in awe.

As soon as the car rolls into park, I jump out.

He's right beside me a moment later.

With my mouth still open—at this point, it's a miracle I haven't swallowed a fly—I move closer. "Are we going in?" I sound like an idiot, but my brain isn't functioning properly right now.

"That's the plan."

"Cain?" I turn toward him. He's standing beside me but not facing the home. Nope, he's watching me intently. Normally, I would feel like I'm a speck on a microscope, but I don't. Not with the way he stares at me. Instead, my heart starts to pump harder. My earlier assessment of him needing to see my reaction, of experiencing joy, is confirmed by the soft look in his eyes as he stares.

"Yeah."

"This is—" I stop because I don't know what else to say. There are no words to say. In the car, it was amazing, but outside, standing in front of it, I just couldn't come up with words. For someone who writes for a living, it's crazy that I'm at a loss.

"Come on."

Cain starts to walk, and as my eyes adjust to the décor, I can see we are making our way up a pathway. Before, it just looked like rocks. He stops eventually and lifts his hand, and as if by magic, the mirrored door opens.

"Welcome home, Mr. Archer," a voice says as we walk into the house.

"Is that the house?" I whisper as if the house can hear me.

"Yes," he answers.

"Is it like Jarvis from *Iron Man*?"

He chuckles. "That is exactly what it's like."

"Wow. Are you like Tony Stark?"

He shakes his head at me. "I sure fucking hope not."

"Why not? This is a talking house. Crazy tech all around you . . ."

"I'm no superhero, Layla." His eyes look darker, and I'm not sure why, but I shrug it off. "This is more like Alexa on crack. Play music."

A sad, peaceful song comes on. "Do you have a playlist?"

"I do, actually. It's part of the opening paperwork. Different songs have different meanings. Eventually, the house learns your biometrics, which will make it anticipate and learn your moods, and when it figures it out, it plays songs that fit your mood."

"How does it know?"

"It can hear the way you speak, and it learns your moods from that. When you speak, the pitch and cadence change. When you talk, whether you're angry, sad, or happy, it will analyze it, and it plays the music based upon how you feel."

"What do you do with this information?"

"If you're asking if we are selling it, we aren't. This is just part of the experience in order for this to be the most self-sufficient, fully running AI in the country. We need this data; we don't sell it. We don't give it to anyone. This data is yours and yours alone."

"I sure hope so. That would be creepy."

"Come on. Let me show you the rest of the house, and you will see that although it's a little larger than the one you're staying in, it's basically the same concept. The only difference is everything is catered to the main homeowner."

He leads me through the house with the same floor-to-ceiling windows, the same modern technology, the same modern furniture, the same all-white canvas. He takes me into the bathroom, and it replicates mine, the only difference being the panel on the wall.

He points at it. "Same as yours. The difference is when I tell the house that I'm ready to take a shower, it will ask me questions in the beginning. Once it gets to know me, it will just settle on what it knows I like."

I take a step forward, looking over the space as I do. "The whole entire house is virtually hands-free?"

"Yes and no."

"Examples?" Pivoting my feet, I glance back in his direction.

Cain lifts his hand, a finger pointing up. "It won't cook your food."

"That's a letdown for those of us without culinary skills."

"Actually, it's a bit more complicated than that. Let me show you." His words are abrupt as he breaks our connection and heads across the living room.

I follow Cain into the kitchen, and when we get there, he opens the fridge. "When I say it won't cook your own food, it will, in fact, cook your food for you. The difference is that it can't food prep. Nor can it do a fancy sauté, braise, or flip your food, etc. But what it can do is you can tell it the time, the temperature you want, and it will alert you when it's done and turn off the stove."

"That's still pretty badass."

"Thank you," he says proudly.

We continue to walk around. He points at each device, explaining how it works. By the time we step out, my head is spinning. There is so much to write down.

Together, we step out of the model home, and as we start to walk toward another home, a car pulls up.

"Expecting company?"

"No," he says, his eyes narrowing.

"Who's that?" I ask.

"It's one of our on-site sales reps. Looks like he is doing a walk-through."

The man is at the car door, and a couple steps out. Cain stops, staring directly at the couple. From across the gravel, I see the woman. She's facing in our direction. There is something familiar about her. I narrow my eyes but can't place it. Then it hits me. "Isn't that the photographer?"

"No."

"Yes. I think it is. Imagine her hair pulled back with a baseball cap and glasses . . . I think it is her."

"You're wrong. But it doesn't matter, let's go. It's too crowded here. We can come back and see this home later."

He pulls me toward the car. I'm shocked by the fact that he's holding my arm but also how hard his grip is on my elbow.

As I step in and sit down and wait for Cain to get in the car, I look at the woman. She is still staring intently at Cain. Weird. The way she looks at him makes chills break out on my legs.

Why is she looking at him like that? Her reaction to him is strange.

The woman is gawking and not like he's the hottest thing she's ever seen. The woman appears almost nervous, or maybe it's anticipation. It's as if she's waiting for him to do something, say something to her.

Before I can press Cain on the woman, he's pulling the car away faster than normal, kicking up gravel as we go.

"Let's grab food. I bet you're hungry." At that, my stomach growls, giving me away. No need to lie.

"Yep." I never did eat breakfast. "Where to now?"

"We're going to one of the restaurants on the premises. Right now, it's open to the staff for breakfast, lunch, and dinner. All the staff have implants or bracelets. And for the time being, the AI is practicing running off the information we fed into the computers. That way, by the time the residents move in, we'll know it's fully functioning."

"And does the restaurant have staff?" I ask, now watching the road as we drive. The trees are beautiful here. I don't think I will ever get over how lush and green it is. I'm used to the city. Sure, I didn't grow up in the city, but I've been there since I graduated from high school. There aren't many towering pine trees to marvel over.

"The staff at the restaurant is minimal. You'll see shortly, but have you ever been to a conveyor belt sushi restaurant?"

"Yes."

"So that's what this restaurant is like. It's like a five-star conveyor belt restaurant."

I turn back to him. He's looking at the road, so I can't tell if he's teasing me, but from my angle, there is no sign that he is being anything but forthcoming.

"How does that even work? Who's in the back? Who's cooking the food? Not a robot, I hope."

"Well, obviously, we have a chef, a sous chef, and a pastry chef. We have all the makings of a regular five-star restaurant. The difference is you can come in and order right away. This restaurant is for people who don't want the long dining experience. We have different restaurants on the premises. Some will be a six-course meal and others that are like this."

"Why so few staff?"

"Everything is automated, including the ordering process. This cuts down on cost, and by cutting down on staff, we limit who's coming and going, therefore more security."

"Makes sense."

It doesn't take long for us to pull in, and this time, there are no mirrors, and there's no glass. The restaurant is modern, but it's still built in the same fashion—to blend.

"No mirrors?"

He follows my gaze and shakes his head. "Not this time."

"It'll do." I playfully roll my eyes.

"I'll tell the architect," he jokes, and I laugh. This is the Cain I like. The playful one. The one who I, for some inexplicable reason, have been lucky enough to meet. Once the car is turned off, I throw open my door and move to stand. Cain walks up beside me, and together, we step inside. Once we do, a voice speaks.

"Welcome, Mr. Archer. Will you be joining us for brunch?"

I stumble back at the sound. My mouth drops open as I stare wide-eyed at the ceiling. From beside me, I hear Cain. "I will. It will be two of us today."

"A hostess will show you to your table," the AI coming from lord knows where says.

A second later, a tall, beautiful brunette comes over. She shows us to a table right by the glass, which grants us views of the chef's station. Then she excuses herself, and I notice the panel on the wall by the table has illuminated.

"Impressive. I'm a little disappointed though. Where's the robot?"

"I'll get right on that." He winks before pointing to the panel. "That's where we order. If you are a resident, your order can easily be given by just telling the computer that you want anything from your regular to something different to make the day special."

His voice is still serious. For a moment, I thought he was over the attitude. I notice right away that Cain is no longer acting like the man who showed me the model home. Ever since we left the model home, he's been cold and strange, and his answers have been a little short. Then I thought he had moved past it when he joked with me in the car, but I guess not because he's back with the salty attitude.

I wonder why he keeps flip-flopping.

Better yet, I wonder what brought the whole change of demeanor on.

What happened between the model home and now to change his attitude?

And that's when I remember the woman who stared at him and the way he drove off. The woman who I truly think was the trespasser.

Could that be it?

Am I reading too much into it? Or should I keep following what my gut says and dig in further when I have the right moment?

Some time passes from ordering, and we both sit in relative silence. I use the awkward quiet to jot in my journal to make notes on what I saw, and when the food comes, I hear a smash against the floor and notice Cain's dish lying broken. When I look up from the floor to meet his eyes, nothing about him is similar to the man I've gotten to know.

Cain jumps from the chair and storms off, and I have no idea what happened, but something tells me there is definitely more to this than meets the eye.

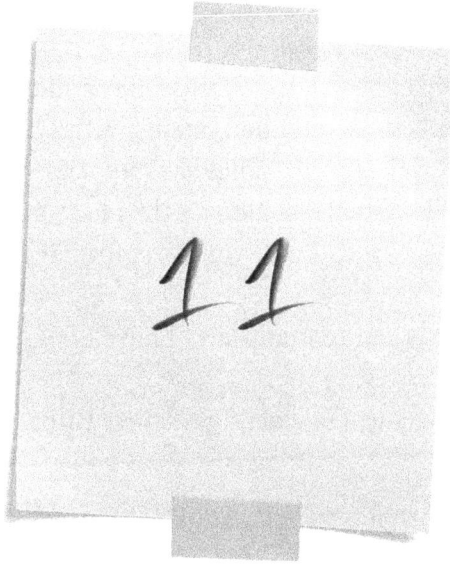

11

Cain

Did she notice the way I reacted earlier?

Is Layla aware of the woman at the home tour? It was like seeing a ghost.

But this ghost is real.

Fuck.

I can't breathe, and blackness veils my vision. Am I dying, having a heart attack?

Fuck. Fuck. Fuck!

I'm having a panic attack.

This can't be happening. I feel myself literally coming apart.

Seeing *her* shouldn't set me off.

Normally, it wouldn't, but . . . since meeting Layla, something has changed.

How can this one person undo years of trained behavior?

Everything is coming apart.

The darkness envelops me.

I'm losing my cool, and I need to get myself back in order.

But here lies the problem. Normally, I can. Order is never interrupted. I don't let chaos in.

However, when Layla is around, my emotions that are usually in check are all over the place.

It's not just the laughing. It's not just the smiling. I'm angry, too.

For as long as I can remember, my anger has been a pot of water, simmering but controllable. Ever since she stepped into my life, my emotions, ones I should control, are all over the place, and now I'm boiling over. It should be easy to calm down. It's something I've mastered my whole life, but nope.

Layla has me tied up in knots, and I have no idea why.

She makes me crazy.

The weirdest part is, I'm starting to crave things I've never craved before.

Like when I was bowling with her, I wanted to see her smile. When we were playing darts, I wanted to make her laugh.

When I took her for the first tour, I wanted to see her eyes open wide with amazement.

I wanted to see my building through her eyes. Which is not something I ever cared about.

For me, I prefer a clutter-free personal life. I like things to be taken care of in an organized fashion. I like meticulous.

That was before Layla awoke this hunger inside me.

It had lain dormant for years. Pushed down to the very bottom of my dark soul.

It's resurfaced and needs an outlet.

Look at me now.

He would be so disappointed in me.

I'm ready to throw it away, everything I built, just to see her smile.

It makes no sense. Despite what I should do, which is walk away from this woman and let someone else continue her tour, I find I can't. The desire to figure out why she makes my pulse pump harder drives me. I need to get to the bottom of it. I need to understand why.

I realize that being this close to her is making me lose my cool. That she makes me want things from her I don't understand.

I want things I've never wanted. I hardly know her, but I'm intrigued. Since this is not something that happens to me, I decide that, despite my better judgment, I won't call my assistant and have her take over the tour. The tour she was supposed to be giving in the first place.

Instead, I walk away from the table, make my way outside, and calm the fuck down.

When I'm standing outside, and the fresh air hits my nose, I suck in a big gulp of oxygen.

I will myself to be normal.

I inhale, and then I exhale.

Continuing this breathing pattern, I remember what he said to me as a small boy when I needed to control my anger.

Pretend you are blowing out candles.

He taught me to control myself. How to act normal. And despite not wanting to think of him, I need to right now because my rage is barely contained.

Time passes, and after a few minutes, I feel her hand on my shoulder.

I know it's her because when she steps closer, I can smell the faint fragrance of her perfume.

It smells like crisp summer days. Fields of lavender. I want to turn around and dip my nose into her neck, linger in her aroma. Again, another thing I never wanted before her. Not true.

There was another . . .

"Are you okay?" Her soft voice is a calming melody in the silence of the morning.

I don't answer her right away.

Instead, I take another deep inhale, and when I feel like I've calmed enough, I turn my head over my shoulder. I look down at where Layla's standing. I tower over her when she's wearing her flats.

"I'm okay." I know I need to say more, but I feel strange right now, open.

It feels like I've been eviscerated, and it's bleeding out all over the floor.

I need to get my bearings before I say anything, and luckily for me, she must understand because she just stands there, staring up at me with her big blue eyes, telling me without words that she'll listen when I'm ready to speak.

Again, this incredible connection; I feel like I know what she's thinking, but how could I possibly? I don't even know her, but I welcome the silence.

When my blood starts to simmer at a normal clip again, I lead us back to the table.

The mess of my outburst long since clean.

A new plate is in front of me. Layla's plate also is perfect.

"I'm sorry for my outburst." I let out a sigh. "My entire career rests on the success of this place. I want to retire to travel, or at the very least have the ability to only accept jobs I'm truly passionate about. This project will more than secure my future and allow me to do that." I reach for the glass in front of me, take a swig, and then place it back down on the table. "I'm tired, Layla."

Her hand reaches across the table, and I allow her to take mine in hers. She gives me a little squeeze.

"I understand. I mean, I don't understand what you're going through, but I understand being tired. I can't imagine the responsibility you're under, but if you ever want to talk about it off the record . . ." Her lips tip up into a smile, one that is meant to reassure.

"For as long as I can remember, this has been my dream. This is how I envisioned peace."

"Will you live here once it's done?" she asks me, and I stare down at where our hands are still connected.

"At first, I'll take a little vacation, and then yes, that's the idea. Why I built my own version of paradise."

"And then?" She drops my hand, and I miss the feel of her. I want to take it back in mine, but instead, I answer the best I can.

"Live in peace, I hope."

She looks at me like she understands, and maybe a part of her does. Maybe because of her job, she understands why I would want to calm down and not work so hard.

But that's not what I'm talking about. I'm talking about shutting out the monsters and being peaceful for once.

I know it's a pipe dream, that you can't shut up the monsters that are already inside you, but I'm hoping that here, behind the gates, I'll be able to.

"Is there anything else bothering you?"

"No."

"Are you sure?" she asks, her eyes narrowing ever so slightly. By the way she's watching me, I can tell she's trying to ascertain the truth to my words.

I'm not going to lie. I'm concerned about how she's acting.

Needing to change the subject, I lean back casually and decide to turn the topic away from me and onto her.

"So, I obviously know you work for *Concept and Space* magazine, but tell me how you got that job?"

Her cheeks turn an adorable shade of pink, and something tells me this isn't the kind of question she wants to answer.

"I applied," she answers with a shrug. "I got it."

There's more to this story than she's letting on.

"Not buying it. Talk. You already know my deal."

She inclines her head, sucking her cheeks in. The look basically says *are you kidding me.* "It's my job to know your deal."

"Semantics."

She lets out a huff. "Fine. I hate it."

That takes me by surprise. She's been so involved and enthralled, I can't imagine her faking that reaction.

"How is that possible? Your reaction here—"

"This place is different."

Her answer gives me pause. "How is it different?"

"I don't have to understand architecture to understand this place. I wasn't lying when I told you it was spectacular. It's like a living, breathing entity of its own. It feels like you're fully immersed in this world. Like by breathing, the building breathes with me."

I can't help but stare at her because she's a person who has admitted that this isn't her specialty, yet she has captured the full essence of The Elysian.

"If you could work anywhere, do anything, what would you do?"

"You truly want to know?"

"I do." I lean forward in my chair, my elbows resting on the wood table.

"I want to be an investigative journalist."

That's not what I expected her to say, but it makes sense. I see the way she watches. Observant in her stares.

"I think you would be great. But I also think you aren't as ill-fitted for this style of writing as you think."

"How do you figure?"

"The way you described The Elysian. You understand, Layla. Not many do. But you grasp it, and the description you used was perfect. I think you would excel at anything you want, but if your true passion is breaking stories, I can help you."

"How?" Her eyes are wide. It's the look she gives when she is in shock. Has no one ever offered to help her before? Even I had help, *once*.

"I have some contacts back in New York that I'd be happy to introduce you to."

"Thank you so much. I'll take you up on your offer. But not anytime soon."

"I don't understand."

"I need to nail this article first. I can't concentrate on anything else until I do."

This time, it's my turn to reach my hand out and take hers, a show of affection I'm not used to, but I find with this woman, I'm doing all kinds of things that aren't typical for me.

"Layla. You have a gift. Not just a way with words, but you see more than is on the surface. I have no doubt that you will nail this article. And that your bosses will be clamoring to promote you. I have no doubt that whoever I introduce you to in any field will want to hire you. You're tremendously special, Layla."

At my words of praise, her pupils dilate, and her chest rises and falls with the heavy breaths leaving her body. She likes my words. She enjoys my praise. I watch as her back straightens and how she blooms underneath it, how she exudes confidence. I like the way she reacts to me.

And most of all, I like the way I feel about her reaction.

It's a heady aphrodisiac.

And I want to bask in it.

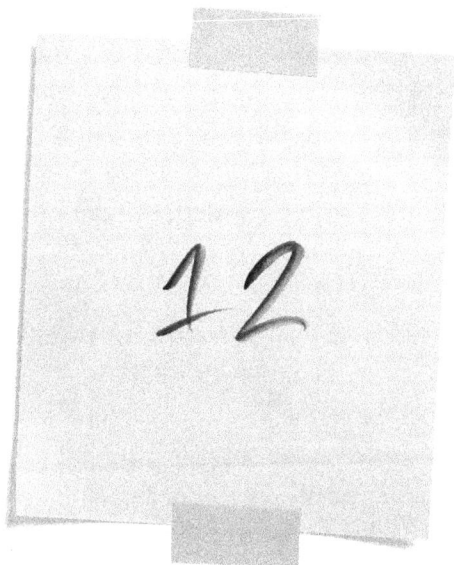

12

Layla

After we are done eating, Cain leads me back to the car, and we set off to the residential home area.

We park the car in front of the model home that we didn't enter earlier. The one he rushed away from. *Too crowded*, he said, but I am not sure I am buying that.

Maybe it's the investigator in me, but I feel like he's hedging or holding out on all or part of the story. He said nothing was bothering him, but that woman made him tense.

Who was she? And what does she mean to him?

She was extremely pretty.

There's no taking away from that, even if there was something vacant behind her eyes. And then there is the matter of her creeping around the property in an area no one should have been in.

Crossing my arms at my chest, I cock my head to the left and look at Cain's profile.

The lines of his jaw are set. It's rigid, reminding me of stone. Cut marble. Almost like a sculpture of a Greek god.

It's unnerving the lack of emotion on his face as he drives.

I wonder what he's thinking about.

Is he thinking about the questions I might ask? Or maybe he's thinking about the woman. A heavy feeling weighs on my chest. I hope he's not. I hope he is thinking about me.

Do I occupy the space in his mind the same way he occupies the space in mine?

The air around us is stilted in silence. I can hear the faint hum of his breath.

I wonder who will break first.

Apparently, it's him. A cough leaves his mouth, and he turns to me. "Are you ready to see the larger model?"

"I'm as ready as I'll ever be."

I wonder what's different about this model than the other. Off the bat, I can't tell. It does appear bigger. But I can't be sure because of the reflective mirror on the outside, so I imagine the space goes deep instead, or maybe I could be wrong. I guess I have to go inside and see.

Reaching my hand out, I fling the car door open and then step out, heading toward the house.

I have to stand here and wait a few seconds before Cain walks over, because I can't enter without him.

I still can't believe he has a chip embedded in him. I wonder if it was painful.

"What?" he asks, and I turn my attention to where Cain is making his approach.

The sound of the gravel beneath his feet gets closer. His eyebrows are tilted, and I realize he's asking me.

I give him the look of confusion, scratching my nose, letting him know I have no idea what he's asking.

He lets out a chuckle. A sound I feel doesn't come naturally to him, but it's a beautiful sound, nonetheless.

"I was asking why you were making that face," he clarifies.

I grimace. "I didn't realize I was making a face."

"Yes, there was a little line between your eyebrows as if you were thinking really hard."

"So now you know me well enough to know my lines? It's just a facial expression."

"Normally, I'd say no, but for some reason, with you, yeah, I do."

Cain lifts his wrist up to the sensor board on the side of the house, and the door swings open. He moves aside so I can pass him.

"That's rather presumptuous of you, don't you think?"

"Presumptuous . . . That's probably one of the nicer things people have said about me."

"Yeah, not a lot of people have very nice things to say about you."

He's now standing beside me, but soon he walks in front of me and turns around to look over his shoulder, his right eyebrow raised. "Checking up on me?"

I suck in my cheeks, thinking of how to respond, and then I let the right side of my lips pull up into a smirk. "That is my job, after all."

"That it is. That it is," he says.

Instantly, when I walk in, I can see the difference between the models. Although also modern, the color scheme in this house has more tones of gray. This one feels more industrial.

I follow him around as he shows me the different nooks and crannies of this house he built.

He beams as he talks. His level of pride for his project is pretty extraordinary. I don't think I've ever met anybody who's had this amount of pride.

The thing is, I think most people who know Cain Archer confuse his pride with arrogance.

That's not how I see it at all.

He's not arrogant. He's quiet and thoughtful. All of these things make him seem rude, but to me, he's an introvert.

He doesn't associate well with people. I can understand that.

His phone rings, and he holds his hand up. "Take a look around the house. I'll follow you."

I give him a nod, and then I set off to see what I can find. At first, I don't see anything different in this home. A few seconds later, I'm surprised that Cain is right behind me.

I thought he'd give me space, but apparently, he's decided against it, because as I'm staring at the wall, he's lifting his wrist. I let out a gasp as a secret door opens, and I see that there's actually a closet behind the wall.

I also see a safe that stretches from the floor to the ceiling.

Interesting. Small crevices and small secret compartments.

He places his phone down for a second. "We like to utilize all empty space," he tells me and goes back to listening and speaking to whoever has called him.

I wonder who this house is built for, if it has a resident yet. Is it built for someone in mind?

As I walk, my brain wanders a million miles a minute to figure it out. That's when I see another closet, and I wonder if this one also has a compartment behind it.

He gives me a shake of his head, telling me no, but then he takes his hand and reaches it out, and I don't know what to do, but I allow him to take my hand in his, and then he is pulling me through the house.

He's not speaking, but I don't need words to enjoy the view and to understand what's happening.

I'm sure that when he's done, he'll tell me, but then he opens the wall again. I walk through.

This is no small crevice. This is a room. "This room is sound-proof." His voice behind me has me jumping. "Sorry about that," he says, and I shrug. "Always work," he says, referring to the phone call from before.

I nod in agreement, understanding there's always something that pops up.

"So, this is soundproof?"

He walks me inside the room and then lifts his hand up, and the door closes. The first thing I noticed is that the walls are padded. A shiver runs up my spine.

"Why would you need a padded soundproof room?" I ask.

"We build homes to accommodate all needs."

I bite my lip, thinking about his words. All needs? I can't wrap my head around it. "You're gonna have to give me more details than that. Why would anybody want this in their house? Is this a safe room?"

"No, actually the safe room is in a different room, located some-where else."

"Now I am really confused."

"Not to give away too much information about the confidentiality of the resident who might buy this, but there are a lot of uses for a soundproof room."

This sounds shady, as well. Why would anyone need a soundproof room? I need to get to the bottom of this, and something tells me he won't give me a straight answer on it.

"Examples, please." I give him a flirtatious smile. "It will help me write my article." I place my hand on my hip, and I wait patiently for him to tell me what I want to hear because, ultimately, I'm a dog with a bone, and I'll keep asking until he does.

"It can be used for a music producer."

I lift my eyebrow, giving him a look that says *yeah, I'm sure that's exactly what this room is used for.* "Since there's no equipment in this room, and I don't see any place for speakers, I doubt that very much. I don't even see a place to install electronics, but maybe I'm wrong. Maybe the system runs through this room, as well. Is it all tied to the AI system that I can't see?"

He takes a step closer, and I take a step away, my back hitting the soft material that runs the length of the walls.

"As you said before, it could be a safe room."

"And as you said before, it's not."

"Is that what you need it to be, Layla? Do you need it to be a safe room?"

"I don't think so. I feel pretty safe right now."

He closes the distance, and our bodies are close. I crane my neck to look at him. His eyes seem darker in this room, his pupils larger. We're almost touching, but we're not. "And if it were a safe room. A room to be . . . loud in . . . to scream . . . do you have a word you would use?" he asks as he leans down, his face getting closer to mine.

"Word?" I ask, my voice sounding breathless. My heart racing faster.

"A word for when a couple's sordid fantasies become too much."

His breath fans my face, and I think he might kiss me.

I move closer.

A sound echoes through the space, and I'm so lost in the haze of

99

my desire that I don't realize what it is, but Cain steps back, and I realize it's the house alerting us that the door has been opened. Cain moves away from me, and I feel out of breath, out of sorts, and out of my mind. I can't believe how close we came to kissing. I can't believe how much I wanted him to.

I feel dazed and a bit confused.

My brain is in crazy chaos from this man. I feel like I'm running on a treadmill, and I can't catch my breath, and worse, I can't keep up with the pace he is setting.

I do take a deep inhale, willing myself to calm, and then when my heart rate starts to subside, I realize Cain has walked not just out of the room but down the hall.

Following, I listen to see what he's doing, and when I find him, he's having a conversation with a man I don't know standing next to the front entrance.

He looks up, his face still stern. The expression he always makes for everyone else but me is present again.

I don't like it.

I yearn for my Cain to be back.

He isn't *your* Cain.

He isn't your anything.

You are solely a reporter writing a piece on his project, and when you leave, he will probably forget you were ever here.

Stop, Layla.

I need to keep my head clear. No overanalyzing. No wishing for things that can't be. This is a job.

Once I have my feelings reined in, I head to where Cain is standing.

Together, we walk out of the model home, and then as if we are strangers, we are back in the car. Both of us are silent on the drive.

The scenery is the only thing keeping me entertained since Cain seems a bit off.

The moment we shared has passed, and I don't know if we will get it back.

When I get to the house, I don't say goodbye, just give him a small smile and then exit the car. And he says nothing as I do. Just stares out the windshield, knuckles gripping the steering wheel. I want to ask what's going on. I want to know what's happening with the switch.

The worst part is me. *My reactions.* I go between being hot for the guy to fearful of him.

Now, I'm in my house, the haze from the almost kiss and almost dirty talk finally starting to lift.

It's like I'm completely blind when he's around. I only see him. I can't stop thinking about Cain, and as I'm about to call Mara because I need someone to talk to, my phone chimes.

I glance down, and it's him. Cain.

Cain: Be ready tomorrow by ten.

Good, I'll have time to work on my article tonight.

13

Layla

I will never get over how fresh the morning air is here in the mountains. Crisp with an aroma of pine. It reminds me of my childhood. Back when I used to lie in the grass beside the small trees my parents had that separated them from the world.

A hedge of them. To keep the privacy. Something they often needed as they screamed and fought. But I found solace outside alone, lying on the grass and looking up at the sky.

I inhale deeply.

I'd forgotten that I did that until now.

Tilting my chin up, I watch as a formation of clouds drifts across the sky. White and billowy rays of sunlight streak out from behind them, warming my face and making me smile.

I hear him before I see him. The sound of his footsteps crunching on the gravel give his presence away. "Good morning," I say before looking down and in his direction. I want to soak up the sun before I have to start work.

"Good morning, Layla."

Dropping my chin, I meet his gaze. He looks good today. Not that he doesn't look good every day, but he's wearing jeans and a black T-shirt today.

I like casual Cain a lot.

He's tall and lean, and his perfectly sculpted arm muscles are emphasized by the cut of the shirt.

I want to thank the manufacturers for making it. "Where are we off to today?"

"Impatient?" Cain places his hand in his pocket as I step closer to him.

"Never . . . yet always." When I'm standing beside him, I need to crane my neck to look him directly in the eyes.

"It will be worth it." His voice sounds raspier than normal, almost a tease, and I swear my knees feel wobbly at the sound.

"Promise," I practically purr, and as soon as the word leaves my lips, I want to scold myself. Sure, I've given up pretending I'm not affected by him, but jeez, can't I be less obvious?

"Always."

"Fine. Lead the way. But only if you promise to feed me after." I move toward the car and grip the door handle. From behind me, I hear Cain's footsteps as he heads to the driver's side of the car.

I pull the door open at the same time he does, and we both get in.

"Hungry?" he asks as he buckles his seat belt and turns on the engine.

"Always." My stomach chooses that exact moment to growl. Nice touch, Layla.

He chuckles. "Well then, I'm going to take you someplace special."

"Hop to it." I've gotten used to not having a clue where we are going as he drives. This place is huge and confusing. No matter how I try to keep my bearings, I can't.

He turns onto dirt paths that aren't roads, and it only takes me about three seconds before I'm lost. I'll need a damn map, GPS, or compass to find my way around here. Luckily for me, Cain is a fantastic tour guide.

When the trees clear, yet again, I'm stunned. Days later, I'm still shocked that this man can leave me speechless with his designs. He's a genius.

I throw my hands up in the air. "How do you do it?"

"Do what?" he asks.

"Make every building more beautiful than the next. What is this place?"

Then he does it. The thing I love most, he smirks. My belly flutters. Is it normal for a man to affect me like this?

Especially one who I barely know.

"This, Layla . . ." The way he says my name is even more deadly. The way his tongue drawls out the last *A*, I could listen to it on repeat and die a happy woman. "This is the hotel on-site."

Despite my current status of drooling from auditory porn, his words break through my fog. "You have a hotel?"

"Where else do you think visitors will stay when they come?"

"For some reason, I didn't imagine visitors were allowed," I mutter. In all the times I have spent thinking about this place, never had that thought crossed my mind. But it makes sense. I don't have anyone in my life but Mara and a cousin, and if I lived here, they would just stay with me, but I guess I'm not like most. If I had a large extended family, I could see the need for a hotel.

"Of course, they are." He shuts off the car, swinging his door open. "And they have a state-of-the-art location to stay in."

I move to leave the car, as well, and once I'm outside, I look toward him. "Like where I'm staying?"

He laughs while shaking his head. "Nothing like where you're staying."

Taking a few steps, I make my way over to where he's standing. "What's the difference?"

"The hotel is not fitted with AI in the same way. With frequent turnover, it's just not feasible."

"Soooo," I draw out, "what you're saying is my accommodations are better." Playfully, I bat my lashes, and he continues to chuckle.

I will never get over this swoon factor from that damned chuckle.

"Only the best for you. Come on. Let me show you." He reaches out and takes my hand to pull me toward the building. Willingly, I follow, loving how his hand feels wrapped around mine.

I'm pissed off when he drops it the moment we step inside the automatic doors, but my annoyance is soon replaced by awe once I'm standing in the grand foyer.

The ceiling must be twenty stories high.

But it's the chandelier that has my eyes widening and my mouth falling open.

It looks like a waterfall is falling from the sky, but it's not water, rather individual illuminated glass lights. The illusion is remarkable.

"I'm impressed." I turn to face him until our gazes lock. "I have done endless research on lighting. I consider myself quite the expert." I wink. "And never have I imagined a chandelier to cascade down like a river plunging to a pool below."

Cain stands in front of me, momentarily speechless. His large brown eyes widen. I think I surprised him.

"Come on," he finally says, and then again, he takes my hand and pulls me toward an open glass elevator. Because we are the only people here, we don't have to wait for it, and when we step inside, I can't help but grin at him. "Nothing is better than watching you," he says, and while I know he's talking about my reactions, there's something else in his tone which leads me to believe he's talking about something else. Dare I say this tangible pulsating attraction between us.

When the elevator stops, I lurch forward a bit, and Cain's arm shoots out. His large hand brackets around my waist.

For a second, I can't breathe.

His fingers touch the exposed skin between my blouse and my skirt.

My heart thumps rapidly in my chest. It beats so hard that I'm afraid it will explode.

Should I turn around?

Should I look at him?

I'm about to when the elevator door opens, and he quickly drops his hand. A cough escapes his mouth. "After you."

The hallway is serene, with soft, gray carpet, and the walls are glass windows facing the branches of the trees cocooning us.

The light fixtures are flush mounts. I have to stifle a laugh as I realize after all my bitching over articles I've been forced to write in the past, I'm now well-versed on the matter.

From the corner of my eye, I catch Cain strolling over to a large black door. Then he steps back and waits for me to enter the room.

The moment I do, a gasp escapes my mouth.

Inside, it's not much different from the homes, but what sets it apart is the view. The hotel is built within the mountain, set amongst trees.

Decorated in soft grays and whites, it's tranquil. But it's the balconies that deserve the standing ovation. Each room has a balcony cocooned in branches. "It reminds me of a tree house." There is no hiding the awe in my voice. My words come out breathy and low.

He takes a step toward the glass door that leads outside and pushes it open. "That was exactly the idea." Turning toward me, he reaches his hand out, and I press mine into his. "You really do understand."

My cheeks grow warm. Is the heat spreading over my face from the compliment, or is it because Cain's fingers lightly dance over my skin as I make my way out onto the terrace?

"It feels like heaven." I'm not sure what I'm referring to.

The balcony? The view? Or the man standing close enough I swear I can feel his body heat?

All of the above.

Side by side, we face the trees. A gentle breeze has the branches making a soft swishing sound around us.

Here. At this moment. I see it. I see the possibilities. I see the world he's creating.

I open my mouth to tell him, but my tongue feels heavy, and I can't seem to find the right words.

"I know," he says, and he gives my hand a squeeze. As crazy as it sounds, I think he does know. My emotions bounce around like an old-fashioned pinball machine. "Come on, let me now show you the rec room," he says, breaking the heavy mood.

I welcome the distraction. I'm not ready to think about how I feel about Cain. Taking a deep breath, my chin tips to look up. "So even the hotel has a rec room?"

"Yep. Have to have guests happy, too." Cain leads us back out of the hotel room, and we begin to walk through the large hallways again.

"Other than steel beams, is it just glass that's the main material in this building?"

"On the outside, yes. Obviously, between each room and the interior spaces are drywall. But other than that, yes, all exterior walls are glass. That way, the guest feels immersed in branches."

"It must be amazing when it rains."

"Most people think it would be scary."

"Rain isn't scary. It's beautiful," I say dreamily.

"It is."

Then we are back on the elevator and heading down to the lobby. When we arrive at our destination, we are no longer the only people in the lobby.

Barbara is standing with a clipboard in her hand, tapping her foot as she reads from it.

"And who do we have here?" an unfamiliar voice says, and I turn to see a handsome man with short, dirty blond hair and a scruffy face move closer to me. When he's standing directly in front of me, he lifts his hand to shake mine. I'm about to, but Cain steps forward, blocking the man's path.

"No one for you to concern yourself with." Cain's voice booms through the empty space, causing Barbara to cross the distance until she stands in front of us.

"Now, now, boys. Layla, why don't you come with me? Scott had to ask Mr. Archer a question regarding the lower-level gym. Didn't you, Scott?"

"I did," the man I now know as Scott says.

"While you talk, I'll bring Layla to see where the bar is going to be. Ready?"

"I am."

Without a backward glance, Barbara starts walking me in the direction of a glass door. Once inside, I see it's not complete yet, but I would have to be an idiot to not know that this, in fact, isn't a bar, but just a plain room.

"Okay, so if you aren't going to show me where I can grab a drink, why don't you tell me why you led me here?"

"Be careful."

"With?"

"You know what."

I glare at her; my temper barely contained with this conversation. "I can assure you I don't."

Her lips thin. "Mr. Archer."

Now I'm furious, but instead of snapping, I inhale deeply and will myself to calm. "What about him?"

"Why are you getting so close?" She basically spits out the question.

I narrow my eyes, shooting her a cold and angry look. "I'm here to tour the property for my article."

"You need to know he's not like other men. You don't know him like I do."

"Again . . ." This time, there's no hiding my red-hot anger. "I'm not here for him. I'm here for The Elysian."

"I'm just warning you. He's not a good man."

"From what I see, he's not the monster you make him out to be."

"He's not showing you his true self. I don't know why, but what you're seeing isn't the guy the rest of us see on a daily basis."

"What does he do normally?" I place my hands on my hips in challenge.

"The man doesn't let anyone in. He has no one. I've seen him disappear for days in his office working on projects, not a care in the world if he talks to anyone. What you are seeing now is a fluke because you are different from his daily routine. Sure, you are pretty, but you don't have what he needs."

"Are you . . . are you jealous?"

"No. It's not like that with us. I just want to warn you. This won't go anywhere. You're not safe to pursue this further than this silly article."

"Silly? Fine. Got it. Consider me warned. Now, if that's all . . ." And with that, I leave, heading back to Cain. Back to my tour.

When I return to the hallway, Scott is no longer there, and Cain is on his phone. He looks up at me and crinkles his brow in concern as I walk by and out the front doors toward the car.

Striding up next to me, he ends the call, shoving the phone back into his pocket. "Why the frown? What did Barbara say to you?"

This man is too perceptive for my own good, but I wave him off. "Oh, just typical women talk. Everything is fine. Where are we off to? What's next on this grand adventure?"

"Lunch."

Later, when I'm in bed and ready to call it a day, my phone chimes. A text from Cain on the screen.

The text I open asks me if I'd like to go to a fundraiser The Elysian is holding at the grand opening of the new lounge in town. It's VIP and invite only. He wants me to be his plus-one. Since my time is coming to an end, he says having insight into all the new business coming to town could help my article.

Of course, I want to go. I want to see this, but that's not the reason I'm saying yes. The reason is I'm not ready to walk away.

I'm still desperate for this, to figure out why I feel this way.

He responds, telling me to be ready tomorrow at eight o'clock to finish my tour. He then tells me that someone will help me prepare for the opening later tomorrow as well. Once he stops texting, I place my phone down, my eyes growing heavy, and I fall asleep thinking about him.

At eight o'clock on the dot, I'm dressed and ready to go. I don't know where I'm off to today, but I know that tonight, I have an event with Cain, but I'm not sure what he'll be showing me. Or when.

This morning or this afternoon.

He was vague.

Which doesn't help with the anxious feeling that unsettles my belly.

I'm nervous and excited for tonight.

I don't want to read into it, but it seems out of the ordinary for him to invite someone he barely knows to an event. Especially when, in the past, he always had women who looked like models on his arm.

That's the part that makes me nervous, but being able to spend more time with him, on his arm, nonetheless, makes me excited.

I start to pace the foyer of the house I'm staying in.

Sitting would be smarter while I wait, but I have so much energy inside me, nervous energy, that I can't sit still.

There's a knock on the door. A chuckle escapes my mouth.

Always punctual.

I swing the door open, but I'm shocked to see it's not him. There's someone I've never seen before standing on my doorstep.

"Hello. I'm Stuart. Mr. Archer sent me to escort you for your spa treatments today."

"I'm going to the spa?" I ask, and he nods.

To say I'm shocked would be an understatement. Sure, I expected to go to the spa at some point during my stay, but just to tour it. I didn't expect to be participating.

I follow Stuart outside. This is new. The Wrangler is not there.

I've grown fond of that car.

It must be Cain's car.

Instead, today, there is a golf cart.

I'm not sure how this will drive on these roads, but I guess I'll find out soon enough. That's when I see the wheels. Yeah, there won't be any problems.

These must be some state-of-the-art wheels meant for off-roading.

They are huge.

We start to drive, and it's surprisingly a smooth ride. "How long until we get there?" I ask, merely to make conversation.

"It's just up the road in the clearing."

He continues to drive, and we weave in and out through turns.

About five minutes later, the road opens, and there are no more trees. There is, however, a beautiful building made of wood.

It reminds me of a tropical jungle. These trees look like they were planted here to make the change in habitat look natural. Like a rainforest you would find in Hawaii.

Then I hear the sounds around me. The sound system must be placed in the trees.

I'm instantly transported to the rainforest with birds chirping, the sound of running water, and the smell of rain.

It's tranquil.

When I look closer at the building, I notice it's not closed in. There are no walls.

It's an open building, or at least, that's how it appears.

I can't imagine they can be open year-round in this location, but it must have walls that they place during the winter and remove during the summer.

Stuart gets out of the golf cart and leads the way to the main reception area.

Behind the desk is a pretty brunette. She looks a little bit younger than me, and her smile is contagious as she beams up at us.

"You must be Layla." I can't help but smile back at her, and I nod. "Yes, that's me."

"Well, boy, do we have a lot in store for you."

"I can't wait." I grin back. "I'm actually surprised I'm doing this."

"You will be one of our first. Mr. Archer called down and told us how important you are."

My stomach flutters at her words. *Stop. You're being ridiculous.* It's probably innocent and not at all what I'm hoping.

I'm sure he means I'm important because I'm writing an article about this place, but somewhere deep inside, I hope it's for other reasons.

Except I told him I wished I could get a massage, and he opened this place for me. He said it was closed . . .

This must mean something.

The woman behind the desk hands me a piece of paper, and when I look down, I can see that it's a typed-out itinerary of all the things I'll be doing here.

Jacqueline walks around the desk and motions for me to follow her. She leads me into an atrium full of flowers and trees.

I take a seat in one of the comfortable-looking chairs in the middle of the space.

The next thing I know, she's bringing me a glass of champagne, and then she's pouring what looks like fresh orange juice into the flute.

"In the corner is a robe. Please, at your own pace, relax, change, and when you are ready, your masseuse will be here."

"This is where I'm getting the massage?"

"It is."

Jacqueline presses a button, and the massage bed rises from the floor.

"This whole atrium is for me?"

"It is."

"Wow," I say, dumbfounded.

"Press the button when you're ready."

As soon as she leaves, I remove my clothes, and that's when I notice there's a locker door behind the robe.

I place my clothes inside the locker and put my robe on.

I take another sip of my mimosa, then walk toward the button.

I'm blown away by this place, and if I remember correctly from the sheet that I left at the table with my drink, I have a full day.

A massage, facial, and then there is a dress fitting.

Hair and makeup begin at four thirty.

Cain is picking me up at six.

The trouble he seems to have gone through for me to make this the most perfect day makes me feel special. This is an amazingly incredible gesture. The only problem with today is that I only get to see him tonight. This would be even more spectacular if I could spend the day with him.

I pick up my phone and swipe a quick text to him.

Me: This is a complete surprise and shock. Thank you for this special treat. You didn't need to make this happen.

Cain: Making you happy is exactly what I needed to do. See you tonight. Enjoy.

Is tonight his way of sending me off with a proper goodbye? One last cherry on top to get me to write the perfect article?

No. This is more than that.

Regardless, it doesn't change the fact that tonight might be the last time I see him.

I don't want it to be. Maybe it doesn't have to be. Maybe I could broach the topic of seeing him again. That's what I want. I wonder if it's what he wants. I can't read him perfectly, so I'm not sure, but it feels that way. It feels like he wants to spend time with me. Why else would he have volunteered himself to take me on this amazing tour?

It could be because he's the architect, and he wants me to see his vision.

No. No, it's more than that.

Anybody here could've taken me on the same tour. But he wanted me to see it through the lens that he sees it. That's why he asked me so many questions.

As I'm lost in my thought, the door opens, and a woman walks in, and I know it's time for my massage.

I lie down on the table, and when I'm done, I hand her the robe, and she turns back around to start.

Hours pass, and I spent them sleeping and relaxing. I let all the thoughts I felt inside me drain from my body.

I didn't realize how much anxiety I was holding over this article. How much nervous energy over this man I've gathered.

But as I lie here, listening to the soothing music and the soft sounds, I allow this paradise to suck me in, and I'm sad that I'll have to leave.

After my facial and light lunch, I'm led in a clean robe to another room. An immaculately dressed woman stands in the center of the room with a rack of gowns beside her. There is also a very stylish older man in a suit.

"Hello, Layla. My name is Elise. I am the stylist here at The Elysian. This is Roger, and he is the on-site tailor. Mr. Archer has chosen all the dresses behind me. Pick the one you love the most for tonight's event, he said, and he wants you to know that you are welcome to take anything you want back home with you when you leave."

I refrain from letting my mouth hang open. What an incredible man. All of this is here for me. Then I see Elise reaching over, and she opens a chest. "He made sure to choose all the pieces of jewelry himself from The Elysian vault. Every piece he has chosen will work with any of the gowns behind us." At this, I am left completely speechless.

I want to say it's all too much. Because this isn't normal. Who leaves ten gowns for a woman he doesn't know and lets her borrow priceless jewelry?

I don't voice any of this because maybe this is normal. Maybe that's why there is a stylist, a tailor, and a jeweler on staff. Maybe this is how the people of this society live, and who am I to judge? Instead, I'll enjoy it.

I take a step toward the racks full of dresses, thumbing through each piece, each more beautiful than the next.

Then I pick one.

It looks like a dream. With white gossamer falling in ripples to the floor, it's everything that the word *paradise* brings to mind. Almost like a cloud of heaven.

The top is a white, form-fitting corset, and I turn to try it on.

Stepping behind the curtain that Elise has established for me, I drop my robe and step in, taking care not to touch the material in a way that could damage it.

Once it's on, I step out, and she gasps.

"This is the perfect gown," Elise gushes. "Perfection. Now to find you a piece of jewelry."

I look down, and I see each piece glimmering back at me, but ultimately, I go for just the plain tennis necklace.

Of course, it's not plain. It's probably twenty carats' worth of diamonds and likely costs more than my apartment, but it looks beautiful as Elise places it around my neck.

As I stand in the room in the gown, Roger touches the material, looking to see where he can nip and tuck it. But other than a few inches from the bottom, it's perfect.

"How did you know what size I was?"

"That was all Mr. Archer." Is it weird that he knew the size I was or that he knew my height?

I guess not, seeing as his job is to understand the measurements required to make a building, and maybe that's how he looks at me, as if I'm a work to be constructed. Either way, it doesn't matter because he did an amazing job.

I step out of the gown so it can be tailored, then head to get my hair and makeup done.

Two hours later, with perfect makeup and hair swept off my face into soft waves flowing down my back, I'm ready.

At six o'clock on the dot, I hear the telltale signs of his shoes, which is weird because up to now, I haven't with his preferred system settings.

I peek over my shoulder, and this time, I can't help how the breath rushes from my chest as I gaze at him.

If I thought Cain Archer was handsome before, casual, working Cain has nothing on this version.

He's dressed in a tuxedo, and this one is cut to perfection, fitted close to his body.

My cheeks warm as I take in the weight of his stare as he glides his gaze over me, tingling at the way he looks.

It's a heady feeling, and I want to explore it.

I don't want today to be the last time I see him. I want to spend more time with him and get to know him.

I want to bask in the way he looks at me because even though I don't know him very well, I want to, and I feel that I'm falling for this guy.

This is dangerous.

We don't come from the same worlds. We're nothing alike.

Not now. There is no need to let these conflicting thoughts run wild. Not tonight.

Not when he is looking at me like this.

I tamp down all the thoughts and decide that if tonight's the last night I have with him, I am going to enjoy every single minute of it.

14

Layla

There is no moving past the way he is looking at me right now. It is unlike anything I have ever experienced before. He looks at me like I am the only person in the world. Like I am the air he breathes. And for a brief second, I believe it.

It is like the world revolves around me.

It's crazy to see someone stare at you like you mean something. He doesn't blink for a minute. His gaze is unwavering. But then he must notice himself because his head does a little shake as he crosses his arms in front of his chest. I wait for him to speak.

"You look stunning."

From the heat in my cheeks, I know I am blushing.

"It's all because of you."

He shakes his head. "No, it's all because of you." His words are definitive, leaving no room for objections. Not that I would anyway. Something tells me he doesn't like that. I've watched how he reacts with other people. Although, he seems to be amused most of the time with me, so maybe if I teased him, he would smile. It's not worth the risk, though, so I don't.

"Thank you."

"Are you ready to go?"

"I believe you did tell me six, so yes, I am completely ready for you."

"Do you always do as you're told?" I can hear the mild innuendo beneath his words, his voice husky with meaning.

"Not particularly."

His lips tip up. "Interesting."

"What is?"

"That you just follow orders with me." I'm not sure how he wants me to respond, but at this point, my entire body is hot. I'm not sure I can actually find words to leave my mouth.

I grab my clutch off the table. "I am ready when you are, sir," I say, essentially ending this line of conversation. I start to walk out the door, and I hear a faint chuckle behind me.

I'm glad I'm entertaining him. Truth is, I'm entertaining myself. I'm basically a melted puddle on the floor from just looking at him.

I act like a complete moron around him.

Hell, even I can see the humor of the situation. If the roles were reversed, I'd be entertained, too.

Behind me, I hear his steps, and then I feel the weight of his hand being placed on the small of my back.

Shivers run down my spine. Goose bumps break out on my skin.

It's not just my brain that is affected, but my body as well.

I'm hyperaware of him, and as we step toward the car, our bodies touch.

Calm down.

At least I won't have to jump up into a Wrangler in this dress.

Instead, a really nice Mercedes is parked outside the house. A man stands in a suit with the door open. He must be the company driver.

"Is he with you?"

"This is Reginald, and he works for The Elysian. He is one of the many drivers on staff if one of our residents needs a car service."

"Another service you provide. "

"I think, Layla, you can see there is very little we won't do for our residents." This is a good tidbit to add to my article, and I wonder if I'll remember it after tonight. I will.

"Does this get booked through the concierge?"

"Mentally jotting down notes, are we?"

"Always working."

"And that's why I respect you." His words and praise shouldn't get to me, but they do. They make me feel important. I feel seen.

I never knew how much I enjoyed praise, but since meeting Cain Archer, I realize I do. Or maybe it's just *his* praise.

Maybe I enjoy his reaction to me or his approval.

God, do I have daddy issues?

Not that he's old enough to be my dad. It's only a ten-year age gap. That's not much older than me.

Plus, that's the least of my issues.

One being my job.

Leaving being the second.

I need to stop micromanaging everything and just enjoy myself tonight.

Reginald opens the door for me, and I step in and sit down. The distraction is exactly what I need to stop my ever-present inner monologue. Placing my hands on my lap, I tap my fingers at the material of my dress. A few seconds go by, and then Cain's walking around to the other door and enters like the gentleman he is.

Prim and proper, he's not the rugged architect walking through the paths on a hike.

Now, he's all suit.

I don't know which version I like better, the laid-back version or this one.

No.

I do know which version I like the best. I like the version that plays darts, laughs like we are kids, and knows how to bowl. That's the version I think only I get to see.

It takes us about thirty minutes to get to our location for the fundraiser. The event is for the key investors of this development.

When we walk in, the first thing we do is grab two flutes of champagne, and then we start to walk around.

The location is much like The Elysian. It feels like I've walked into a midsummer night's dream.

The lights are dim, candles illuminating the space. Vines hang from the ceiling, intermixing with the lights.

Cain introduces me to everyone we come in contact with.

He exudes confidence in every introduction, demanding respect. I watch him as he schmoozes. He's something otherworldly, and the way he works the room, it's truly a sight to be seen.

At one point, he smiles at me and tells me he has to speak to someone, and as I watch him cross the room nodding at other people, I notice a presence beside me.

"You're here with Cain Archer?"

I turn to the voice, and I see a woman who looks to be in her mid-thirties. She has long, wavy, brown hair, bright green eyes, and heavy makeup. Her dress is skintight.

"I am."

"He's quite extraordinary, isn't he?" she coos.

"Oh, it's not like that," I say, waving a hand dismissively at her underlying statement.

"I didn't think it would be with you," she responds, looking down her nose at me.

Something about her cut feels a little deep, but then again, she looks like a model who's probably now a housewife.

A trophy wife, and I'm just a struggling, poor journalist, a little out of my element.

"I wish we could keep him."

I turn to face her, and I see that she's not talking to me anymore. Now she is talking to the next Barbie. Another trophy wife, maybe? Are these the residents who'll be living in The Elysian? The idea that a woman like this would be the resident of such a spectacular home doesn't sit well with me.

Will she ever appreciate the house? Or does she just like it for the technology? Does she understand the work it took for Cain to make it into this paradise?

I internally chastise myself. I might not be better than her if I'm judging her, but as the two women speak of Cain, degrading him down to merely a handsome face to look at, I realize I understand why Cane is so closed off. If everyone looked at me like I was merely a good face despite my genius, I, too, would be closed off.

"Do you think there's anything we could do to keep him here?"

"Besides getting on our knees?"

"I bet that's what he likes. For a woman to crawl to him."

"I *have* crawled to him," the brunette says, her lips sucked into a coy, flirtatious smile.

The idea of either of these women being with Cain sets my blood on fire. I feel like I'm practically sizzling with anger.

I take a deep breath, plastering a fake smile on my face, and then I excuse myself.

Without another word, I head off.

I start to take a loop around the space, glancing at the faces surrounding me, listening to their conversations.

This event is for the donors, the people who invested in The Elysian. I can hear them talking, and apparently, if this is a success, they will have Cain build properties like this all over the world.

A part of me is excited for him, but another part feels it's wasted on people like this.

I continue to walk the space, and then from across the room, I see Cain. He doesn't see me at first, and I watch him. He's talking to a group of gentlemen.

His face is stoic as per usual, and then he catches my eye.

His head tilts to the side, and our gaze's lock. The way he looks at me is different than how he looks at them. He takes a deep breath, and it's like he can breathe for the first time tonight.

Maybe I'm reading too much into it. Maybe I'm seeing things that aren't really there, but it feels like when he sees me, he's different.

God, I hope so. I truly hope so because I want to be different for him.

I want to be more.

15

Cain

There is nothing I hate more than this dog and pony bullshit. I despise every moment of these types of events. Every aspect of it is worse than the next. Plaster on a fake smile. Pretend to laugh at their jokes. Seem engaged.

It is a test of my will to be here.

Granted, I have trained for this my whole life. Faking a smile and pretending to care have been my constant companions.

They're the shadows that follow me everywhere I go.

Until her. She's like the sunlight after a long storm. The darkness that has surrounded me for thirty-five years breaks open when Layla is nearby.

From the first moment I saw her, I could feel the warmth she exudes. I continued to put myself in her orbit to see if the light would fade. But if anything, it's flourished. Why is she different? Why do I want to hear what she says? Why do I care to hear the answers? Is it just that she's the first person to make me genuinely laugh?

She's special.

Unlike the women before her, it's not about Layla's looks.

It's about the way she looked at me.

Most people shy away and back down, but she looked me right in the eye when she met me, and I could tell she wanted to know the real me. She challenges me. *Understands me.*

That's it, and here, now, it's more pronounced as I listen to the men. All they talk about is money and finance.

Their wives are worse. They are staring at me like I'm fresh meat. I'm just a quick, noteworthy fuck to these women. I'm an orgasm. That's it. A novelty.

My gaze finds her. She's surrounded by women, and by the look on her face and the way her brows are pinched in, she doesn't like what they have to say.

As I watch her, she turns in my direction, and I catch her eyes. They're now narrowed, not angry. No, now they remind me of the look she gives when she is concerned. And that's why she is special. The concern is for me.

"Excuse me, gentlemen. If you don't mind, I have a pressing matter to attend to."

I make my way across the room, trying to find her. But as I walk toward where I last saw her, more people stop me. My back goes ramrod straight as a woman slithers up beside me, her hand touching the shoulder of my tuxedo.

"Mr. Archer," she draws out, her tongue jutting out to lick her lips.

If this were any other event, I would remove her hand from my shoulder, but I remind myself that this is part of the game. The bigger goal.

I can't be shortsighted. I am trying to change the world.

I lower my head to meet her eyes. She is not unattractive. A typical man might find himself lucky to have a roll in the sheets with her.

But I am not a typical man.

That's not to say I don't have basic needs.

And yes, sometimes I have an itch I need to scratch. Maybe this lady would be the perfect distraction in another place, another time. But right now, I only have one woman on my mind. And that's the woman I'm going to seek out.

"We need to talk about my residence."

I arch an eyebrow. "What about your residence?"

"I was wondering if you could take me on a tour. I forgot the layout, and I wanted to see—"

I hold my hand up, stopping her right there. "I'm sorry, Mrs . . ."

"Mrs. Murphy." Of course. The very married Mrs. Murphy. The wife of one of the biggest donors of this establishment.

I tread carefully, not wanting to insult her, yet not giving a fuck if I do. My partners would have my ass, and although I normally don't care, I need this project to go off without a hitch.

"Mrs. Murphy, please schedule an appointment with me for next week. I would be honored to show you the ins and outs of your residence."

She beams at me, and I have to refrain from showing any negative emotion. Again, something I've grown accustomed to at these occasions. Refraining from showing emotion is second nature to me. If anything, it's a ploy and an act when I do let the walls break.

I say goodbye to Mrs. Murphy and go off in search of Layla. I find her standing in the corner, observing the crowd.

She looks regal where she stands. Like a goddess sent down from heaven.

Her presence torments me because I want so badly to be a normal man for her. To be able to spend quality time with her. But I have too much baggage, too many secrets, too many skeletons in my closet. If I'm not careful, and if I don't keep every aspect of my life locked in tight, I run the risk of everything falling out. I can't mitigate the damage if that were ever to happen.

So as much as I want to pursue her, I can't. Tomorrow will be the last time I see Layla. And because that is the case, I intend to make the most of this final evening. I cross the room on a mission.

One sole destination in my view.

And despite the consequences of this decision, I don't care.

16

Layla

'm standing in the corner of the room. The need for air and to escape is overpowering.

The crowd. The people.

This party is a lot to handle.

It's not that I'm upset to be here, not at all. It's actually quite the opposite. I know it's important for the article that I'm in attendance. My presence here will give me the opportunity to see who the investors are and who the residents will be, but at the same time, I want to leave already.

I peer around the room, looking for Cain. He's nowhere to be found.

Then on my third sweep of the room, I do catch him. This time, there is a woman beside him. Another woman. However, unlike the last time I saw him, when it seemed to be merely a business conversation, this one looks different.

Nothing about this conversation is innocent or professional. My eyes narrow at the vision before me. This tall goddess has her hand on his shoulder.

I know I have no reason to feel jealous. But I can't help myself.

My stomach sours at how she touches him. The familiarity she seems to have with Cain makes me tense.

Stop looking.

As many times as I tell myself to look somewhere else, I can't. Instead, I find myself staring for far too long.

Anger coils inside me.

It's irrational.

I know this. But it doesn't stop me from feeling it.

Taking a step to my left, I position myself in a location where I can no longer see him.

There's no reason to make a show of it. I know I don't have a shot with him—not with women like this hanging on his every word—so why torture myself? Standing around gawking at him is the equivalent of looking at a dessert buffet if my mouth is wired shut. We are just acquaintances. He invited me as a business courtesy.

From where I'm now positioned, I'm able to take in the bar's ambience. The low lighting and chandeliers that hang above it. They spared no expense. My stiff shoulders drop in relief now that the looming shadow of Cain and whoever he's talking to is no longer front and center.

Finally, I can do what I'm supposed to do. I'm able to think.

Mentally, I take notes.

I only had one drink, so my memory should be clear tomorrow when I'm able to record this.

This party is spectacular, and I try to remember every small detail.

I'm lost in thought when I feel a presence standing in front of me. With my head tipped down, the shadow he wields eats up the distance between us. There's no need to look up to know who it is. Only one person would cross a room and stand in front of me. But despite the fact that I know he's there, I don't lift my gaze.

The emotions swirling around inside me are confused, and I'm not ready to look at him because I know without any measure of doubt that Cain Archer will be able to read me.

He always does.

And right now, I'm not sure what he will see.

Whether it's jealousy or longing, either way, I don't want him to see the truth. But that's the thing. Cain Archer always sees the truth with me. Which is alarming and sends off major red flags, seeing as we've only known each other for such a short amount of time.

"We can leave," he says, but I don't look up. The façade of indifference hasn't dropped down yet, so even though I'm acting a bit like a petulant child, I'm not ready to look at him.

His fingers touch my jaw, and he tips my face up.

"You okay?" His voice is soft, and I can hear the concern he has.

"Sorry. I was just lost in thought. What did you just say before?" I respond, trying to play it off.

"We can go. Are you ready?" Cain looks toward the door, and I shrug at his words.

"Sure."

He nods at me, and then he drops his hand and takes mine. He places my arm in the crook of his and begins to walk. It feels like he's making a point as he walks proudly toward the exit.

I can feel eyes on me, and I can't help but smile.

It might not mean anything, but it makes me feel better, nonetheless.

I don't like the emotional response I just had. As we get into the car and I move toward the window, I realize that putting as much space between us as possible is maybe for the best. Sure, it felt great to be on his arm, but comparing myself to other women is not something I do.

I'm not this person.

I'm confident. I know my worth.

Surrounding myself with these people, even if only for the night, has changed me.

I can't imagine how Cain lives this way. I peer up at him, narrowing my eyes and trying to read the expression on his face. He doesn't seem as affected by it as I am. He must be used to it.

I turn my head, and I notice him staring at me.

"How do you do it?" I ask.

And not surprisingly, he knows exactly what I'm talking about.

"I won't lie, I hate it. But unfortunately, as my team likes to remind me, it's the nature of the beast. I have a vision, Layla."

"A wonderful vision," I add. "Truly innovative, but this"—I gesture to the gathering of people—"I don't know if I could do it."

"It means more to me than everything, and I will walk through fire to see it happen."

His determination is to be respected. "I don't think I could do what you do."

"But you do, don't you see? We aren't that different. We are two sides of the same coin. You're here, just like I was there."

"It's not the same. This place—"

"When you came here, on the drive, you didn't know that yet. You did what you had to do to succeed. To obtain your goal."

"I did."

My words hang in the air. Filling the space with thought. By the time we pull up to the home I'm staying at, I'm not sure how we will end it.

I hop out of the car, but he scoots over as if to follow me.

"What are you doing?"

"Being a gentleman and walking you to the door. Reginald, I'll be back in a few minutes."

We are both quiet as we make our approach. I don't need to fish out my key because Cain lifts his wrist and the door opens. Before I can comprehend what is happening, his hand is on me, and I'm pulled into the foyer. Then the door shuts, and my back hits the wall. It's not hard, but it's enough of a shock for me to open my mouth to ask what's wrong. That's until my gaze meets his.

There is no mistaking the look in his eyes as he steps up, caging me in. His arms lift and he essentially has me trapped.

A predator cornering his prey.

Except, in this case, I don't want to escape. I want to be devoured.

I bite my lip, and his gaze drops to follow the move, then he lifts one hand and trails his finger over my wet lip.

My tongue snakes out of its own accord and licks him. That's enough to set him off because a growl emanates from his mouth before he's leaning forward.

When our lips fuse, my knees quiver beneath me.

His hands move to hold my waist, essentially holding me up as he kisses me.

His tongue sweeping against mine.

I follow his lead, reaching my hands around to pull him closer.

He runs his hands up my side and kisses me like I'm the air he needs to stay alive.

I kiss him back just as desperately.

I'm lost to this man.

If he asked me now for anything, I wouldn't ever be able to say no.

But just as fast as the kiss began, it stops.

Cain's chest rises and falls as he breathes heavily.

"I'm sorry," he says, and I shake my head.

"For what?"

"For moving so fast."

I smile, lifting up onto my tiptoes and placing another kiss on his lips.

"Nothing to be sorry for. I wanted you to do that."

Cain's body stiffens, and I'm not sure why or what I said. "I have to go."

"Okay," I mumble, feeling confused and a little bit dejected.

He starts to move, and his hand reaches out, and I know the door is about to swing open, but before he does, he takes me by surprise, grabbing me once more and fusing our lips, taking my breath away.

The kiss, if possible, is more passionate than the last one.

Something about this kiss is final. Like he is hungry for me, but he knows this is it, so he devours me as fast and as hard as he can. It's almost like he's treating me as if I'm a mirage that will disappear in a few seconds.

But it's him who will evaporate.

Because before I can even ascertain if this moment was real, the door flings open, and he fades away.

In a daze, I make my way farther into the house, into the bedroom, and throw myself on my bed.

My heart hammers frantically in my chest. I lie motionless on my bed until I can get my breathing to calm down. Once I do, the whole night flashes behind my eyelids. I feel like a ball of restless energy. It has no outlet. I need to tell someone. I reach into my clutch sitting beside me on the bed, pick up the phone, and dial Mara.

"Hey, girl."

"Help," I respond as a greeting. And then I let out a large, overdramatic groan.

"Well, this doesn't sound good."

I frown. Not that she can see me, but my lips thin regardless. "It's not."

"Spit it out and tell me what happened."

Kicking off my shoes, I start to pace. Unlike in Cain's office, my steps make sounds. Angry, frustrated sounds as my feet slap against the floor. "I kissed him."

"Kissed who?"

"Who do you think I kissed?"

"Well, it's obviously not the hot architect I told you to stay away from, now, is it?"

This time, my groan sounds even more dramatic, if that's possible. I'm doing my best at impersonating a dying animal. "Of course, I kissed the overly hot, completely closed off, emotionally wounded architect you warned me not to."

"How did that happen?"

I scan the room, looking from the chair to the bed. "Um, he put his mouth on mine."

"No, idiot. I know how it happened. What I mean is, walk me through the logistics."

I choose the bed. Plopping down on it, I'm exhausted, but my brain won't allow me to fall asleep right now. "I honestly have no clue. He dolled me up, took me to a party, brought me back home, and kissed me."

"And then your carriage turned into a pumpkin?"

"Basically. He ran out of here like the dogs of hell were on his tail."

I roll onto my stomach and bury my head into the pillow, popping up for air only after I hear Mara's voice again. "Well, with the rumors circling him, he probably commands the dogs."

"Not fair. He's not like that."

"Defending him much? Jeez, what happened to you?"

"I don't know. I'm so confused." Face, meet hands. If Mara were here right now, she would rip my fingers from my face and force me to put my big girl panties on and not die from how pathetic I am.

"Okay, so let me help. That's why you called, right? Tell me the

129

problem. Other than the fact that you're probably horny and he left you high and dry, in which case my suggestion is to masturbate."

"Oh, God, Mara, no. I mean, what do I do? I know he left me high and dry, but do I stay a little longer and take my shot, or do I tuck my tail between my legs, lick my wounds and hide, then go back to New York tomorrow?"

"Truth?"

"Always." *But only if you tell me to stay.* Nope. I can't say that. She will never let me live it down.

"You go home. You go home, you write a kick-ass article, and you chalk this up to what it is."

"And what exactly is it?" Setting the phone to speaker and placing it next to my head, I wait for her to tell me.

"One fantastic mistake that didn't go too far, that you can always remember fondly."

I clear my throat, more like choke . . . "Seriously, that's your advice?" I sound exasperated. Which I am.

"Well, it's not like you're gonna listen anyway."

"What's that supposed to mean?"

"You are the worst at taking advice."

"That's not true."

"Case in point, you kissed him when I told you not to kiss him. I told you to stay away from him, and you didn't listen. Now you're sitting there all emotional."

"Fine."

"Feeling better?"

"No, you totally suck." We both laugh, say good night, and I hang up the phone. Then I lie in bed. I don't sleep. Instead, I toss and turn, thinking of all the reasons I shouldn't pursue him. All the things that can go wrong. The most important one being I'm sure he will break my heart.

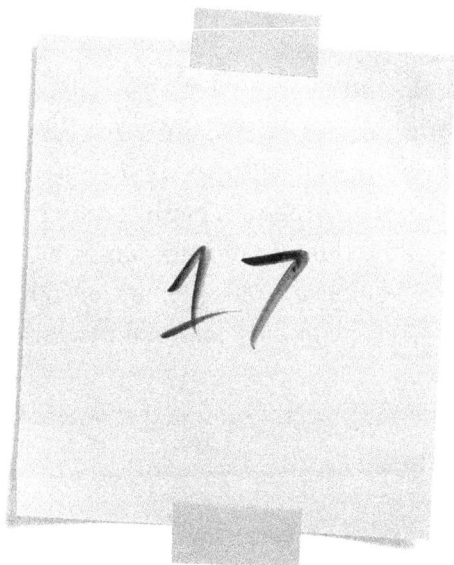

17

Layla

I can't believe today is my last day here.

My heart feels heavy, and there is a lump in my throat.

It could be that I need water, but something tells me it's not. It's as if I'm choking on dust, completely parched, but I know deep down it's the idea of leaving.

This place is special, and I have fallen for it. The peace, the tranquility, and yes, even the weird, crazy AI system in place that's supposed to make the environment more livable.

Despite my feelings, though, I need to head out.

The drive to the city is about three hours long. Yet my body has other plans. It doesn't want to leave this bed. If I could stay here another week, I'm not sure that would be enough either.

Who am I trying to kid? No time would be enough because I feel robbed. It's not like I think Cain Archer is my soul mate, but there's definitely something there that I want to explore. It feels like a grand injustice not to see this thing out.

My chest feels empty, the knowledge that I will never know what could have been creating a crater inside me.

An audible sigh escapes my mouth, but I can't linger here any longer.

It's time to get up and start my day.

Placing a foot on the ground, I stand, stretching my arms out, and then make my way to the closet to pack. I don't bother folding my clothes before just throwing them in haphazardly into the suitcase.

I stifle a laugh at the thought of Cain taking a peek in my suitcase and seeing my mess. Something tells me he would have a heart attack.

Once all the clothes are in the bag, I make my way to the bathroom and freshen up.

After I take a quick shower, I blow-dry my hair, but I leave it wavy, and then I throw on clothes.

Time to go.

Making my way to the foyer, I turn around and get one last look at the magnificent home I've resided in for the past week and say my goodbyes.

I move to open the door, and when I do, I see Cain standing there. His hand is up in the air with a fist formed as if he was about to knock.

"What are you doing here?" I ask, shock evident in my voice.

"Did you really think I was going to let you leave without saying goodbye?" he responds.

I give him a small smile. "To be honest, I wasn't sure." I try to play it off like I don't care either way, but I do.

"What had you hoped for?" His question is simple, but it isn't at the same time. He's asking if I wanted him to say goodbye, but I know he's asking if I want to leave.

Right now, emotionally, I'm not at a place to lay my feelings on the ground. I know Cain isn't the man you hang your dreams on, but at the same time, if I can hold on to this fantasy a little longer, I will.

"I hoped I'd see you, but I know you're busy."

He steps toward me, grabbing my suitcase out of my hands. "Not too busy to say goodbye to you, Layla."

He walks over to where my car is parked, and he points at the trunk. "You mind?"

"Oh, sorry." A soft chuckle leaves my mouth, and I reach into my bag, grab the key, and unlock it.

He puts my suitcase in the trunk, then closes it.

We stand in front of each other. My arms cross in front of my chest as I wait for him to say something. It's a nervous habit, a way to protect myself from this moment. "Thank you for everything. You didn't have to. I should be—"

"Are you in a rush to leave?" He cuts me off. I furrow my brow, not sure what he's asking.

"No. I have no place to be today. Just driving home. That's it."

Jeez, Layla, could you ramble something more pathetic?

He shuffles his weight from the left to the right foot. "Can I show you one last thing?" His hands are in his pocket now. Is Cain nervous? Or am I reading too much into this?

My heart rattles in my chest. "Yes. Of course."

"Great." He smiles broadly, and he looks younger now. It's a good look for him. "Then let's go."

I look over at my car and then at his. He must understand what I'm asking because he nods to mine.

"Let's take yours. If you don't mind me driving. And then you can drop me off at the main office because I have work to do after this, and it's closer to the main road."

"Okay." I reach out my hand and place my keys in his. With our fingers now touching, my body grows warm at the contact.

His lips tip up slightly, and I know he feels this, too.

What does that mean? I have no clue, but overthinking it right now won't help me decipher his feelings. Tomorrow, when I'm back home, I can do that.

I sit down in the passenger seat, and he gets in the driver's seat.

He looks way too big for my small car. His presence is imposing. He's larger than life. A man like him shouldn't be in something so tiny, but it doesn't seem to bother him as he pulls out of the spot and makes his way to the street.

A few seconds later, he's weaving his way through different streets until we're on a road that is barely paved.

The car rattles, bumping up and down on the fresh gravel. Eventually, we pull off, and he throws the car in park. I turn my head, lifting an eyebrow. "There's nothing here."

He throws open his door, but before he rises completely out, he turns over his shoulder. "Just trust me."

Doing as he says, I get out of the car and follow him. We head through thick brush where there is barely a path.

It looks like the type of place where he would take someone to kill them.

Is that what he's doing?

A nervous laugh bubbles up out of my mouth.

Layla, you really have gone overboard with your imagination this time. You're not here alone with him so he can kill you.

That being said, if this were a movie, this would be the perfect murder spot.

"No need for that face. It's just up ahead." Famous last words. In this flick, I'm the silly girl walking toward her death.

But just as I'm about to make a joke about which murder movie this scene is from, the path clears into a large meadow.

Holy hell.

Not only am I in the middle of a little patch of paradise, but there's a picnic blanket set up in the middle of the field.

"What is this place?" I ask, eyes wide, pulse thumping.

"Where I go to think."

I pivot to stare at him beside me. "And you're bringing me here?"

"Most don't know about this place . . ." He shrugs as if bringing me here isn't a big thing. It's huge.

"So, why are you showing me?"

"Because you aren't just anyone, Layla."

It feels like my wobbly knees can't hold my weight. I take a seat, hoping that will help with my weak limbs. Cain sits beside me. The idea that a man like him would be sitting on a blanket in the grass has me shaking my head.

"Everything okay over there?" he asks.

"I'm still just shocked that you did this."

He points at the basket. "You needed to eat."

"I could have stopped by the café on the way out of town."

"Then I wouldn't have been able to say a proper goodbye."

I turn my head to look away from him for a moment. A miserable attempt to rein my emotions in. I wring my hands in my lap, nervous energy coursing through me.

Words are heavy on my tongue. I want to ask him if this is what this is. A goodbye. But I'm too scared to. Because this moment is perfect. I don't want to tarnish it if he tells me something I don't want to hear.

From beside me, Cain riffles through the basket, and eventually, he must find what he is looking for because he reaches his hand out.

It makes me laugh as he smiles at me. "Scone?"

I bow my head and then smile. "Yeah, I'll have one." I reach out and grab it, then take a bite.

We sit in silence while we both eat.

It's not awkward like you would imagine, but rather peaceful. The sounds of nature play around us.

After we are done eating, Cain reclines back onto his elbows, his face tilting up to look at the sky.

"What will you do when you get home?"

His question is open-ended, and I'm not sure what he's asking exactly. Is he asking about the article, work . . . life?

Does he really want to know the details of my everyday life? But then I think about him at the café, and I start to speak. "I'm going to write this article first."

"And then?" he probes.

"Then I'm going to look for a new job."

"I think that's a smart choice."

"Being here has made me realize I should be doing something I love." I tilt my head up and look toward the sky. A light dusting of clouds forms a canopy above us.

"What about here made you think that?"

Lowering my gaze, I look into his eyes. "You," I say honestly.

He crosses the distance between us on the picnic blanket. At first, his lips are soft on mine, coaxing my mouth open, and then it grows more passionate.

The kiss is different.

It's as if he's trying to put into words what he's feeling with a kiss.

He's not the most open man, but I have come to understand him in a short time.

After a few seconds, he pulls, away and the moment is lost.

"Are you done?"

I'm a little taken aback by his question, and I move to stand. When I do, I see a wispy white dandelion, fluffy and in need of a wish.

Leaning over, I grab it in my hand and bring it up to my face.

"Picking my weeds?"

"A dandelion isn't a weed." Cain is standing beside me, and I hold it out for him to look at. "It's a symbol of hope and love. It's a symbol of happiness. Didn't you ever pick dandelions as a kid?"

His head shakes, lips thin. "I can't say that I have."

"It's said to carry wishes. You blow the seeds, and they fly to the sky, bringing your dreams with them." I bring the little white flower to my mouth, close my eyes, and blow.

I hope this isn't goodbye.

"What did you wish for?"

"I can't tell you that." I take one last breath, hoping for a future. Hoping for more with Cain. "I should get going."

My emotions are swirling inside me a million miles a minute, and it's time to leave.

We don't clean up the mess. Apparently, his staff will do that. Instead, he leads me back to the car, and silently, we drive to the main building.

When he pulls up, we both get out of the car.

His mood has grown solemn, and I wonder what he's thinking. Does he want to see me again? Enough with being cautious, I decide to just ask. It's time to put myself out there.

"Will I see you again?" I ask.

"I'd like that."

But his words don't make me feel any better, nor do they calm my confusion.

I can read between the lines that it's an empty promise. With this large scope of a project, he probably has no plans on being in NYC anytime soon. Couple that with the fact that he doesn't make any plans here and now with me.

Cain's brow furrows, and he stares at me intently. Then he must realize something, like the fact that I'm spiraling, because he leans forward and places a kiss on my lips.

"We will see each other again."

He doesn't say when, but it's enough to placate me.

He moves away from the car, and with that, he's stalking away.

I get in the driver's seat and watch him. I can't pull my eyes away as he leaves, and then once I pull the car out and head through the gates, I notice something odd . . . something wet on my cheek. A tear.

18

Layla

"Are you ever coming back to the office?" Mara says through the line. I have my phone sitting next to me on speaker again as my fingers type on my computer.

Halting my movements, I think about her question. "Of course, I'm coming back. I'm just busy."

"You know you can be busy in the office like the rest of us." She snickers at me.

"Mara," I mockingly scold, removing my hands from the keyboard.

"What's really going on?" Her question has me pushing my chair back from my desk, taking stock of my appearance.

I haven't showered in days. I'm a mess, and the smell emanating off me . . .

"I'm in article crisis mode," I say to her by way of an excuse.

"Got it. Basically, you're not fit for company."

Patting my hair, I'm met with a bird's nest of a mess. "That's putting it lightly."

"How bad do you smell?" She laughs.

"I smell like a garbage dump, if you must know."

"And this is because of the article . . ." She trails off, waiting for me to confess the real reason for my stench.

"Yes. What else would be the reason?" My voice is nonchalant, but I don't know if I'm fooling anyone. I'm certainly not fooling myself.

She sighs so loud it's almost like she's here in the room. "Talk to me."

What am I supposed to say? That this has nothing to do with the damn article and everything to do with the stupid man I haven't heard from in over a week?

I'm not sure what I expected when I left, but it certainly wasn't radio silence.

The worst part is that I've been a wreck since I've been home. It's embarrassing. No one needs to see me like this.

I didn't think I was the type of girl who becomes obsessed with a guy I've only known for a week, but here I am every day checking the tabloids.

Googling him.

I actually had to stop myself from setting an alert on my computer to tell me when a picture is posted of him or when his name is mentioned.

That's next-level obsessed, and even though I could chalk it up to the fact that I'm writing an article about him, I know I'm full of shit.

Even now, if I close out the open Word document on my computer, a picture of Cain Archer is staring back at me from the monitor. It's from the last night I was there. Yep, that's how pathetic I am.

It's my screensaver. Well, no, not really, but I was staring at it before, and it's still there now.

I can't help myself.

In the picture, Cain looks down at me, and a genuine smile lines his face.

I have spent countless days searching the internet for any other picture where he's smiling like this, and as of yet, I haven't been able to find one.

I actually haven't been able to find a picture where he's smiling at all.

And trust me, I have looked.

The thought that the smiles were just for me makes me happy. It does things to my stomach that I shouldn't even want to admit.

It makes my heart skip a beat. I feel like one of those hopeless romantics in a romance novel, but that was only on the first day. When I still had false illusions that he would reach out to me.

That he would want to see me.

But seeing as it truly has been radio silence and not one text all week, now those damn butterflies dancing in my stomach are dead. Replaced with slugs.

"Is this about Cain?" Mara's words pull me out of my endless mental rambling.

"What? No. Of course not."

"So, it's not about the picture from the event last night?"

"What event?" I have no idea what she's talking about. "What picture?"

"Um." She goes quiet for a second, and my heart thumps harder. "There was an event for potential residents."

"There was?"

Thump.

Thump.

"Yes."

"Where?"

"It looks like it was in some swanky clubhouse."

Our clubhouse. There is no us in this clubhouse. There is just him. This is his clubhouse.

"Yeah, it looks like an adult playground."

I swear my stomach drops. Yep. It has to be the clubhouse he took me to.

Reaching my hand out, I start to type into the browser of my computer.

The idea of seeing what she's talking about has my stomach knotting and my back going ramrod straight.

I don't want her to be on the phone with me when I do this. "Can I call you back?"

"Are you all right?" Concern is evident in her voice.

"Yep. Fine." I sound way too chirpy, which probably gives me away. "Call you back." I hang up before she can object.

That's when I find the picture she's referring to. The place is immaculate, and it reminds me of when I was there with him. The way we played together, how he looked happy when we did. I scroll through more and more of the party, and then I freeze.

I see a picture, but I need to zoom in to see what I'm looking at. There's the woman I saw at the model home, the same woman disguised under a hat, oversized sunglasses, and holding a camera. I zoom in just to confirm, and yes, it's her. She's standing next to a few people, but she's not paying attention to them.

No, she's looking in the opposite direction. I follow her line of sight to see what she is looking for, and I see it.

On the other side of the image, a group of people are talking, and in the center is Cain. She's looking at Cain.

Who is this woman? And why is she always around?

Obviously thinking of buying at The Elysian, since she was with the realtor, but it feels like there is more to the story than that. It feels like she knows him. That her being around is personal. The part that makes my stomach bottom out is that by the way he reacted to her, it feels like he knows her, as well.

I feel sick.

The smart thing to do is to open my Word document and stop this crazy pursuit of the truth of their relationship. But then I wouldn't be me, so I don't. Instead, I return my attention to the picture, zooming in once more to look at her features.

The way she looks at him has a chill running down my spine.

Is that anger?

Or fear?

She looks rattled and unnerved. I can't pinpoint it. There must be a history there. I continue to scroll more images from that night. Maybe there will be more of this mystery woman.

Maybe I will be able to get a better grasp of who she is. And what their relationship is.

There could even be one where they interact. One by one, I look at each image, and then my finger stops. There in front of me is Cain. But this time, he's not in a group, nor is he alone.

This time, a woman is draped on his arm. Tall and willowy. She looks like a model. Straight out of a magazine. She looks up at him adoringly. Whatever he's saying has her enthralled by his words.

141

I swear it feels like I'm being stabbed in my chest, spearing my heart. I want to pull the girl away from him. But instead, I shut my computer down and step away from it.

I am not the jealous type, but this can't be anything else but jealousy. I'm green with envy, and I hate it.

How can I feel this angry over a man I have no claim on?

We are from two separate worlds, and I guess, like a shooting star, our time was never meant to be.

It's time to move on.

Write this article and never think of Cain Archer again.

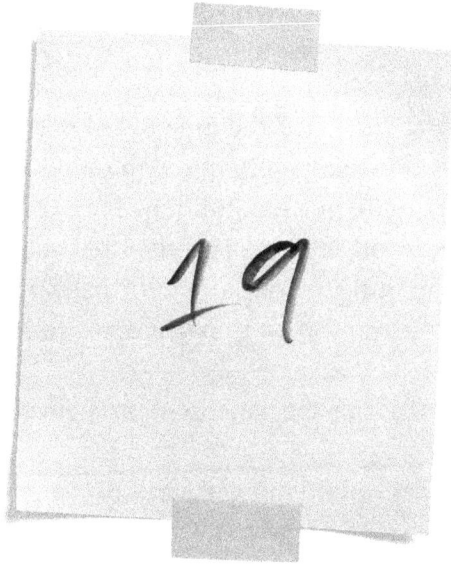

19

Cain

Pacing my office, I try to think about the solution to the question one of my builders had for me. About what to do with the open vacant space on the far side of the property. Nothing is what I want to respond.

My investors won't have that.

The acreage alone is worth millions.

Then, if we add more properties for sale, we can turn an even bigger profit, but I hate the idea of building on it.

That property is special, especially untouched.

Who am I kidding? That property is special because it's where I took Layla.

Speaking of Layla, it's been two weeks, and I have yet to get her out of my mind.

Despite how much I throw myself into work, I can't. I wonder what she's doing.

I think about her often.

Each space I go to has the lingering effect that she was there.

Doesn't matter where I am. Since I showed her every square inch of the property, she is everywhere I go.

Walking over to the window, I peer outside, looking across the vastness of the acreage.

What is she doing?

When Layla first left, I had the urge to tell her to stay. But I knew I couldn't do that. I don't have very much to offer to someone like her. Sure, she makes me more normal. But how long will it last? How long until the novelty wears off and I become the shell of a man I was before?

That's the funny thing about Layla. Normally, I wouldn't care, but with her, I do. I don't want to be in her life just to leave and have her sad when I go again.

This is what makes her special. These insistent thoughts that don't stop in my head.

I've never experienced anything like this before, and something tells me I never will. This is unique to her. I need to know what she's doing. I pick up the phone, dialing a number before I can think better of it.

"Mr. Walker's office."

"This is Cain Archer. I would like to speak to Mr. Walker." I hear the sound of her breathing, and I wonder if I took her by surprise. Normally, I'm impossible to get in touch with, and here I am, calling.

I can only imagine this is Mr. Walker's assistant. The same one who had to jump through hoops to get an interview with me.

"Can you please hold on, Mr. Archer? I'll patch you right through."

The line goes silent, and I wait. Thankfully, no annoying elevator music fills the silence. I have never been one for falseness.

"Mr. Archer. Mr. Walker here. A pleasure to hear from you again, but I must say I'm surprised. Is there something I can help you with?"

"The article."

"What about the article?" His voice rises with concern.

"Is it done yet?"

"It's been handed in for preliminary editing, fact-checking, etc. Why?"

"I would like to read the article," I say matter-of-factly.

"Of course, Mr. Archer, I'll have it sent to you right when we print it—"

"No," I interrupt. "I would like the unedited copy sent. Today." I look down at my watch. "Now, actually."

"Mr. Archer—"

"If you want to work with me or any developer involved with me, the article will be in my email within the hour."

I hang up, not waiting for an objection. I am not one to be trifled with.

With that settled and knowing full well I will get what I want, I move on to my next task. I pull out my sketchbook and start to design the next phase of the project.

Not even thirty minutes go by before I hear the ping on my computer. I place my pencil down, brush off the debris left on my hands, then slide my chair over in front of my computer.

I click thru the emails until I see the one from Layla's boss.

The full article. Complete with Layla's name on the byline.

I start to read, and instantly, I am transformed. I'm no longer sitting in my office.

Now I'm experiencing The Elysian through her eyes. I'm seeing it for what it's supposed to be, for the magnificent space that Layla's words have captured.

When I first met her, I knew she was special, but reading the way she immersed herself in my world, and then how she spun it out in a way that others would want to do the same thing as well, has me stunned.

As I keep reading, I notice the tone of the article changes. In the beginning, her first impressions and her voice in the article were excited and enthralled, but as it proceeds, the spark goes missing from the story. Something has changed, and the ending feels like writing it was a chore for her.

What happened?

Something is different with this woman.

I'm not sure how I know this, how I know in the bottom of my soul that something is off with her, but I know it.

Go to New York. See what happened.

I need to see why the spark is missing from the story. It's clearly there in the beginning. The end doesn't feel right, and I need to know why.

I pick up the phone and call Barbara, telling her I'm going to New York City.

She doesn't offer any comments, but I wouldn't expect her to. I know it's not a good idea. The timing isn't right. There's nothing smart about going in the middle of wrapping up the final preparations to open.

Going to the city right now is a luxury I don't have time for. I cannot afford to leave here at the moment, yet something says I can't afford to stay.

I need to make sure this article is perfect.

That's what I tell myself, but I know I'm full of shit. This isn't about the article; this is about the writer.

No. No. No.

It's about the article. This is the final piece to secure that the grand opening is everything I need it to be in order for it to be perfect. We need to make a splash. Show the world something no one has ever seen before.

"I'll be gone for the rest of the week," I tell her.

That should be enough time to figure out what's going on.

Obviously, I can't be a normal guy. I can't just call ahead and tell her I'm on my way. I have to sit across the street like a stalker. Taking up a table in the coffee shop across the corner from her building, just waiting for a chance to see her.

It was bound to happen. I was always destined for this.

I've never been normal, clearly . . .

This isn't the first time I've let this part of me out, the part I try desperately to push away, but I thought that time of my life had passed.

I thought I had the urges under control.

Wrong.

My mom said I would wind up this way. That there was no escaping the way the men in my family behaved. And here I am, proving her right.

If only she could see me now. Hope she's happy wherever she is.

But my self-deprecating thoughts are interrupted when I see her walk out of her building and to the curb to hail a cab.

She's beautiful.

My breath catches, and there's that warmth radiating through me again.

That's all I needed to feel like this was all worth it. Everything I've done so far was to get me to this point. Where I can see the woman who I've become infatuated with.

I can't let her see the real monster inside. I know it's there, and my feelings for her keep him locked down.

Mostly.

20

Layla

'm back at the office. Finally.

Sitting at my desk, I have the article open in front of me. I'm looking over the notes my editor left on my first preliminary copy.

The article is good, but it's not great. Not yet, at least.

The editor mentioned that the first half was stronger than the second.

Most of the first half was written at night while I was still on the property.

Now I need to go back from the beginning and make sure the tone and voice are consistent throughout the piece.

I start to read from the beginning, and as I do, it feels like I'm back there reliving it.

This part is good, really good.

It's probably the best work I have ever done.

Placing my hands on the keyboard, I scroll down, but I'm not even halfway down the page when I hear the sound of a knock on my cubicle wall.

Looking up, I see Mara leaning over the divider.

She has a funny look on her face. It's almost comical. She looks like a cartoon, like when the cat ate the canary.

"What's got you so amused?"

"You're never going to believe who I just saw walking into the Mr. Walker's office."

I rack my brain for an answer but come up short.

"Yeah, probably not, but by the way you're grinning, I'd have to say the prince of a large country."

"Close." She giggles.

"Spit it out. I don't have all day here." I motion to the pile of papers on my desk. It's a mess, but I work better this way. "I do have work to do, so don't do that thing you do. Just tell me."

She grins. "You ready?"

I roll my eyes. "Jeez. Mara. Come on," I whisper-shout, not wanting the whole office to hear but wanting to know, nonetheless.

"Cain Archer."

"What?"

All of a sudden, it feels like I'm swimming underwater. My hearing becomes muffled. She couldn't possibly have just said Cain is here, could she?

"Are you sure it's him?" I whisper.

"I'm not a complete idiot, Layla."

"Obviously, I know that. I just—"

"I know." She's my closest friend. Of course, she knows how my distance, leaving him, and the rejection have affected me. "It's him. And something tells me he's here because of your article or maybe because of you, so I wanted to give you a heads-up so that you were prepared when he rounds the corner in a few minutes."

"You don't know that he's here for me."

"A recluse architect who never gives interviews shows up at a magazine, and you don't think it's about your article or you?" She has a point.

He's here for me or, at the very least, for what I wrote. My heart hammers in my chest. It feels like a stampede of elephants is running amok.

I will it to calm down, but there is no calming down this torrent of emotions grappling inside me.

Did he hate the article?

Did he even see the article?

That would be a gross violation of Mr. Walker's journalism ethics if he showed it to Cain, but unfortunately, my boss does what he wants regardless of what's right and wrong, so I have to assume that's why Cain came.

I'm so confused, and I could try to figure out the reason he's here and torment myself with all the what-ifs and the whys, but the truth is, the only way I'm getting an answer is when he comes out here and tells me.

A strange, nervous energy cycles through my body, and I feel my knees shake. How long do I have to wait?

I catch my reflection on the computer screen, and I'm thankful that today, unlike last week, or the week before, I took the time to make sure I looked professional and at my best.

I try to concentrate on the article in front of me. I try to focus on work, but instead, I'm really watching the archway where the hall connects with the management offices.

I remain at my desk, and then I see them. My boss and Cain are rounding the corner.

Mr. Walker makes it outside my cubicle, and Cain is standing behind him with a grin teasing his lips.

I move to a standing position, and I catch Cain's eyes as he sweeps them down my body again.

Thank God I cared about my appearance today.

"Layla," my boss says, and I peel my gaze off Cain and look at Mr. Walker.

"Yes?"

"Mr. Archer is here to see if you have any more questions for him before you finalize the article. I have let him know that you are at his disposal and vice versa until you feel you have enough information to write the end of it."

"Can we go somewhere quieter to talk?" Cain asks.

I bite my lip, my mouth still parched from his unexpected arrival.

"After you," he says, and I grab my purse from the bottom desk drawer and walk us to the nearest elevator.

We wait in silence for it to arrive, and then when it does, it's jam-packed, so we're still unable to speak.

Once we're in the lobby together, we maneuver toward the exit. Luckily, it's not busy at this time of day, so it only takes a few seconds before we step outside into the New York City air. The temperature outside is staggering compared to the buildings near arctic air-conditioning. Goose bumps break out against my skin the way it does when you spike a fever.

Sure, it's from the weather . . .

It has nothing to do with the fact that Cain is here in New York City. Standing next to me in broad daylight. *Nope. Nothing.*

We continue to walk, my heels clacking on the pavement as I try to keep pace with him. We pass a hot dog vendor on the way, and the fragrance wafting off the cart makes my stomach feel queasy.

Definitely nerves.

I can't ignore the way my blood pumps faster the farther we walk. Why is he here?

By the time Cain points at a small café, it feels like my heart will explode. "Here," he says, and I raise a brow. "It's great and quiet."

I clear my throat. "You've been here before?"

"Yes. With an acquaintance who owns an advertising agency in the city." His hand reaches out and pushes the door open. "After you." Always the gentleman.

When we step inside, it's exactly like what Cain said: quiet. Not a sound can be heard. It reminds me of the floors in the main building of The Elysian.

But when I move a step in and hear my footsteps, I have to stifle back a laugh. Of course, they can be heard. No one but Cain would install soundproof floors. It seems there is no hostess, but that doesn't deter Cain. He steps up behind me, places his hand on the small of my back, and leads me toward a table in the back of the space.

This time, when he touches me, I shiver.

A full-body shiver that I'm sure he notices. He's polite enough not to mention it.

My body's reaction to him needs to be tamped down.

This can't be okay.

He has me on edge, teetering to fall just from his proximity.

When we are standing in front of the table, I scoot in, and Cain sits across from me. Only a moment goes by before we both order a coffee from the waitress walking by.

Glancing around the restaurant, I notice we are the only table occupied. I'm lost in thought until I hear the sound of the two mugs being set down on the table. Then my nose is hit with the robust smell, and my mouth begins to water.

My hands move to grab mine, and I don't bother with cream or sugar. Instead, I bypass them to drink it black. Not how I normally take it, but my nerves are shot right now, and I'm afraid my fingers will shake if I try to pour some.

From across the table, Cain's fingers move absently on the side of the mug as he drinks.

Finally, I cut the silence. "I don't need your help being a journalist, just like you don't need my help being an architect," I practically spit out.

"Layla." He levels me with his stare. "I'm not here for a damn article."

"You aren't?"

"No."

I go quiet again. Every time I try to speak, my words get stuck in my throat, and nothing comes out. Grabbing the mug in front of me, I take a sip and then try again. "How's the opening?"

"It's coming along."

"Are you ready?" I ask as my leg bounces under the table. It's only been two weeks, but it feels like a lifetime since I've been at The Elysian. Being here with him brings out all the emotions I've tried my best to push down.

"As ready as I'll ever be."

"Will it be weird?"

Cain places his mug down on the table and cocks his head at my words. "Will what be weird?"

"To share your vision with the world."

"It will be." He goes quiet for a second, and then he nods his head. I'm not sure what he's nodding at, maybe something he's thinking about, but you never can tell with Cain. "But coupled with the article and opening, I anticipate it will be successful."

I lean forward and place my elbows down on the linoleum table. "I can't imagine anything you do not being successful."

I can feel his stare through to my bones. There is something different about it. A flash of darkness. "You would be surprised."

I want to ask what he means, but I don't dare to. I'm not sure how much time we have, and I don't want to spoil it by putting him on edge or in a bad mood.

We spend the next hour talking. But it's small talk. It's not like the things we talked about when we were together in the mountains.

We keep the conversation simple, and for the first time since I've met Cain, it feels like we're strangers.

I don't like it.

It's like the light switch he had illuminated just for me went off, and now it feels like I'm everyone else.

Once we're done, we stand, and when we step outside, he stops walking and turns to me. "Would you like me to walk you back to the office?"

"I'm actually not going to go back to the office."

My plan wasn't to work from home today, but after seeing Cain, I'm one hundred percent positive I won't be able to think straight for the rest of the day.

"Where are you going?" he asks as we begin to walk.

"I'm going to head home. I'll continue to work from there."

Cain stops walking, so I do the same, turning to face him on the busy sidewalk. "Then let me take you."

"Okay," I mutter, nervous energy settling inside me. Oh, who am I kidding? It's been swirling inside me since he showed up at the office earlier. Now it's a full-fledged tornado.

"How far is it? Should we grab my car?"

I try my best to remain calm, shouting out all the questions brewing inside me. My fingers absently play with the hem of the shirt. Anything to distract me from his presence.

"I only live a few blocks from here. It's a nice day. We can walk."

We start to head off in the direction of where my apartment is, and although we are companions on this track, neither one of us speaks. I am too lost in my own head, wondering why he's here, and I don't know what he's thinking, but as the time trickles on and we get closer, I know I need to ask.

When we arrive at my building, I use the key to let myself in, and then we walk the two flights of stairs to my apartment.

"Why are you really here?" I ask, breaking the silence and asking the question that has been haunting me for the last few hours.

A sinking feeling inside me tells me it's because he hates the article, that it's because he read it, the early copy, and he saw what my boss saw. Which was the disconnect in my voice.

I bet he wants me to scrap the whole thing and start from scratch.

That has to be the reason he came back. If there's any other reason, he would've been here sooner, right?

And at my question, he grins and steps forward. My back hits the door.

"Because I couldn't get you out of my mind."

21

Layla

'm about to respond.

Ask him if that's how he feels, then why hasn't he called me or acted on it? But his mouth cuts me off.

His firm lips probe mine, coaxing me to open for him.

When I do, his tongue sweeps in. All words are lost to me.

He's essentially shut me up, and I love it.

I love the way he kisses, and if it were up to me, I'd never let this moment end. That is until I hear the sound of a door closing and remember where we are.

In the middle of the hall, kissing like no one is around. But there are people around, and I live here. But despite all of this, I can't find it in myself to pull away, so while my mouth mingles with his, I reach my hand out and shuffle with the keys.

It takes me a good minute to jam the key into the lock and turn it, and Cain chuckles against my lips.

"Bet you wish your microchip worked here." I laugh back, but again, he silences my words as he pushes me into the now-open door of my apartment and into my foyer.

Never separating, Cain guides me against the wall.

The kiss intensifies, his lips growing hungrier as his hands start to roam over me.

He cups my face, and then Cain's fingers glide down my jaw, down my neck, until his hand rests on my collarbones.

He applies pressure, and I feel like I could become lightheaded from the strength of his fingers, but he loosens his grip after a second.

We continue to kiss, and he never lets go of my neck. Instead, his other hand trails down until it finds the exposed skin of my thigh.

The feel of his fingertips on my skin has me moaning into his mouth. His lips stop moving, and he hesitates for one minute, leaning his head against my forehead.

"If you want to stop—"

I shake my head frantically.

Then I feel myself being lifted into his arms, walked deeper into the apartment, and before I know what's happening, I'm being placed on my bed.

I stare at Cain where he stands and wait for him to move, and then he is. Pulling my skirt off, I lift my hips, letting him take it off me. He caresses my thighs, running his hand up to my shirt. In a swift moment, my blouse buttons are flying, and I'm sitting before him in just my bra and panties.

"I need to taste you," he groans, and then his hands reach out, and he's pushing me down onto my back. I feel his hands on my hips as he removes the scrap of lace separating us.

My body trembles with anticipation.

I lean up on my elbows and watch him. His face looks dark, his eyes hooded. He drops to his knees in front of where my butt hangs off the bed.

The hammering of my heart is painful as he pulls my legs apart, opening me up to his perusal. The next thing I know, he's placing my legs on his shoulders.

He leans forward and parts my folds, then his thumb begins to strum my clit.

I lift my hips in answer, and he responds by removing his hand. I groan in protest, but my words die when his tongue replaces it.

When he starts to lick and suck, I think I might die.

My whole body comes alive, my hips rocking back and forth.

"So good," he moans against my damp skin. He sucks harder, and when he nips at me, I swear I'm at the top of a roller coaster, about to fall over the edge.

"I'm going to come."

"Do it, Layla," he challenges. "Come on my tongue." This time, it feels like an order.

His mouth tightens around me, sending me over the edge. A primal moan pours from my mouth.

I can feel myself come apart.

As the thrust of his tongue grows harder, so does my orgasm.

It keeps going and going, and I swear it will never stop. My walls contract, pulsing and gripping, needing desperately for something to fill me.

"Fuck me." I'm riding the edge of oblivion, panting and not being able to control myself. "Please. I need you."

He pulls away, and then I watch through hooded lids as he removes his clothes, pulls a condom out of his pocket, and sheathes himself.

He crawls up my body, and I wrap my legs around him as he aligns himself with my core.

One powerful thrust and Cain Archer is fully seated inside me.

He holds still, not moving an inch, but the need to have him do something has me lifting my hips.

His cock thrusts in and out.

"Just like that."

He slows his pace at my words, dragging his cock slowly in and out of me. He's trying to torture me, and it's working.

He gives a little laugh as I squirm under him, trying to speed him along. And then he pushes back inside me.

"You're not in control here," he practically growls out.

His hands grip me under my thighs, and he lifts me to get a better angle, fucking me again. I wrap my arms around his neck, and he kisses me. Our mouths collide in a frenzy of passion.

"Feels so fucking good," he says through gritted teeth. He readjusts his hands to cup my ass. "I need to feel your tight pussy when you come."

His dirty words are my complete undoing.

He pumps into me mercilessly as he brings me closer to the brink. Then I'm falling over the edge, and he's groaning right beside me.

He collapses into my arms.

I've never felt anything like this in my life, and the thought scares me.

Maybe Mara is right.

I could lose myself completely to this man.

The question is, do I care?

And as he places a soft kiss on the skin of my neck, I think to myself, *No, I don't.*

I would happily get lost as long as I can feel this way, even if only for a brief time.

22

Layla

When I open my eyes the next day, I find Cain lying beside me with his hand thrown over his face. The early morning stubble on his chin reminds me of all the things we did yesterday. It was incredible, but now I'm supposed to go to the office.

How can I leave him here?

I let my eyes wander over his face, down his collar, and then I see his exposed chest. The blanket lays over his hips, but that perfect V is visible.

I can't leave.

I grab my phone, careful not to wake him, and fire a text to my boss, telling him that I'll be working from home to finish this article.

Then I'm removing the blanket and crawling closer to him.

With the blanket off his body, I can't help but stare.

"Morning," he mumbles, but I don't respond. Instead, I lick my lips and take him in my mouth. At first, as I lick him, he doesn't move. But as I continue, I hear him moan. "Now this is how I want to wake up every day."

His words spur me on, and I become even more enthusiastic about my early morning task.

I bob my head up and down, and he grows even larger, if that's possible.

"Off." I look up at him, confused. "Inside you," he groans, and then his hand reaches out next to the bed where my box of condoms is. He sheathes himself, and the next thing I know, I'm being flipped and rolled onto my stomach. He moves fast.

His hands land on my ass, then he thrusts inside me from behind.

There is nothing sweet or nice about this.

He owns me as he pumps fast and hard.

"Mine." His words make my body quiver. I moan at what he says. "Good girl."

Then he pulls himself out and slams back in. He continues this pace, and soon, we are both falling over the edge.

Both of us lie on the bed, breathing heavily, trying to regulate our breathing.

"When do you have to go to work?"

"I actually emailed my boss. I'm working from home today. I thought we could hang out together while I finish the article."

"Is that what you really wanna do? I won't get in the way?"

"Yes, I want to spend the day together. And no, you won't be in the way. I do have to take breaks."

"Sounds like a plan. We can do that."

I realize I don't want to work, and I just want to spend the day with him. "And right now is break time. Let's get dressed," I say.

"Then grab food? I know how you don't like missing breakfast," he responds.

"I think that's a solid plan."

After we shower and dress, we go to the kitchen, and I realize I have nothing to eat. He laughs. I love the way his face lights up in amusement, but somehow not shock, that I have nothing to cook.

"Let's go out."

Together, we leave my apartment and head to the coffee shop just across the street for breakfast sandwiches. Once we finish a quick meal, we find ourselves on the street corner. Cain turns to me. "You lead the way." I'm quiet for a second, and then he shrugs.

"I showed you The Elysian. Now it's your turn to show me your city."

"Okay. I can do that." I try to think of where I want to take him, and the first thing that comes to mind is the small gallery that's only a few blocks away from my apartment.

I have to assume Cain has been to New York City many times, so I don't want to take him anywhere that would be super touristy.

Plus, that's just not the type of man he is.

I don't think that's something he would enjoy.

Knowing him, I know he'd like to see a place I like to go to.

Taking his hand in mine, I lead us down the block, and when I see the eclectic sign, I motion to the door. He steps forward and opens it.

"This gallery is my favorite in the city," I tell him.

"Then I can't wait to see it."

"The paintings here are not over the top. They are watercolors, but the palette is grays, whites, and black. I think you'll love it."

"I'm sure I will."

"There is an eerie presence to them, almost like New York City during the rain. I don't know why, but it reminds me of your buildings. How the mountains reflect off the glass-mirrored walls. It makes you fall into the space. That's what it's like here. It feels like you're surrounded by a rainy day in the city."

Walking around, Cain is silent, then he walks up to one painting in particular.

This one is muted shapes and colors, but if you peer closely, you can tell it's a home.

He points at the artwork in front of him. "This."

"I know."

He doesn't say what he thinks because I know he came to the same conclusion I did. This painting depicts his vision of The Elysian to perfection.

"I need to have this," he says, and I nod in agreement.

"It would look beautiful in the hallway that leads to the solarium, wouldn't it?"

"It is exactly what I'm looking for." He continues to stare at it, and I watch him.

I wonder if this is what it looked like when he watched me looking at his buildings. A sense of pride weaves its way through me that I'm

161

able to give him this. "I am going to speak to the curator," he says when he walks off, leaving me standing in the center of the gallery.

I walk up to the next painting. Again, it's a building, but this time, when you look at it, you can see two figures inside, entwined in an embrace.

It's not obvious to the unobservant eye; a person would have to stare until the lines separate, but it's a pair of lovers.

It makes me think of last night, of the way he grabbed me in his arms.

The way he kissed me and the way he made love to me after.

A warm feeling spreads through my limbs, and I wistfully think of how I can't wait for him to touch me again.

I could spend the rest of my life allowing myself to worship him and letting him do the same to me. Still, as I stand here looking around the room at all the images, I realize that maybe I'm in over my head.

He's here buying a painting to bring back to the mountains, and when he leaves, I'll be left here with this mounting obsession I have toward him.

It's only growing stronger. If I feel this way after only one night, what will happen if he stays longer?

I'm lost in thought over my mild obsession when I feel a hand grab my arm and pull me.

Next thing I know, the object of said obsession has me cornered in a small, dark alcove.

His mouth is on mine before I can object.

Lips, teeth, mouths colliding.

His hand grabs my hair and pulls my head back to expose my neck, and then he's sucking on the vein.

It's like he wants to devour me, and I want him to.

Maybe this isn't one-sided. Maybe he also feels the way I do.

As if reading my thoughts, he groans into my neck. "I can't get enough of you." He nips, and then I feel his hands sliding under the material of my skirt.

I pant into his neck. "We can't."

"Sure, we can." And then his finger is inside me. I let out a sound, but it is cut off by his mouth as he swallows my moans.

His fingers thrust inside me, and I can feel myself coming apart.

I'm about to fall over the edge when I hear a voice in the background. Cain halts, and I squirm against him, begging him to take me over the edge.

I pull my head out from his neck and implore with my eyes that he continues.

He doesn't, though. Instead, he grins, removes his fingers, and licks them clean.

I want to scream and shout, but I don't. I push down the need growing inside me as Cain steps away from me and goes to talk to the curator. It takes a few minutes for me to pull myself out of the haze.

Inhaling and then exhaling, I right myself.

And when I'm no longer hot and bothered and feel more normal, I step out from the alcove and join them where they are standing in front of the painting.

They must've reached some sort of arrangement because they're exchanging business cards, and Cain is taking my hand and leading me out, back into the New York City streets.

"Where to now?" he asks.

"Let's see where our feet take us," I speak. "When I first moved to the city, it was one of my favorite things to do. On a Sunday afternoon in the middle of the summer, I would walk and walk and walk with no direction and see where it took me."

"Then that is exactly what we should do." We start our path with no destination, and as we walk, we hold hands and speak of nothing important.

I tell him about my coworkers, and he listens. I talk about Mara and how we met that first day when I started to work at the magazine. How we were instant friends. And how she's the only person I can complain to about how much I hate my job.

I expect Cain to say something, maybe object, because obviously, his passion is architecture, but he doesn't. He just listens, and it's refreshing. As someone who works in the field of journalism, I feel all I do is listen, so it's nice to be the one speaking for once.

Soon, we are by Madison Square Park. Across from us, I can see the familiar hamburger stand, and my mouth waters. Cain is looking at me, and then he smiles softly. "Someone is hungry."

"Aren't you?"

His lips tip up into a wicked smirk. "Not for burgers."

"And what, pray tell, are you hungry for?" I ask in a coy manner, knowing full well what his answer will be.

He pulls me closer, nuzzling his mouth in my neck. "You. I'm hungry for you." His breath tickles my skin, and goose bumps break out.

It takes every ounce of strength inside me not to tell him just to take me home and finish what he started at the gallery. My stomach growls, and I'm happy I've made the right decision to track forward on my quest for a greasy burger and fries.

It only takes us a few minutes, and we find a small table. Once we have the food, I take a bite of my burger, and it's delicious, the taste bursting in my mouth. I let out a groan.

"If you keep making that sound, I won't let you finish."

"Let? And just how will you stop me, Mr. Archer?"

I know I'm playing with the beast. I'm toying with him, and I shouldn't aggravate him. Because I can tell he's only moments away from throwing me down and ravishing me on this table in front of guests.

Maybe that's what he likes. Maybe he likes the audience. I'm about to speak when I notice something. Cain's flirtatious grin is gone.

He looks like he's lost in thought, and I wonder what he's thinking about. There is definitely a noticeable shift in him.

His shoulders are tight now. The bone in his jaw is rigid. But the way his eyes are narrowed has me wondering what happened.

"Are you okay?"

That's when I notice that he's not looking at me. He's looking above my shoulder.

I turn to follow his line of sight when I see her.

The photographer. The lady from the showing. The woman from The Elysian.

Why is she here? Is she following him? Does she mean something to him?

Maybe she's an ex and obsessed with him for some reason.

Maybe he broke her heart, and she can't get over him.

Did he hurt her?

My mind is racing. I want to ask him, so I turn away from the woman and look at Cain to do just that, but when our gazes lock, he looks different.

I've never seen him this closed off before. A black cloud has fallen over him, and my body tenses with fear.

I dare not mention it now.

It looks like he could explode right on the spot.

I'll have to ask him later.

23

Cain

Hand in hand, we walk through Madison Square Park as I lead us to a nearby table to eat the food we just purchased.

Ever the gentleman I am supposed to be, I pull her chair out. But the funny thing is, when I do it, I don't need the inner voice prompting my every step. With her, I just want to. She takes a seat, and I sit beside her.

We begin to eat, and as we do, we are both quiet, but that's the thing with Layla. It never feels awkward or like I need to find words to fill the silence, and the better part is, she doesn't expect me to.

She takes me for who I am.

And it is one of the things I appreciate the most about her. I never have to be fake with her, and I never want to be.

The man I am is better when she is around, so I gravitate toward her.

As we continue to eat, I look at the buildings around me, often being inspired by my surroundings.

That's when I see her.

Again.

This isn't once. Or twice now. Fuck, this isn't even the fourth time I've seen her. She's treading on dangerous ground.

I've let this go too far.

I narrow my eyes, but she doesn't avert her gaze away from me.

Instead, as I stare at her, I shake my head, tapping lightly on my throat. Implying without words that she is not welcome.

At the movement, her eyes widen. She understands what I'm saying, her own hand lifting to the scar on her throat.

But she doesn't leave. Instead, she hardens her stare.

As though she isn't afraid of me.

It's a bad choice.

She should be.

She has observed my hate before, and she should not make the mistake to think me weak.

I am not one to be trifled with, and she needs to learn her place.

"Are you okay?" I hear from beside me.

I turn to see Layla watching me, and then she pulls her gaze from me and looks in the direction I was just looking in.

I know she sees her.

I know she wants to ask me.

When she turns her attention back to me, the questions are silently written all over her features.

"Yes," I grit out, trying to keep my voice neutral. For the first time since I've known Layla, I will my lips to part. I make myself throw down the façade I've mastered throughout my life. "Of course." I reach across the table, taking her hand in mine. "But—"

Her eyes widen. "What?"

I drop her hand and stand abruptly. "I want to get out of here." Layla is quick to join me.

"Is there a reason?" Her voice dips, and her gaze darts back to the woman. The bane of my existence.

"Yes."

Moving in the opposite direction, Layla tries to catch up. Her steps are hurried as if she thought I would leave her. Spoiler alert, I'm never going to do that. Then she stops abruptly, and I halt my movements to turn back and see what she's doing.

A part of me thinks she's about to confront her, but then I see Layla reach to the sidewalk. She's grabbing a damn dandelion. She looks at me and then back at my stalker. Layla closes her eyes and blows at the flower. The wisps spread through the air. The *wish* moving toward the sky.

"What did you wish for?" I ask.

She shakes her head. "I can't tell you that, remember?"

"Give me a hint, then."

Her movement is subtle. Her gaze drifts back across the park to where *she* sits, still watching us. "I'm just happy you're here with me." She doesn't go on, but I don't need her to. I know what she wished for. For us to be together. For no obstacles. No drama. *Just us*. I can give her that.

"Let's go," I say again.

"Where?"

"Home." I lean closer, brushing my lips to her ear. "I want to fuck you." She shivers at my words, and I know they have done their job. All thoughts of the stranger across the park are long forgotten, but just in case, I add, "I want to feel your sweet pussy squeezing my cock." I draw the words out slowly, and I feel her gasp.

With that, I pull her along the sidewalk with me.

I can feel her pulse beating rapidly as we head back to her place. She's excited.

Desperate for me. And that's okay.

I prefer it this way because if she knew the truth, if only she knew the wolf that walked alongside her, she'd run.

⚔

We're not even out of the foyer of her apartment before I'm pulling her toward me and lifting her up.

Her back hits the wall, and with my free hand, I'm pulling my cock out of my pants.

I am a man possessed.

I need the oblivion only she can give me.

Seeing *her* at the park brought out the monster in me, and only sinking inside Layla will quiet the beast.

Once my dick is out of my pants, I use my hand to push the lace aside.

"Wait. Cond—"

"Nothing," I grit. "I want nothing between us."

I feel fucking possessed. I should get a condom, but I can't find it in me to care. I need to feel her. All of her.

"I'm cle—"

"I know you are." I take her lips in mine.

"Are yo—" she tries to say as I line myself up, teasing her entrance.

"Yes." And with no other words needing to be said, I thrust inside her.

Once I am fully sheathed, I let out a long breath. I hold myself still, not moving an inch until the need to thrust forward is overwhelming. So, I do. I pull out. Then I slam back in.

"Fucking perfect. You are fucking perfect."

She's so tight and wet. I can't slow down.

"Oh, God."

I pick up my pace at her words, dragging my cock in and out of her greedy pussy at a punishing pace. I can feel her tightening and clenching every time I push back inside. She's close and so am I.

Reaching up with one hand, I can't stop myself from wrapping my fingers around her luscious neck. Just a little bit. Just a little bit tighter.

I take out my frustration on her body. I pour my emotions into each thrust of my hips.

My body says all the words I can't say. I start pulsing my hand tighter around her throat.

Layla gasps, her hands on my shoulders trying to give equal compression, but she's no match.

"Please." There's that magic word from her pouty lips. What I'm not expecting is what she says next. "More."

And then, with that word, the sounds of Layla coming apart, and a final thrust, I purge myself of the day. Of the woman. Of everything but the feel of her tightening around me. Of the series of pulses her body gives me, and when I can't take much more, I feel my own orgasm rushing to a head, and then with Layla, I tip over the edge. Falling over the abyss, finding my release.

My monster has met its match.

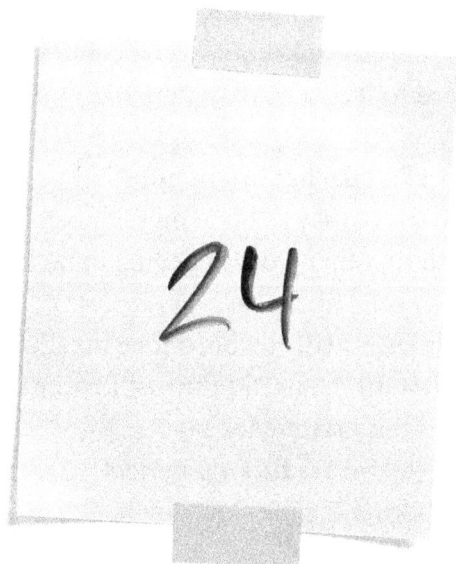

24

Layla

He's like an animal. I d^pon't know what set him off, but I would be lying if I didn't admit, if only to myself, that I love the way he touches me, the way he fucks me.

Because that is what this man does. There is nothing sweet about him right now, and I don't even care.

When both of us come down from our high, he pulls out of me, and the moment he does, I miss his presence right away.

Then he moves his hand from my throat, unwraps me from around him, and brings my feet back down to the floor. They aren't there long as he picks me up bridal style and makes his way down my hall, into my bathroom, and turns the shower on. Once he does that, he sets me down, and I work to remove my clothes that he left on, and so does he, and then we are stepping into the hot water.

I expect for him to say something, maybe explain to me why he took me so savagely against the foyer wall, but instead, he grabs the shampoo from the wall.

"Can I?" he asks.

"Yes." I watch as he lathers it in his hand and then steps up to me.

"What are you doing?" I ask dumbly as he starts to wash my hair.

"Taking care of you." His voice is low, and I can almost not make out his words over the sound of the water pounding down on us.

"Why?"

I tilt my head up at him. His eyes seem different now. They are no longer heated with passion but rather sadness.

Is he regretting what happened? "I was rough," he mutters.

I lift my hand and place my hand on his chest. He looks down at where my hand touches him.

"I liked it."

"I hurt you." He touches my neck, and when he does, I feel the tender skin.

In the moment of passion, his hand was wrapped around my neck. "I'm okay."

"Would you tell me if you weren't?"

"Yes," I say with a force I didn't know I was capable of.

His face grows more serious, if that is even possible, and he continues to stare at my neck. A bruise must be forming. I lift onto my tiptoes, suds of soap running down my face, and place a kiss on his lips.

"I promise you. I'm okay."

Lifting my hands, I wrap them around his torso, and he must believe me because I feel his body relax into mine.

After a few seconds, I pull away, and this time when I look at him, I can see the change. He's found the peace he needed, and it makes my own shoulders uncoil.

Despite the change of mood, Cain continues to take care of me, wash me, and then, when the shower is done, he wraps a fluffy towel around me and leads me to my bed.

We both lie in bed, and this time when he kisses me, it's slow and sensual. There is no rush. No frenzy. No, this time, it's everything it should be at the moment, exactly what we both need as he slowly makes love to me. Worshiping every inch of my body with sweet, slow caresses.

The connection we have doesn't need words. We rise and fall together as if our bodies have always belonged together.

Sometime later, my eyes flutter open, and I realize I must have fallen asleep. Rubbing the sleep from my eyes, I look around the room.

I can't find Cain anywhere.

Did he leave?

I start to sit up, feeling myself sink at the notion that he did, but then I hear a sound in the kitchen.

Standing from the bed, I see my robe laying on the edge of the bed, and a smile spreads across my face as I realize Cain left it there for me.

Slipping the robe on, I make my way into the kitchen, where I find him.

He's dressed in his pants and no shirt, and my face warms at the sight. He's chopping up vegetables when I come up behind him and wrap my arms around his waist. "What are you doing?"

"Making us dinner."

"I am hungry." I snuggle in closer.

"I figured you were."

"What are you making?" I drop my hands and step back; he turns from the counter to face me.

"Well, it was slim pickings in here."

Crossing my arms at my chest, I do my best to give him my most over-the-top eye roll. "Yeah, well, some of us are super busy writing articles on this super weird architect."

He lifts his brow. "Super weird, huh?"

"Yep."

"Does he have any redeemable qualities?"

Lifting my hand, I mockingly look at my nails as if this conversation is boring me. "Nah."

"Nothing?" His hand reaches out and trails his index finger across my neck. "Are you sure?"

"Oh, well, there is this thing he does with his tongue."

His movements stop, and I want to beg him to continue. "Do tell."

I roll my eyes. "What did you find in my pathetic kitchen?" He drops his hand, turns to grab something off the counter, and then lifts a box of store-bought dried pasta. I grimace; who knows how long that thing has been in my pantry.

"Pasta and a few vegetables."

"Simple. Plain." I shrug.

"Not because of me," he chides as he moves back to his chopping.

Cain looks like a natural in the kitchen. Is there anything this man can't do?

It's almost annoying how perfect he is. "Curious minds want to know if this were your place and had actual food, what would you make?"

"Still pasta, but something with artichokes and lemon. Not just cheese."

"Again. Busy here." I motion dramatically, hands flailing, to myself.

"It's fine. I'd happily eat shit to be able to spend time with you." His words take me by surprise, making me feel warm and fuzzy inside.

Cain moves back toward the counter, lifting a spoon, and I watch him stir the sauce.

"What's your favorite food?" I ask.

"I don't know." He moves away from the sauce to the other pot, and then he adds the pasta to the boiling water.

"Well, if you don't know that, how about what's your favorite dish to cook, then?"

"I don't know," he says again.

I sigh. "You're not really helping me here, Cain."

"As long as I'm cooking for you . . . anything will be my favorite."

At that, I swear I melt.

This isn't good.

Any time I spend with him will make it harder when he will eventually leave.

I smile up at him.

Play it cool. Don't show him how much his words are affecting you. Because that's the thing. I'm falling for him, and I'm scared because I know he's going to leave. What will happen to my heart then?

I move away from him and go to grab a bottle of white wine from the fridge.

"Do you want some?"

"No, thank you," he responds, and that's when something hits me.

"You don't drink, do you?" He had a glass at the party, but I never saw him lift it to his lips.

"No. I don't."

"Is there a reason for that?"

"I don't like to lose control," he says before he turns around again.

I sit at the small table and watch him. I like how he meanders through my kitchen like he's been here a million times. It feels right, and another pang of worry creeps in. His eyes lift, and when they meet mine, he smiles.

"Need help in there?"

"No . . . I want to do this . . . for you."

I take a sip of the crisp, cold wine. As I sit at the table, I pull my computer closer to me.

Guess it's time to finish this article, and we can put a bow on whatever this is before it becomes too much.

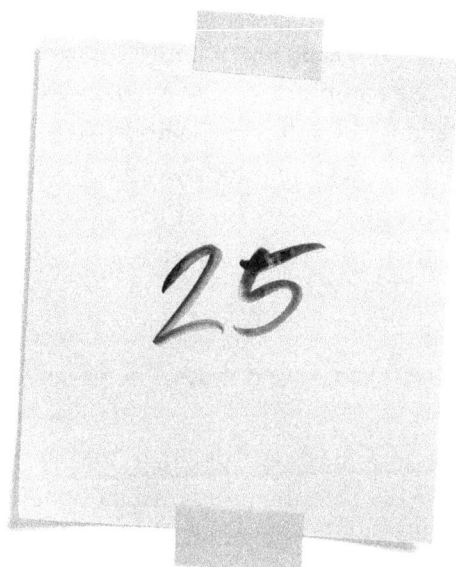

25

Layla

After we are done eating, Cain volunteers to clean up the mess while I sit in front of my computer again. Finishing the last part of the article means that this happy chapter is going to end.

I'm not ready for what happens after publishing but making Cain proud of my work drives me to finish the task. A new sense of inspiration flows through me as my fingers hit the keyboard at an alarmingly fast pace. The emotions that The Elysian evokes pour through me. Hopefully, this article will allow everyone to see and feel it, too.

Everyone, but especially Cain.

I'm not sure how long I sit there, but at one point, I notice Cain place a bottle of water in front of me. I take a sip and then I'm back at it.

He keeps himself busy as I check my notes, reread phrases, remaster sentence structure. I have no clue what he's doing, but he's keeping close and not hovering; I appreciate it.

Having him here could be a distraction, but he's not like that. He understands what I need. I feel comfortable in my skin around him. I don't need to be a hostess to a guest.

He just fits into my life.

I continue to type, and soon, I realize I'm done. Everything that I felt that week is in the article. None of the unhappiness of walking away from him that last day has seeped back into the writing.

I look up from the computer, bleary-eyed, and scrub at the wariness inside me. The moment of truth. Was he here just because of the article, and now that it's perfect, will he walk away for good?

In the quiet of the apartment, I hear his footsteps as he approaches me. I turn my head to him; his hair is disheveled, and his eyes are glassy. I woke him.

What time is it?

I glance over at the clock, and that's when I see it's after one in the morning.

"Did I wake you up?" I ask. Although, it doesn't take a rocket scientist to know the answer since the moment I stopped working, he came in to check on me, but for some reason, I want to hear him say it.

"I am here because of you. I'm also up because of you." His words do funny things to my stomach, making me feel a surge of energy, but there's no time for that. Instead, I turn from him and look back down at my computer.

"Do you want to read it?" My voice is practically a whisper, and he takes the seat across from me.

"Yes," he answers.

I slide my computer across the surface of the table, the squeaking sound jarring at this time of night. It sounds like nails on a chalkboard.

I hope he likes the changes.

As he reads, I fidget with my fingers under the table, needing an outlet for my anxiety. I care what he thinks about this piece more than I want to voice.

He is his property. In turn, this piece is about him. To someone who doesn't know how he feels about the development he constructed, they might miss it, but he won't miss anything I've written here.

The Elysian is Cain Archer. And Cain Archer is The Elysian.

Time seems to stand still as I wait for him to read. I can't tell what he's thinking. His face is neutral, the stoic look he gives when you can't ascertain what he means. Finally, he closes the top of the computer.

The sound of it shutting has my hands shaking in my lap. I lift my eyes to look into his. At first, he gives nothing away. Then the right side of his lips tip. Instantly, I let out the breath I didn't realize I was holding. My shoulders uncoil.

"It's phenomenal." His voice is laced with pride. "The changes . . ."

"Did you like them?"

"How can you even ask that?" He leans forward, cocking his head to the right. "Where did the changes come from?"

At first, I don't understand what he means. He saw me typing, so they came from my head, but then I understand what he means. He means where I got the inspiration to write this. "They came from you."

He doesn't stop staring at me as he thinks of how to respond. "What do you mean they came from me?"

"Having you here brought back the memories of seeing you, talking to you, smelling you. That brought it all to life. I remember the colors and the sounds." My cheeks become warm, and I look down.

"Don't get shy with me. You never need to be afraid to tell me anything."

"When I wrote the last part before you were here, it was hard to think about it. I didn't anticipate missing you, and I couldn't connect when you weren't with me. It felt vacant, hollow when I tried to sit down and write. But then when you got here, it all came back to me. I felt full if that makes sense." He doesn't speak, and I fiddle with my hands, trying to backtrack. "I probably sound crazy since we haven't known each other long, but I do care about you, and having you here . . ." I feel like I'm being cut open as I try to put into words how I feel. "Having you here has made me realize how much I care, and I know you need to leave now that the article's done, but—I wish I could keep seeing you," I let this rush out before I lose my nerve.

He takes a deep, long breath, and my leg bounces under the table, anxiety coiling in my belly. I laid myself out, and now, I have to deal with the consequences.

"I'll admit I'm not the relationship kind of guy. I've had dates and short-term flings, but I've never been interested in maintaining anything else . . ." His words trail off, and my heart jackhammers in my chest. I'm waiting for the other shoe to drop, for him to tell me that this was fun, but it's time for him to go. "Things with you are different, though." My pulse becomes erratic at that. "I can't promise you anything. I can't promise much since we're not in the same location, but . . ." He reaches his hand out, and I take it in mine. Then he pulls me out of the chair and places me on his lap. "I'd like to try to make this work with you."

I curl into his chest, letting him wrap his arms around me, and I let out a breath. I realize for the first time we parted at The Elysian, I feel light, like anything is possible.

Maybe it's his words, or maybe it's the fact that my article has made him proud, or maybe it's everything combined, but I feel good, and I relish in the moment.

I sit in his arms for a few minutes, but then his phone rings.

At one in the morning, who the fuck is calling him? I lift myself up from his lap, and he fishes out his phone.

Looking down at it, his once smiling face has now dropped back to the sullen look he always gives when he doesn't like something.

"I need to take this," he says, and then he walks out of the room, and I'm left confused and alone.

I watch the clock across the room as I wait. One minute turns to five, turns to ten. It's an eerie feeling, waiting.

Feels like the detonator of a bomb and I'm counting down the seconds before everything blows up.

I hear the footsteps before he returns to the dining table. He crosses the space, pacing back and forth for a few minutes, but he doesn't say anything to me. He just paces back and forth. His whole demeanor is off.

"Who was it?" I ask.

"I need to go back. Tonight. Now. Something I can't avoid."

"When will you—"

He lifts his hands up to stop me. "I don't know. I'll be in touch . . . Just . . . I have to go now."

And with that, he walks out of the room, and I'm stunned. I should go talk to him, but I am welded in place.

At the sound of the door opening and closing, my happy bubble bursts. Cain fails to say anything about returning, and I'm awash in heartbreak.

I fall forward onto my table, my hands bracketing my head. I'm completely enchanted by a man who I don't know anything about.

This isn't good.

These feelings I have for him aren't good at all.

26

Layla

Three days.

Not a single solitary word from the man who said he wanted to try with me.

Just walked out the door, left me alone, and now I have to pick up the pieces of my life.

I've returned to writing for my own personal joy. I don't give a damn if Mr. Walker puts me on an article about drapes or lounge chairs for your pool house. I have to get back to something that interests me to keep my mind off Cain.

I throw myself into an editorial I wanted to pitch to the *New Yorker* years ago but put down when I got the job at *Concept and Space*.

Only an in-depth and hard-hitting story would draw me away from my misery.

Murder it is!

This is the type of project that gets me excited to delve into, which is why, three days later, since I decided to throw myself into writing it, I've barely eaten or slept.

Sure, at first, my insomnia was because of the way Cain left, but then I turned my sleepless nights into something productive.

I'm at my office cubicle, typing away at my computer, when Janet appears like the ray of darkness she is.

"Mr. Walker wants to see you," she states flatly as she glares at me. My God, this woman can make bread stale.

I can only imagine this is about the article. I submitted it to him two days ago.

With a sigh, I stand from my chair and head over to his office.

"Take a seat, Layla," he says, pointing at the empty chair. Once I'm sitting, I pull out my pen and pad, ready for him to tell me about what my next project will be. Instead, he smiles broadly at me. "They loved it. I loved it."

"What? The article? And who's *they*?" My mind is spinning; what is he talking about?

"The PR team at The Elysian. Of course, we would have run with the article regardless, but the whole team not only approved it but also gushed over your work. You have a bright future here, Ms. Marks. Now, with the project complete, I have to think of what you will work on next. Maybe I'll send you to LA. There is a new development property there that could piggy-back nicely off Archer's space. I was going to send Jon, but off the excitement of this project, it might be better if you go instead."

My stomach drops. If he sends me away . . .

What does that mean for Cain and me?

Who are you kidding? The man hasn't even called you. It's time to get over this little obsession. It's time to move on and figure out what you actually want to do with your life. For example, the article you are re-searching right now behind your boss's back.

Maybe this is when I tell him I quit.

Say I hate it here, and I don't want to write about concepts or spaces any longer.

No.

I can't do that. Not until the article comes out.

I need to be able to use the success of the piece to leverage myself for a new job.

"What's wrong?" he asks, and I give myself a shake and look up at him. "You're pale. You look sick. Maybe you've been working too hard.

Why don't you go home? You deserve a break to recover from your successful writing adventure."

I nod to him, but my words have dried up, my tongue heavy with emotion. I stand from the chair, the sound of the metal against the concrete floors grating against the silence of the room. "Thank you," I mutter. "I'll see you later." Not waiting for him to respond, I head to my desk to grab my stuff.

Janet just glares at me as I walk past her desk with a slight nod and wave. Maybe Mr. Walker is right; home is a good place to be right now.

"Where are you going?" Mara asks, and I freeze, looking up from where I'm hunched under my desk, unplugging my laptop, to find Mara looking down at me from the cubicle divider.

"Home."

Her eyebrow furrows. "Not feeling well? I noticed you looked off. I figured you were pulling all-nighters to finish the article, but you turned that in already. You okay?"

"Yeah. I'm just not myself."

No. I'm the pathetic girl who let an unattainable, commitment phobic male make her feel less than worthy.

I've become a miserable, pathetic fool, and I recognize it's not healthy.

The whole walk home, I think about what I need to do. I need to put this whole business with Cain behind me. It's time to move on. Time to think of it as a fantastic one-night stand that lasted a bit longer than it should have.

It was a fling.

Yep. That's exactly what it was.

I straighten my back and decide to no longer think about it.

Of course, that bitch, fate, has a way of laughing at what we choose for ourselves because no sooner than I step up to my apartment door do I notice a monstrous flower arrangement at my door.

Bending my knees, I grasp hold of it, and then I haul the giant arrangement into my apartment. Once settled, I walk over to where I placed the flowers on the kitchen table and pull the plastic down to look for a card.

I don't need to read it to know it's from him.

The universe is mocking my decision to move on from my infatuation with Cain Archer with the largest, most stunning bouquet.

Who else would send me flowers? Especially after my boss mentioned how fabulous the article came out.

I should probably assume it's from my magazine, but there is no way anything this beautiful would come from the place I work. Especially since the details and blooms are immaculate.

No. These are all Cain. And when I pull out the card, I see his words: *I'm sorry I've been absent. I miss you.*

I'm not sure how to feel, if I'm being honest. Radio silence for days and then this card that doesn't explain where he's been hiding.

I need to think of it as the kind and thoughtful gesture it is, even though he has Barbara who can make flower deliveries for him.

And for fuck's sake, I deserve a better apology.

After the days we spent together entwined in each other's arms, I should expect better.

Shouldn't I?

Am I asking and expecting far too much from this man?

I barely know Cain. He has closed himself off to other relationships based on our conversations, so why should I expect more communication from him?

Sure, when I'm with him, it feels like we can talk, but maybe that's the trick. Is it the same feeling for him? Only when we are together, does this magic happen? When in his presence, my gravitational pull toward him blinds me to anything else. But once I pull away, it's like the real world suddenly comes into focus, and I remember just how much of a mystery he is.

Twenty minutes after the delivery, my phone vibrates on the counter. Finally, it's Cain.

Grabbing it, I swipe at the screen and answer. "Hello."

"Layla." That voice. My legs shake and my hands tremble. Damn treacherous body responds, and he only said my name.

I take a deep breath to try to regulate myself before I speak. "Hello, Cain."

"Did you get my flowers?"

The blood-red floral arrangement beckons to me from across the room. Walking over, I let my finger touch the silky red petals. There must be over one hundred roses, tightly pulled together to form a dome. The bouquet sits with a round, black suede box with gold writing. My heart flutters in my chest as I breathe in the sweet aroma that permeates the air around me. "I did. Thank you. They're lovely."

They are incredible, but are flowers enough? It doesn't take away from the fact that he hurt me.

"I'm sorry about the last few days." His voice is low, sullen.

"Do you want to talk about it?"

"There was a huge issue at the place, and I've been tied up. I didn't want to leave you like that, but I didn't have a choice. I've been going crazy being here alone and thinking about you."

As he continues to apologize, I wonder if I should forgive him.

Then I remember how this is casual; why shouldn't I enjoy more time with him? Why should I let this be ruined by something out of his control?

Plus, I miss him, too.

"I'll come visit the first chance I can get away. Maybe over the weekend," he promises, and when we hang up, I smile.

See, there's nothing wrong. It's just business keeping him away. Not everything is as bad as it seems.

27

Layla

'm not surprised. Cain isn't coming.

However, this time I can't be mad. Unlike last time, when he left me without a backward glance, he at least called and told me about it.

Apparently, this weekend, his reason is valid as there is another issue needing his attention. He didn't go into detail about what was wrong, but with a grand opening looming, I can understand.

Cain is closed off, so even if I wanted him to open up to me, that's not really in his nature. It doesn't make me happy, but I can understand.

I'm not one to open up either. I don't have very many people in my life. Which is one of the reasons I gravitate to him.

Besides Mara, my best friend, I have a cousin, but don't have anyone else I consider a close friend.

I look across the living room and grin at Mara, who is sitting with a glass of wine.

When I told her Cain canceled, she showed up, bottles of wine in hand, and said we were getting drunk.

And that is exactly what we are doing. Drunkenness is on the schedule for tonight, and I'm already on my second glass.

Mara might be on her third. I've learned not to keep up with her.

The TV is on, but we're not really watching it. It's on for background sound as Mara tries to grill me.

And the more I drink, the looser my lips are getting.

"Tell me again, how big is his di—"

"Mara!"

"What?" She shrugs nonchalantly as if she didn't just ask me a gigantically personal question. "You still haven't answered. It's a legitimate question. How am I supposed to know the advice to give you if you won't tell me what he's packing?"

"Shut up." I throw a pillow at her playfully.

"You almost knocked over my wine." She gestures to the glass and almost accidentally spills it herself.

"But did it kill you?"

"No, but I will tell you, if you spilled it, I would have killed you."

"Har. Har. Har. It was you that almost spilled it."

With a roll of her eyes, Mara places the glass down on the coffee table in front of her, and then she's leaning back on the couch. "So, if you won't tell me about his, um, package, how about you tell me about the sex?"

"Pass."

She lifts her eyebrow in challenge. She knows me and all my hard truths, so she lays down the gauntlet. "Did you have '*The*' conversation?"

"Better question. I can answer that. We did talk. Well, kind of."

"What the hell does that mean? You actually talked to him about the fact you hate your parents and don't talk to any other people?"

"Yes. I did."

"My God, you are going to marry him," she chides playfully.

"Hardly."

"It took me years for you to tell me you're estranged from your family. You've known this man for one month."

I shrug.

"You love him."

"No."

"But you're falling for him."

This is a tricky question to answer. I can see myself falling for him, and by the way I felt this past week, maybe I already am.

Who am I kidding?

The moment his lips touched mine, I fell. Love? No. But serious obsession, yep.

I'm lifting my wine to my mouth when I see a picture of a familiar woman. The wine in my mouth spits out.

"What's wrong?"

"Shh. Make that louder."

Mara moves quickly to grab the remote and raise the volume.

"The body discovered in the woods this week has been identified as Cynthia Richards. Investigators are tight-lipped, but our sources indicate details of this case are similar . . . "

I don't hear the rest of what the anchor says as it sounds like I am drowning. Like there is water in my ears. I can only catch certain words.

My hands are shaking.

"Killed some time in the last twenty-four to thirty-six hours."

It's her.

Chills run up my spine, and my heart ricochets in my chest as the newscaster keeps talking.

Eerily similar to a cold case.

Could be a copycat.

What the hell?

They start to talk about The Compass Killer's MO and all the cases years ago.

Young, beautiful woman. Early twenties. The slice across the neck. The only problem that doesn't make sense is this victim is older, in her mid-thirties.

I remember the cases. I ran across them again as I started researching my other article.

They happened seventeen years ago. But I remembered the original news stories from when I was a kid. I remember watching the story as it unfolded.

Even though I was young, it became one of the stories that made me want to look at journalism as a career.

But that's not what has a pit forming in my stomach. It's the fact that I have seen her.

Not once. Not twice. Three times she appeared.

The woman with the camera.

The woman from The Elysian house tour.

The woman we saw at the park.

Her name is Cynthia Richards. And now she is dead.

I can't deny that a whole host of questions are popping up, and the only person I need to ask is Cain.

"What's wrong?"

A part of me wants to tell her, but I can't. It's probably nothing. She could have just been a woman buying a property.

Maybe everything was a coincidence. Or maybe . . . it's not.

No, stop that line of thought.

I'm sure nothing was going on between them. But as I push away the thoughts of this, I can't help the nagging feeling that this is the story I should be investigating.

28

Cain

'm here in NYC, sitting in an upscale bar facing Layla's building.

Perhaps I shouldn't be, but it's too fucking late. The damage is done, and now I sit, wait, and observe.

Watching everyone enter the front door, hoping none of the men coming and going are there for her. Staring at the window in her apartment, the light is on, and I can see shadows walking back and forth.

I don't think she's alone.

Is she with another man? *Probably.* Considering I'm the asshole who just walked away from her without explanation, I'd deserve it.

Unfortunately, old business had to be settled.

My gaze scans the upscale bar. Small, private rooms are off to the side. Banquet tables along the back. It's a welcoming space. They are certainly perks to this bullshit; the only problem is I hate this pretentious kind of lifestyle.

Then when my perusal lands on a group of women on the other side of the waiting room, I stifle a groan. These are the kind of women I could live without. None of them are my type. Face it, none of them hold a candle to Layla.

Already halfway through a bottle of tequila, their loud and

boisterous voices ring through the air. Practically screaming as they toast a girls' night out that has just begun.

As I lean back in my chair, I notice them taking shot after shot, and then one of them notices I'm staring. One of the women must mistake my annoyance for interest because now, she's smiling at me.

I won't lie and say the women are unattractive, but I am not interested at all. The lady waves me over, displaying an empty glass, and beckons for me to join her. She puffs out her chest and gives me a seductive look.

It's funny how little they matter to me. I may have walked over there and gotten laid tonight, but that was before Layla.

I pull my attention away from the women, but then I sit there, thinking about what I'm going to say to Layla. I don't get reckless. I don't do impulsive. Why the fuck am I here then, staring at her window, wanting to catch a hint of her through the open curtains?

Interrupting my train of thought, I hear feet approaching. The sound is low and light, and I know right off the bat it's one of the loud women. The brazen one who offered me a drink appears at my side.

I look up from my seat.

Her large, red lips are puckered as she seductively leans forward to give me an ample view of her cleavage. "Hey there," she coos. I don't respond. "Would you like a drink? We're celebrating."

"I can hear," I deadpan.

She lifts her hand playfully to her chest. "Oh, no, were we being too loud? I'm so sorry. Let me be so kind, and make it up to you," she drawls out.

Her hand reaches out and touches my arm.

I grab her wrist in a knee-jerk reaction. Her mouth twists up into a smirk.

"We can sneak into the bath—"

"Not interested." I don't let her finish that sentence. I remove her hand from my arm and drop her wrist.

She gasps, but I don't give a flying fuck. I hear the tapping of her shoes as she storms off back to her table.

With a shake of the head, I think about my Layla. How easy it is to be with her. How I don't feel like this with her. Indifferent to the world around me.

With her, I actually feel.

Reaching into my pocket, I grab my phone and call her.

"Hi," she answers, and just hearing her voice has me smiling. Which is insane. For years, I've perfected how to fake my reactions, and with her, it's instinctual. At first, I thought it was because she reminded me of my past . . .

Layla is the first person to elicit a genuine emotion from me in seventeen years, and I like that it has nothing to do with my past, it's just her.

"Hello, Layla."

She's quiet for a second. "I-I wasn't expecting your call. Is everything okay?" Her voice is soft, and she sounds concerned.

"I'm actually heading back to the city."

"You are?"

This time when she speaks, I only hear the excitement that radiates from her words. When I look up at her window, I see her move toward it. As if she just knows I'm here for her. We are two magnets. Different in so many ways, but like attracts like.

I should tell her I'm coming to see her, but I don't, instead opting to lie.

"I have work to do in Lower Manhattan, but I hope that maybe we can see each other while I'm there."

It's necessary to omit details. I don't know her. I don't know how far I can trust her. Not really. She might see my monsters and run if I let her see too much.

"Will you be working the entire time?"

"Hopefully not."

The lie feels bitter on my tongue, and then this strange feeling weaves its way through me.

And I wonder if this is guilt.

"Well,"—she sounds dejected, but I don't stop the course—"if you're free, call me."

"I will."

I feel like shit when we hang up. I've never felt like this before. Hmm. Maybe once before, but I was wrong. No, that was different. I turned my back on her and hadn't thought of her again until I recently saw her.

My mind starts to remember, but just as it does, I receive a text.

Looking down, I see the message from a name I haven't seen in a long damn time.

Only one sentence is typed, but it makes my back go ramrod straight.

We need to talk.

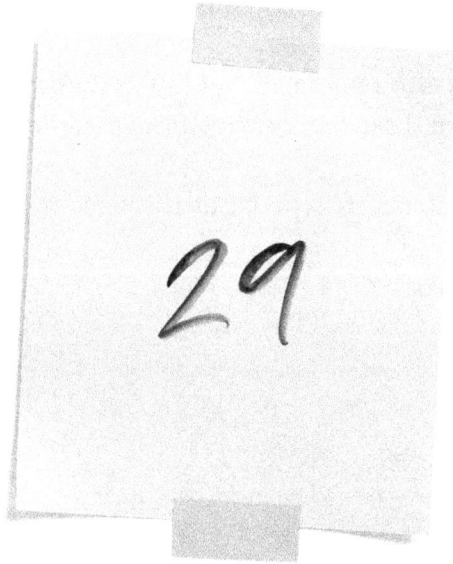

29

Layla

Watching a clock never makes time go by any faster, yet here I am . . .
Still watching.
Still waiting.

Time moves slower when you're anxious, but in my case, it feels like it stopped altogether.

I know we didn't have actual plans to see each other, but that doesn't stop me from waiting.

Especially since the call came in yesterday and it's been radio silence until a few hours ago. When he texted that he's actually in NYC and he's coming over tonight.

Walking across my living room, I take a seat on the couch and grab the remote. Scrolling through the channels, nothing catches my attention.

Not a damn thing. "Ugh." I groan before standing up, shutting the TV off, and heading back into my bedroom and the closet.

I'm wearing a dress, but I put this on hours ago when the possibility of going out to dinner was still an option.

It's late, and I have eaten a bowl of cereal at home since I realized we weren't eating together.

Now in the closet, I wonder what the appropriate clothing is if we aren't going out. I want to look good, but I don't want to look desperate. If we aren't leaving, a dress looks desperate to impress him.

There is only one solution. I call Mara. She answers on the third ring.

"What's up?"

"Nothing . . ." I groan.

"That doesn't sound like nothing. Spill."

Walking out of the closet, I cross the room and make my way into the living room.

Still dressed to go out, but knowing Mara, this conversation could take a while. Girl can talk.

"I have nothing to wear."

"Um." She's quiet for a beat. "Who is this? Because this is not my friend, Layla."

"Real funny." I sit down and lean back in the chair.

"No. Seriously. In all the time I've known you, you have never cared about how you are dressed."

"Are you saying I'm a slob with no fashion sense?" I lean forward, placing my elbows on my knees.

"Of course, I'm not saying that. Jeez, Layla."

"What are you saying, then?" My voice is low, and I feign annoyance. She laughs. "I'm glad you find me so funny."

"I love you. So shut up and just tell me what's wrong."

"Well, which is it? Do you want me to shut up or talk?"

"Pain in the ass. Spill."

I move back to standing.

"I have nothing to wear." I groan, starting to pace in the living room.

"And where are you going at this time of night, young lady?"

"Nowhere." I flop down onto the couch.

"Explain."

"I have company coming." Biting my lip, I close my eyes and wait for the onslaught of questions. Mara equals a dog with a bone. Funny how I'm the one who wants to be the investigative reporter. She would be perfect at it.

"And this company is?"

Wonder if I lie if she will catch on. It's not like she can see me.

She'll know.

Mara always knows.

"Cain," I mutter.

"Girl . . . you are holding out on me."

"Nothing to tell. He's back in town for business—"

"And you're his booty call."

My fist clenches on my lap. "It's not like that." My tone is harsher than I want.

"Girl. No judgment. I'm just saying."

I know she's not judging me, but it does feel a bit on point, seeing as I haven't heard from him in days.

I have too much energy to stay on this couch. I hop up to stand and start to walk. "Sorry, I'm being sensitive."

"No worries. Now, tell me what the problem is. If you don't have clothes . . . well, problem solved. Open the door wearing nothing."

"Mara . . ."

"Layla."

I stop pacing in front of the window and place my free hand on my hip while looking out into the city.

I'm not that high up, only on the second floor, but luckily, my apartment faces the courtyard behind the building.

There is nothing to see at this time of night. No one is outside, so it's just blackness.

"I'm not opening the door naked."

"But you could," she jokes.

"You're not being helpful."

"Okay. Okay. Put on lingerie and attack him."

"You're ridiculous." I laugh, but I find that I am walking back toward my bedroom, and before I know it, I'm sorting through my lingerie drawer.

I'm going to do it.

Why not?

We're both adults.

"I've got to go," I tell her, now with my mind made up.

"You're making the right choice."

I laugh. Of course, she knows what I'm about to do.

If I were with her, she would be waggling her eyebrows at me.

"Bye . . ." I trail off dramatically, and I can hear her giggling as I hang up.

I'm pretty sure she also said, "Get some," but it cut off halfway through the last word.

Walking over to the drawer, I grab a black lace sleep dress.

It's not overly sexy, but it's better than nothing, and then I walk back into the kitchen and pour myself a glass of white wine and wait. The glass is almost empty when I finally hear the knock on the door.

Now sporting a tipsy booze walk, I don't bother covering myself with a robe as I make my way to the door and open it.

As soon as I do, I know I chose right.

Cain's eyes go wide. I'm in his arms before he can even say hi.

Practically mauling me.

His lips are on mine, and I'm being picked up before I know what's happening.

30

Cain

I come up for air, look into her lust-filled eyes, and ask, "Is that how you answer the door for everyone?"

"No, just you. Well, and the pizza guy."

She laughs, legs around my waist, letting me hold her. I've missed this. This closeness we've created has been an ache in my chest the entire time I've been away. When I smack her sweet bottom, she gives me a moan, saying how much she likes it just a bit rough.

I squeeze her ass more, I say, "You are mine, woman. Now apologize. Say you won't do that again for anyone but me."

"And just how do I apologize, Mr. Archer?"

I carry her back to her bedroom. I sit down on the edge of the bed with Layla still wrapped around me, kissing my jaw, down my neck. I reach up and grab a handful of her soft locks and tug her back so I can look at her.

"Ride my cock, baby, like the good girl I know you are."

She lets out a long, sexy sigh at my words and starts tugging at my belt. Layla tears at my button and zipper, desperate to get to me.

I waste no time helping her free my length as she takes off her sexy black nightie that barely hides anything.

As much as I want and need her, I know that at this moment, Layla is mine. No one will ever see her this way but me.

"Layla. You're mine. Only mine."

"Yes, yours," she answers, sliding down on my rigid cock.

Her beautiful, soft flesh envelops me. She's pulling me into her with every move. I never want this feeling to end.

I've come this far in life.

Rebuilt who I am. Stepped out of the shadows. Found my light. The woman who brings me into the sunshine.

No one will come between us again.

I'll never lose this feeling of being whole as long as I'm with her. As long as the only hands on her are mine.

"Give me everything." I reach up and wrap my hands around each side of her neck, giving her a little squeeze.

The sinister side of me wants to reach further, push harder. Once I have a taste of the darkness, it's so difficult to stay away.

"Harder. More. I trust you," she rasps out.

And it's that trust that fills me with hope and banishes the wicked thoughts that have consumed me of late.

Moving my hands down over her arms, giving her breasts a brief squeeze that makes her clench, I wrap my arms around her in a full embrace.

"I've got you, baby. Come."

Together we fall.

I know I've done the right things to protect us. Protect these moments.

I just want to grant her those dandelion wishes she holds dear.

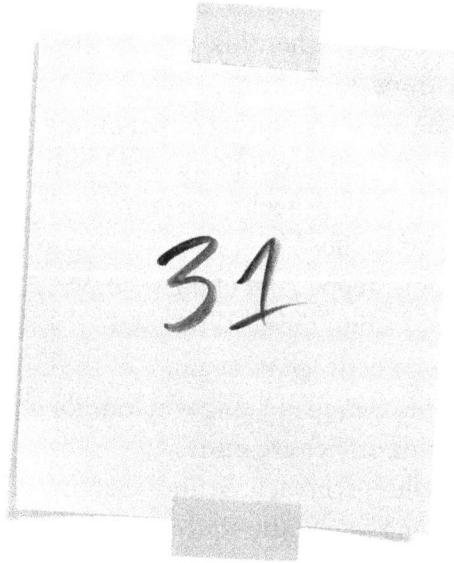

31

Layla

No matter how hard I try, I can't find a comfortable position. I toss and turn, yet minutes go by, and I'm still awake. The clock beside my bed screams at me with each passing minute. Nothing will settle me. Looking over at where Cain is sleeping, I watch him for a minute.

The way his chest rises and falls with each breath he takes.

He looks so at peace.

Must be nice.

I consider waking him but shake off that notion. Cain always seems stressed. And overworked. I can't possibly disturb him.

I allow myself a few more minutes of watching him. He's unlike any man I have ever dated before. Are we even dating? We haven't discussed it. But I guess, do we need to?

It's obvious we both like each other. We've even discussed not being with other people, but despite these conversations, why shake the boat right now and ask him what we are doing together.

I don't need a label.

Something tells me Cain doesn't either.

After a few more seconds, I stand from the bed. My feet hit the cold wood floors of my apartment. I'm careful not to disturb him, tiptoeing past the bed and then out to the living room. Once there, I grab the remote and sit on the couch. I keep the TV volume low enough that he won't hear it but loud enough that I can listen. This inkling to turn on the news hits me in the stomach. Ever since I saw the story of Cynthia Richards, I felt the need to look into it some more. Things have been crazy, so I haven't had the opportunity. But I'm interested to see if maybe there's been more news on it or if anything new has come up in the investigation. I know I need to talk to Cain about it, but our time is so sporadic, I don't want to ruin it.

Once the TV is set to the news, I have to watch through a few different story cycles before the one I have been waiting for comes on. An update on the copycat serial killer. Is there enough evidence to call it a copycat? I wonder.

Holy fuck.

My hands start to shake, and my stomach bottoms out.

The TV has another image on the screen.

They no longer think Cynthia's death is a copycat.

On the bottom of the screen, the text reads, *"He's back."*

The Compass Killer is back.

There is another missing woman.

And another body.

I catch a few things as the older male news anchor speaks.

This time, the MO is spot-on with the original killings seventeen years ago.

But the killing followed the pattern: Blond hair. Fair skin. Petite stature.

"Originally, it was believed that Cynthia Richards's death was caused by a copycat, but recent evidence and the presence of a second body have led the detectives to believe that The Compass Killer is back."

"John, why did they not originally think Cynthia was the work of The Compass Killer?"

"I believe, Hailey, her age threw off the detectives. Although the manner of Cynthia's death and the evidence left on the body, the north arrow of a compass, was accurate, she was significantly older than the previous victims. This is why I believe they referenced a copycat."

"Interesting observation, John. And you might be on to something. But why did he return? He's been dormant for years, and why Cynthia? The age has to mean something."

"She would have been the perfect age seventeen years ago."

"A little bit younger, Cynthia would have been eighteen at the time. The Compass Killer tended to prefer to kill women between the ages of twenty to twenty-three."

"Maybe it's personal," the woman says, and I think about what she just said. If Cynthia's killing deviated, it could be a crime of passion . . .

Cain.

Bile crawls up my throat.

No.

I shake my head.

They said it was part of a serial killing. Cain is many things, but he isn't a serial killer. I'm sure there is a perfectly reasonable explanation for how he knows her.

It feels like my heart is pumping too hard. Reaching across the side table, I grab the pen and paper I keep there to jot down notes.

Two new bodies and another woman missing. All from the Upstate New York area, but the bodies were discovered in New Jersey. This time, the woman went missing yesterday. The problem is, she fits The Compass Killer's MO.

Two killings and maybe a third in only a matter of weeks.

He's escalating.

But why?

Okay, what do I know?

Cynthia lived in New Castle, right outside the city, but she grew up somewhere else. This woman is more upstate. Where did they say Cynthia was originally from? A different town . . . Maybe Somerset, New Jersey.

This new woman fits the same age demographic of the serial killer. They all do, except Cynthia.

Same age.

Same build.

Same light complexion with blond hair and blue eyes.

There is a type.

I remember when the story first broke when I was a girl. They thought it was a coincidence.

Hell, I fit this. Even as a girl, I thought that.

I remember thinking at the time how lucky I was that I was so young because I had all the other characteristics, such as blond hair, blue eyes, and a petite build.

I continue to watch the news.

They have nothing else to go on. No other leads. The police don't think it's a copycat. It's on the news that there is a connection, which means the evidence must be strong for the police not to assume.

I'm lost in the show when I hear footsteps approaching from behind.

Turning over my shoulder, I see Cain.

He's standing by the wall, peering at the TV.

His eyes look vacant. Almost as if he's sleepwalking, and his posture is stiff.

"Cain?" My voice trembles around his name, and I don't like the sound of it anymore.

He doesn't say anything. He just stares at the TV. They're talking about the new missing woman.

He's transfixed, barely blinking. The only way I know he's alive is I can see his Adam's apple bobbing as he swallows.

Is he awake?

"Cain?" I try again, standing. I make my way over to him, but when I reach out to touch him, it's like he suddenly comes alive, his hand darting out and capturing my wrist in his.

The grip is too tight.

"*Cain.*"

I remember reading once that you shouldn't ever wake someone who is sleepwalking, and you certainly shouldn't touch them.

"You're hurting me," I say, our eyes not meeting as he stares past me. The vacant look is still there, his pupils large yet unfocused, but from where I'm standing now, it doesn't feel like he's sleeping.

It feels like he's in a trance.

Like he's transfixed by what he's watching and can't pull his attention away.

"Cain."

I can feel his body shake, and then his head does as well. As if he's righting himself, and then his gaze meets mine.

The hollow look is now gone.

That was weird.

He drops my hand abruptly, and I move it around to make sure I'm not hurt.

"You okay?" he grits out through clenched teeth.

"Yes."

"I'm—" He peers down at my wrist and then reaches out, but I step back from him. "Sorry. I wasn't myself."

"You could have hurt me."

"I would never hurt you." He steps closer to me, but I'm still rattled.

When I don't say anything else, he glances over my shoulder. He's watching the TV again, the news still on. The images now from a vigil being held for the missing girl.

"What are you doing?" All warmth is missing from his voice.

"I'm watching the news."

"Why?"

"As you know, I don't want to work for *Concept and Space* forever."

"And . . .?"

"I want to investigate the death of Cynthia Richards," I spit out, and his jaw tightens at that. "I'm hoping it could lead to another position. One I want."

"This isn't your story," he grits out through clenched teeth.

"It could be. Don't you see that—"

"No."

He's angry. Is it because he knows her more than he lets on?

He said Cynthia was someone who wanted to live in The Elysian, but is there more?

"Cain, did you know Cynthia? Was she someone to you? We never talked about why she was always around—"

"Can't you just leave anything alone?" He walks away from me, his long legs eating up the space with little effort.

He starts to pace, his fists clenching.

There is more to the story with Cynthia. I can tell.

"Did she mean something to you?" I ask again. "You can't deny that we ran into her a lot. It's just odd, and she was always acting strange. Is there something I should know? Were you—" Why is this so hard? "Were you two sleeping together?"

"You have no clue what you're talking about. And because of that, you need to fucking drop it."

I stumble back.

In the time I've known Cain, I have seen him tense with his employees. I have heard of his temper from his assistant, but never has he used that kind of language, nor has his anger been pointed at me.

I shiver.

All the stories are true.

Cain Archer is what they say.

I feel my body shake.

My arms cross over my chest to comfort myself.

Then, as Jekyll replaces Hyde, Cain moves toward me, pulling my trembling body into his arms.

"I'm so sorry, Layla. I was asleep . . ." He places a kiss on my head. "And I just woke up. Sometimes, I don't know what I'm saying when I'm asleep." He kisses my temple. "I haven't been sleeping well. Not without you. I miss you." Kiss.

And then he's lifting up my chin.

His fingers on my trembling jaw. "I'm so sorry for scaring you." He places a kiss on my nose. "It will never happen again. Please forgive me."

"I'm okay. But Cain, if it does . . . I won't be here. I understand you were sleepwalking. But never again. If that means you go see a sleep doctor, so be it."

"I'm sorry." His lips find mine, soft as I remember in our sweet moments. "How can I make it up to you? Anything you want to do this weekend, I'm all yours. Let me make it better."

"It's fine, Cain," I say.

"We can spend the whole day doing anything you want. Whatever you want to do."

"I just want to get out of the city and head to the shore, but since that can't happen, I'd settle for a day in bed."

He smirks and kisses me again. This time, his mouth opens, ready to consume me, and I surrender to my need for him.

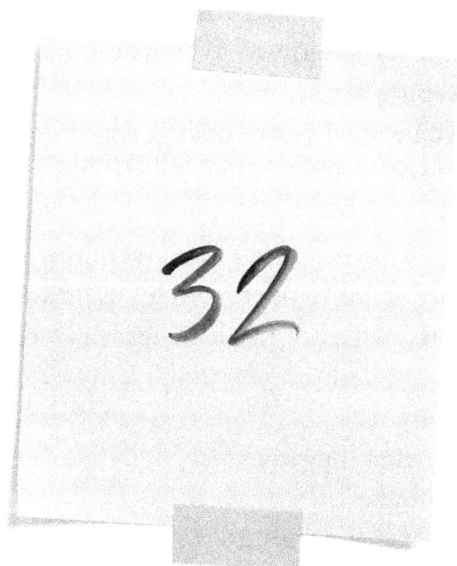

32

Cain

I shouldn't have come. I should have left well enough alone and not tempted myself. But here I am, playing with fire, and I just got burned.

My past has come back to haunt me, and in turn, I hurt her.

She plays it off like I didn't, but I did.

The worst part, I was lost at the time.

The darkness inside me took over. It was like I was in a trance, and only when I snapped out of it did I realize what I had done.

Walking back and forth across her small living room hasn't sated the beast. It's still roaring up inside me.

Anger.

Fear.

The idea of Layla being like one of those girls.

My knuckles turn white from how tight I am making fists.

This isn't how it was supposed to be.

Right now, I need to keep my head in the game. No distractions. Stay focused on building. Instead, I'm pacing her living room, trying to calm the fuck down.

Layla Marks is an unexpected plot twist.

Turning to face her, I cock my head to the left and take her in. She fell asleep on the couch.

I look down at her. She's so small, so fragile.

Someone could hurt her—snap her in half—and she wouldn't even be able to put up a fight.

In sleep, she's peaceful, and for a moment, I wish we could stay like this forever. It won't happen.

It can't. My life is too . . . it's not even about my life. It's about her. She's too pure, too good for me.

Even without me in her life, she needs to be protected.

The idea of me leaving and her being in this city alone has my heart thumping harder in my chest. Girls like Layla can easily get swallowed up in New York City. Like the woman in the news.

Layla could be one of those girls.

She's not much different than the victims. Petite, blonde, fair skin, and light eyes. The only difference is the age.

My chest tightens, and my heart races at the thought of Layla being in Cynthia's shoes.

The Compass Killer.

At first, they thought Cynthia's death was a copycat, but now, with the presence of more bodies, they are no longer at that angle. They aren't studying Cynthia close up anymore. They don't care about her or the people who were in her life. Now, they only care about the serial killer.

That's what the news is saying, at least.

According to the news, the cops aren't giving many details, but to call him the killer means the women were sliced.

My hands clench again, and my limbs start to shake.

I need to calm the fuck down.

Layla stirs, and I stop pacing. I'm probably going to wake her with the way I'm acting. I need to get some fresh air.

What time is it?

One o'clock in the morning.

Fuck it.

I pick her up and carry her to her bed.

Once I put her down and tuck her under the covers, I grab her keys.

Then I'm in the foyer, opening the door, locking it, and leaving.

It might be one in the morning, but the need to walk the streets and calm myself is overwhelming.

I have no direction in mind, so I just head to the left. Cars pass. No matter the time, the city is alive.

There aren't too many people out and about, though. I would have thought that since it's a Friday and the start of the weekend, it would be busier. But I guess there are no clubs or bars around this area.

My arms hang by my sides as I leisurely walk the streets. Each block helps to regulate my pulse.

But then I hear it.

A scream.

And the blood in my veins pumps faster.

Heavier.

Where is it coming from?

Up a few feet ahead is an alleyway, and I pick up my pace. When I make the turn, I see a woman being manhandled in the alley.

"Get the fuck away from her," I bellow, and the moment the little shit takes me in, he's running off, scared.

"Thank yo—" the woman starts to say, but she sways on her feet and then faces me.

Her eyes are smudged with leftover makeup, and her clothes are disheveled. She looks as high as a kite. "T-Thank y-you." Her words come out slow and sloppy. Yep. She's definitely wasted.

I don't have time for this shit. When she goes to thank me for the third time, probably because she doesn't remember the last two, I wave her off.

"Get your shit together, because I won't be there to stop the next guy."

I'm pissed and annoyed. I took this walk to calm myself down, and now, I'm even more annoyed.

Starting to walk more, this time, I don't pay any attention to the side roads. I just keep my head straight and go as far as I can until I lose this anger.

When the sun peeks from behind the buildings, I know it's time to head back to Layla.

A smile spreads across my face. Just thinking about her calms me down.

I'm pretty far away, so I take out my phone and make a phone call to a business associate who owes me a favor. A big one.

"What?" Sleeping and pissed, I don't know what I was expecting from Matt, but here we are.

"I'm cashing in your debt from saving your ass on the LA job you dropped the ball on. Wake the fuck up."

The groan he gives me can't be missed. "Fine, what do you need?" Matt grumbles.

"I need your house."

"I was planning on going—"

My footsteps halt. This fucker better not give me a hard time. "Going nowhere," I inform him. "You were planning on going nowhere is the only answer I want to hear."

"I wasn't going anywhere, Cain."

"Good, I'm glad we got that settled. Have it cleaned." I don't bother waiting for him to object. He will do what I ask.

He owes me, after all.

I am not a man to go against.

Matt knows that better than anyone.

33

Layla

"Layla."

I hear my name, but I don't know where it's coming from. A part of me thinks I'm still dreaming, but when I hear, "Layla, it's time to get up," the baritone voice has me fluttering my lids open.

I lift my hand and rub my eyes, allowing myself a moment before scanning the room.

Is Cain still here?

Or was last night a dream?

Sitting upright, I spot Cain standing across from the bed by the window that faces the courtyard.

He's dressed in gray sweats and no shirt as he leans against the wall, arms crossed as he watches me.

I allow myself to ogle his body; each muscle on his chest is cut like rock. No one should look this good in the morning. I'm sure I don't.

"I'm up." I groan, and he saunters over to me, taking a seat on the edge of the mattress.

"Morning." He inches closer, his gaze heavy on me. It makes me feel warm and tingly with how close he is.

"It's too early. Why are you waking me?" I cover my eyes with my hands.

I feel the bed shift underneath me, and then Cain's warm hands are taking mine and lifting them off my face.

His fingers then touch my chin, forcing me to look at him. The way he stares at me is intense this morning. "Because you need to pack a bag."

Still locked in his penetrating stare, I notice that his deep brown eyes look different in the early light of the morning than they did last night. Today, they seem clearer.

He was definitely sleepwalking last night.

"Come on, up you go." He stands from where he's sitting and reaches his hand out to help me out of bed. The moment I stand, and the blanket falls from me, I realize my mistake. I'm naked, and Cain is staring.

"You need to go get dressed, or I can promise we are never leaving."

"I'm okay with that." I step closer to him, my breasts touching his warm skin. Lifting my arms, I place my fingers on the corded muscles of his chest. He lets out a sharp inhale of breath as I trail a pattern over his skin.

"None of that right now." His fingers wrap around my wrist, and then he pries my hand away. "As much as I want to, and I *do* want to, we have places to go."

Cain steps back, and I let out a playful whine before heading toward my closet.

"Where are we going?" I ask.

"It's a surprise."

"I need to know so I can pack the right stuff."

Cain glances in my direction and lets out a sigh. "Fine. We're going to Cape May."

Staring back at him, grinning from ear to ear, I move quickly to grab my suitcase. "For how long?"

"A long weekend, but don't worry about anything. I already handled it. You aren't expected next week in the office."

Opening a drawer, I throw on a bra and underwear before I remove a black cotton dress from the hanger and slip it over my head. "Don't you have work?" I ask him as I get dressed for the day.

"I took off, too."

"Seriously? You rearranged your entire schedule and mine just so we can be together?"

"Yes, seriously." He walks over to me and lightly smacks my ass. "Now, get a move on."

I'm in a state of shock as I pack.

If that weren't enough, when we walk down to the street, I see a convertible parked in one of the spots in front of the building, and that seems to be the car Cain is walking to.

"What are you doing?"

"It's our ride," he says as he pops the trunk and puts our suitcases inside.

"You drove down to the city?"

"Nah, I rented this one. I figured it would be better."

"Hell yeah!" I step into the car, then wait for Cain to get in.

It takes us about twenty minutes to get out of the city, but once we are, we speed off in the direction of our destination with the top down.

As we are cruising down the highway, the radio plays one of my favorite tunes, and I let loose. Closing my eyes, hair blowing in the wind, lyrics flow from my lips.

Okay, screaming at the top of my lungs.

I can't remember the last time I sang like this or had this much fun. It feels like I'm in college all over again.

Halfway through the song, I open my eyes and look over at Cain.

He's watching the road, but his eyes quickly dart over to me. There is a large smile on his face, and I think he's chuckling.

He looks young at this moment. In all the time since I've known him, this is the first time I've seen how truly carefree he be. Reaching across the console, I grab his hand and hold it.

Once the song is over, he lowers the music a bit when the station turns to a slow, soft beat.

"Talk to me. Cape May. Do you go there a lot?" I say now that the car is quieter.

It's not necessarily easy to hear.

"Not for a while," he answers. "Have you ever been?" His words are muffled by the wind, so as the traffic slows, I press the button to bring the top up.

"You don't mind, do you?"

"Nope."

Once the top is up, I can hear much better. "I've never been to Cape May. My family didn't vacation often."

"Neither did I," he says.

"I guess we have that in common. My parents are dicks. They never wanted me. I was an oops baby, so they treated me like shit. I'm okay with never speaking to them again." I laugh awkwardly. "What about you?"

"My childhood isn't worth mentioning. I'd do anything to do it all over." His gaze is on the road, so I can't see his eyes, but I can tell from his grip that he's not happy.

"What do you mean?"

"Nothing." His knuckles turn white. "Forget I mentioned it."

Knowing full well that he won't go into it further, I decide to change the topic. "Tell me one of your favorite memories."

For a few seconds, Cain doesn't speak. I watch him as he drives, focused, but his jaw has tightened, making his side profile appear more pensive.

Maybe this wasn't a good idea. My childhood sucked, but I still feel that mine, in comparison, was rainbows and sunshine.

I understand why he doesn't want to talk about it. But he has to remember something fondly.

Times stretches in silence, and then he finally speaks. "I was young, a teen, and things were bad. I needed to get out of the chaos of my life . . ."

I squeeze his hand, telling him I'm here and will listen without words.

"When the noises in my life got too loud, I needed to get away. I had nowhere to go. The house where we lived was a mess, and I couldn't go to the cottage." It looks like his hand trembles, but I can't be sure. "I finally walked out, and I went to this small library in town. That's when I read *Brave New World*. I found a tiny nook, tucked away, hidden. The library was really old, like hundreds of years. It was one of those old stone buildings. No one knew I was in there, and for the first time in forever, I found peace. After that, I went back a lot."

My heart lurches in my chest. His favorite memory is one that doesn't include anyone else. Just him.

I can feel the tears forming in my eyes. He doesn't have anyone. I might not speak to my parents, but at least I know that's by choice. My decision, not theirs.

I squeeze his hand again; I'll be there for him. I'll be what he needs.

A sudden realization hits me. I'm falling for this complicated man.

"I'm sorry you never had anyone," I finally say, and from the corner of his eye, I see him look at me. "But I would very like much to be your someone. If you'd let me."

He gives me a small smile, then goes back to driving.

We both fall into silence, and then I reach across the dash and turn up the music, changing the mood from heavy back to light.

Soon, we are pulling up to this cute Cape Cod-style house that's right on the beach and only a short drive from town.

He puts the car into park and then walks me up the front steps. He raises the welcome home mat and finds a key, and then he's pulling me through the door.

Room by room, we go through the house.

"It's perfect, and I'm one hundred percent in love with this house. It's exactly my style and what I'd wish to one day own."

"Glad you are happy with this space," he responds with a smirk playing upon his lips.

When we get to the bedroom, we start to unpack our stuff amid glances and touches as we pass each other at the closet door. Everything is so easy with him when we're both relaxed.

"I have to make some calls, but I'll find you in a bit."

"Sounds good."

I step toward the window and look out at the ocean.

This is the life I want someday. Could this ever be our everyday? If so, I need to know how to keep it. I need to learn more about him to find the key to making him stay.

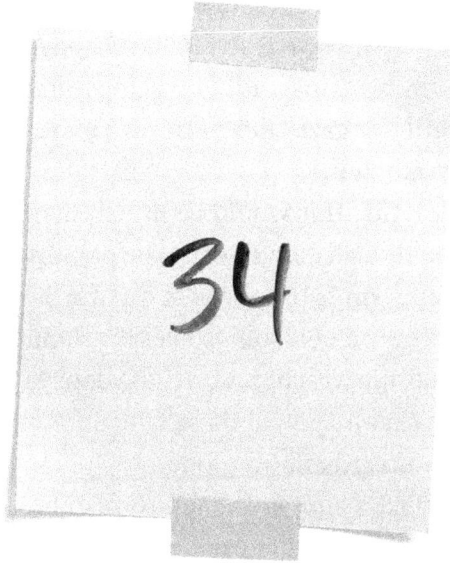

34

Layla

We walk around Cape May. Past small boutiques and shops, tiny cafés, and outdoor restaurants. Just two ordinary people. Like we are a regular couple on vacation.

That's because we are.

This isn't The Elysian. But it could be . . .

Imagine. Together in our personally designed paradise.

Sightseeing around Cape May is everything I needed. As we walk from store to store, I can't stop smiling. Cain must notice because he's staring at me, and he looks happy.

"It's nice to see you like this," I say to him.

"Like what?" He inches closer to me, his arm reaching out and pulling me to him until his arm wraps around my waist.

I crane my neck up and look into his eyes. "Happy." The look he gives me is intense; it feels like he is peering into my soul and demanding I give him everything. I would, too. All he would have to do is ask.

I avert my gaze, needing a second to calm my nerves. "You should build this."

"Build Cape May?" A soft chuckle leaves his mouth.

With a shake of my head, I laugh as well. "No. Build a version of The Elysian on the water. Have it styled like Cape May."

Cain turns me in his arms until I'm facing him. Finger on my chin, he tilts my head until our gazes meet again. "You really understood the concept of The Elysian, huh?"

I nod. "I think I did. This would be *my* Elysian. I love it here. This is my style. Smelling the salty air. It would be paradise for someone who loves the water." Cain's smile broadens at my words. "What?"

He just watches me before looking over my shoulder. "Nothing. Let's go in here." Cain pulls me with him inside the door to a shop that's open.

Inside, I notice that it's got all these cute odds and ends. Things to use for the beach, postcards, snow globes.

It's more than just a souvenir shop. It also has cute clothes and hats—big straw ones. One looks exactly like something Mara would wear.

It's a straw fedora with a hot pink grosgrain ribbon. It's perfect for when she goes to the Hamptons. "This one."

Cain lifts a brow. "I didn't peg you for the fedora type."

"Oh, it's not for me. It's for my bestie, Mara."

Cain takes it from my hand and leads me toward the register. "Tell me about this bestie."

"I know I told you she works with me. Mara is the only person in my life that I consider family. I'm lucky I at least have her. And this"—I point to the hat—"is something she would love. She's fun. Eccentric. Sometimes *nuts*. And she's the best person to have in your corner."

"Then you must get it for her."

"That's the plan. What about you? You going to buy anything for anyone?"

"You know what, I think I will." Cain walks over to the mugs and buys a Cape May mug that says Exit 0 on it.

Furrowing my brow, I gesture to the mug. "Who's that for?"

"My assistant, Barbara. I guess she's the closest thing to family that I have."

The only family he has is an assistant who is petrified of him. My heart breaks a little at that thought. I hope she's worthy of him. It makes me sad that he's alone, but it's probably one of the reasons we initially gravitated toward each other.

Maybe together, we can heal each other's past scars.

"You don't have anyone else?"

"As we discussed, my family was very dysfunctional, and I got out at a young age. The only person I ever considered family was a man who lived in the same town as me. He was a firefighter who used to show me the station and trucks."

"You spent a lot of time with him?"

"Not a lot . . ." His voice trails off, the tone low and almost hollow. Thinking of the past hurts him.

I can understand that.

It might not be the same, but I know how it feels not to have the support of your family.

I reach out and touch his hand. "But he cared for you."

"He did."

"Do you still speak with him?"

"Not often." When he says that, his jaw tightens. It almost reminds me of the eve of a storm, when everyone dashes around and starts to close the shutters, except the shutters, in this case, are the darkness inside of Cain.

What happened to you, Cain? What happened in your past to make you feel like this?

I don't ask the questions lingering on my tongue. I don't dare spoil the mood. The same way I don't mention Cynthia. Our time here is limited, and I'm scared. I know that the truth will catch up to us. It's inevitable.

But not today.

Instead, I ask him other, more neutral questions. "Where is the guy?"

"Gone." He drops my hand and takes a step toward the register.

Strange choice of words. First, not often, then gone. But that would mean he's still alive. I wonder why they don't speak, but again, I know I don't want to push and dampen the mood. I keep all my questions that are begging to come out inside.

I pay for my hat; he pays for his mug, and then I grasp his hand to turn out of the store. As we continue our walk down the road, I see exactly what I'm in the mood for in the block ahead.

I pull him along with a giggle until we are standing in front of an old-fashioned ice cream store.

"Ta-da!" I say with a goofy flourish, pointing at the red-and-white-painted exterior of Freezies Ice Cream, being slightly over the top to make him laugh.

His brow lifts in surprise. "You want ice cream now?"

"I most certainly do, my dear sir!"

He smirks, shakes his head, and pulls open the door. "Then let's get you some."

The inside is exactly what I would expect. It feels like I'm transported back in time to the 1950s. Black-and-white-checkered floors lead to an old-fashioned, large, red countertop. Behind it is an older gentleman wearing a red apron, black bow tie, and matching black hat. We walk in and straight to the counter.

"Hello, what can I get for you?" the man, with a name tag that reads Richard, asks.

"May I please have a soft serve vanilla ice cream in a waffle cone?" I grin so large my cheeks hurt. "Thank you."

"I'll get that right away. And for you?" He gestures toward Cain.

"Nothing for me," he responds.

"Party-pooper." I stick my tongue out.

Five minutes later, cone in hand, Cain and I sit on a bench facing the water. It reminds me of little diamonds the way the sunlight reflects off the waves.

I'm licking the cone when I notice Cain watching me. His eyes are hooded, and I instantly realize how I'm licking it.

"See something you like?"

"You can say that."

I incline my head in question. "Why didn't you get one?"

His gaze drops to my lips. "That's not what I like . . ."

I let my tongue leave my mouth again, this time licking very slowly. He practically groans.

"Stop that," he scolds.

"You don't like it? Here, take a lick. It might cool you off." I reach the cone out, but he doesn't, so I continue to lick.

When I pull it back, he smiles lazily at me, then leans forward, swiping his tongue against the ice cream on my lips.

"It's good, right?"

"Delicious."

"Told you."

"What makes you think I was talking about the ice cream?" he says, and I take another lick to stop myself from climbing him like a tree in public.

Once we're done flirting over my cone, we walk back to the car and drive back to the house. When we arrive, I see there's another car in the driveway.

I narrow my eyes at Cain, who only smiles. "What are you hiding, Mr. Archer?"

"Wouldn't you like to know?" Would I ever. Not just about our mystery guest.

I want to know all of Cain's secrets. All of his hurts and happiness. I want to deep dive into his mind and find those hidden pieces. There has to be something that will point me in the right direction of keeping us together.

When we walk inside, I see a chef there who appears to have been cooking the entire time we've been in town. As we step inside, the cook is packing up to leave, but the table is set with full serving pieces and lit candles.

"This is my surprise? This is too much, Cain!"

Wow. He really thought of everything.

He's so generous and knows the many ways to my heart. I don't want to leave him after this trip. There's no chance of that happening after our magical day.

I've already fallen for Cain. Completely head over heels.

"I'm going to head upstairs and get changed into something nicer." I take a step, but his hand wraps around my upper arm.

"Layla, you don't have to change." He turns me to face him. I lift my hand, motioning to the table lit with candles and the chef-prepared meal.

"I am not dressed for this."

A smirk spreads across Cain's face. "You could be wearing nothing, and you would still be perfect."

"You would like that, wouldn't you?"

"I would, but that's not the point."

I lift my brow, stepping farther into the room and closer to the table. "Then, what is the point?"

He moves closer to me. "The point, is I'm just happy to be here with you. I don't care what you're wearing. If you want to freshen up and put pj's on, that would still be too much."

"I'll be back," I say as I head off to the master bedroom.

Once in the closet, I slip on a sundress but opt for no shoes.

Casual, right?

Picking up my phone, I dial Mara. "Hey."

"Hey yourself." Her excited voice greets me through the line. "I tried calling you. What's the good word?"

"I'm away." In the floor-length mirror, I glance at my reflection. The dress is pretty. It's a simple, sleeveless, white eyelet slip that falls to my upper thighs.

"Say what?" she asks as I start to walk out of the closet and back into the master bedroom.

"I went away with Cain. He surprised me."

"Oh . . ." She pauses for a minute, then coughs. "That's nice."

She no longer sounds as cheerful to hear from me. Something is off with her voice.

"What's wrong, Mara? You don't sound like yourself."

Mara takes a large breath, and I brace for her to speak. "Listen, I'm thrilled for you, but it seems so fast."

"It's not that fast. I've known him for almost two months."

"It's still not that long, and although you might have known him that long, you haven't spent much time with him. Collectively, fewer than two weeks."

I know she just doesn't want me to get hurt, and I can see where she's coming from, but she doesn't understand.

"You don't get it. It might have only been two weeks or two months. Hell, it could be two years, but there is a feeling I get when I'm with him. I can't walk away, Mara."

"And herein lies the reason I'm still single."

"And that reason?" I ask without missing a beat.

"Because I'm a horrid pessimist. Don't listen to a word I just said. Go enjoy every minute of your fairy tale. You deserve it."

I can't help but grin. "I love you, Mara. I'll call you tomorrow to check in."

"Okay. Love ya, girl."

I hang up feeling much better than when we first got on the phone. I know she's not wrong. Cain and I barely know each other, but I know how I feel, and I'm not willing to run from this feeling.

After freshening up, I head back down.

Cain has everything set up, complete with wine and candlelight. I smile, thinking about Mara's words about a fairy tale.

Who knew how appropriate they were?

This is a fairy tale.

Prince and all.

Taking a seat, Cain pours me a glass of wine, and then we are eating the amazing food set before us.

The chef has prepared scaloppini chicken with broccoli rabe, orzo, and a lemon wine sauce.

It's amazing.

"What's next?" I ask him between bites.

"With what?"

"The next project. This one is almost done. Opening is soon. What will you do next?"

Please say something closer. Something local.

I hate the idea of not seeing him again for long stretches of time, but I know I can't say that. It's too soon for me to demand or ask anything like that of him.

"I haven't signed on to anything yet, but I have a few options," he tells me.

"Where?" My hand trembles, but I clench my fist to stem the shake.

"One is outside of London, and the other is in New Zealand."

I feel myself deflate. I can't eat anymore. My stomach is in knots.

It feels like a boulder is sitting in my belly, and I can barely swallow. A lump starts to form in my throat.

219

"What do you think I should do?" he asks me, and I take a breath. I need to keep my emotions in check. I can't have him seeing how I feel.

I shrug like it's no big deal.

It's too soon to beg him not to take a job outside of the US. I can't say anything. All I can do is plaster on a fake smile and pretend it wouldn't kill me to have him so far away.

"Both are exciting options"—I raise my glass—"but personally, I think New Zealand would be a better choice for you."

"Why, Layla?"

"The land. The landscape. The beauty you could create. Can you imagine integrating the buildings and homes with the untamed wilderness? Normally, I would be wary of someone disturbing the serenity of the culture, but with you, I know it would be in very talented hands." I lift my glass. "We should celebrate. Cheers!"

He smiles back at me, but it doesn't meet his eyes. I had forgotten what his fake smile looked like. The last few were genuine, but this one isn't.

He doesn't want to go as much as I don't want him to. Or maybe I'm reading too much into it. But I don't think I am.

We continue to eat, and we both avoid any conversation that revolves around him leaving.

When dinner is over, Cain stands, reaching out his hand. "Come with me. I want to show you something."

He leads me outside through the doors to the deck, and once there, we both lie down on a daybed that is set up facing the ocean.

The night sky is illuminated only by stars.

I lie in his arms, staring up into the sky. "They are beautiful," I whisper.

"Growing up, I loved looking at the stars."

"You did?"

He pulls me closer into his chest, my head resting on his heart. "Always." I listen closely, soaking up the idea of him opening up to me. "I loved to read about them."

"In the library nook?"

"Yeah." His hand moves to my shoulder, his fingers trailing over my exposed skin. "See that one over there? That's Cassiopeia."

"Wow. And what's that?"

"That's Polaris. The North Star." The pattern he's making changes from a circle to a triangle. "Do you know why the North Star is so important?" He traces the shape over and over again.

"Isn't that the one that always leads you home?"

"Yes, North will always lead you home," he agrees, dropping his hand from where it is and then moving until he's rolling me on top of him.

He places his mouth on mine. "It's time to go to bed," he whispers against my lips.

"But I'm not tired," I groan.

"Who said anything about sleeping?"

And then he's pulling us both up to standing.

Who needs to rest, anyway?

35

Cain

Together in bed, with our bodies entwined, I think about our conversation earlier.

At dinner, Layla wasn't acting like herself. She was clearly upset. Sure, she smiled, but I know her. She's bothered by the far away options I have in front of me. Thinking I won't pick her. Her mind says it's too soon for me to do something rash like that.

The thing is . . . there's no choice to be made.

I've never felt anything in my life but pain, and with her, I feel everything that is joyful.

I'm not willing to let this go. Not now, and maybe not ever.

If I tell her this, I may scare her off. I'm not willing to chance that yet. Instead, I move my body until I'm lying on top of her, and then my mouth meets hers.

I kiss her softly at first. Sweet kisses that tell her without words how I feel about her.

As our lips touch, all the things I'm not ready to say pass between us. Slowly, I let my body speak the rest of my devotion to her.

Worshipping her body.

Each thrust of my hips saying she's everything.

Grabbing her, pulling her toward me, and as we both fall apart, I can't stop burying myself into her neck and whispering, "You belong to me."

Trusting she will never know that everything I've had to do is for this moment with her.

The next morning, I wake up to an empty bed. Reaching my arm out, I find that Layla's side is cold.

Usually, I'm such a light sleeper. Strange that she was able to get up and I didn't even stir. I had zero clue she's been gone, most likely for an hour or more.

Occupational hazard, working with clients in all different time zones, I wake at every sound. My childhood taught me to always be on edge, and it's worked well in later years.

But here with Layla, I find myself able to relax for the first time in my life. A peace I never thought I would experience, let alone with a woman.

I stand from the bed and make my way into the bathroom to brush my teeth and do my morning routine and dress for the day.

Then I go in search of Layla.

Walking from room to room, I find her in the small, little office that faces the beach. She's sitting behind the desk, and her laptop is out.

"No working," I chide as I step inside, and she closes it the moment she sees me.

"I'm not working on anything for work."

I lift one eyebrow. She's lying.

She stands abruptly. "Let's go for a walk."

Looking toward the window, I notice the sky is gray. "Where do you want to go?"

"Down the beach?"

"It looks like it might rain, Layla."

"A little rain has never killed anyone, Cain," she chides playfully.

"As far as you know. Fine. If you don't mind the rain . . ."

She shakes her head. "Growing up, I always loved the rain."

Opening the door, together, we walk out onto the patio and then out toward the beach.

"I didn't."

I don't explain to her what I mean. There's no need with Layla.

Now standing in front of the water, I stop. Neither of us is wearing shoes, and the sand is damp beneath our feet. We are close enough to the ocean that we could get wet with the next wave.

I turn to face Layla, and her lips part into a smile. "Why can I already see that about you?"

"Maybe, just maybe, you see the real me."

And it's true. No one has ever understood me the way Layla does. There is no need for words with her. She can see the pain that lives inside me, and her own pain gravitates toward it. We are twin souls.

I might hide my monsters from her, and every once in a while, they find their way out, but deep down, I know she would accept me, even if she saw them.

"I hope I do get to see you," she whispers softly.

Reaching my hand out, I trail my fingers up her chin, tilting her head up so that our gaze can meet. "You do. Trust me. What you see is one hundred percent real."

"Everyone has secrets."

"That is true." I nod. "And yes, I have them, too, but that's not what I mean."

Her jaw trembles beneath my touch. "What do you mean?"

"I can't breathe when you're away from me." Her crystal-clear blue eyes are locked on me. They look glassy like my words might make her cry.

"Thank you." She goes up on her tiptoes and places her mouth on mine. I part my lips and so does she, then I skate my tongue against hers. The kiss ends as fast as it begins.

"What was that for?" I ask against her lips.

"Letting me in."

"I can't promise—"

Her finger presses against my lips, silencing me. "It's okay, I understand, but what you show me is enough."

"And what's that?"

Then her hand is no longer on my face, and it's resting on my chest over my heart. "That beneath this exterior there's a heart."

"And it beats only for you."

As I hold her in my arms, safe and warm, I can feel the familiar feeling of rain striking down from above.

Drip.

Drip.

Drip.

The winds start to pick up. Layla's blond hair whips around her face. She looks beautiful. Natural. At peace.

She looks happy.

And I know it's because of me.

As the hair clings to her face, she reaches her arm up to protect herself. As if her small hand could stop the rain. "We should go in."

"No, please." She steps in closer, and I wrap my arms around her shoulders.

When she's enclosed in my warmth, I lean down to see her eyes. "You want to stand out here in the rain?"

"I do."

"And do what?"

This time when she smiles, it touches not just her mouth but her eyes. "Dance with me."

"Let me get this straight. You want to purposely get drenched so you can dance in the rain?" I shake my head at her. *This woman.*

Her head bobs up and down. "Yep."

"Why?"

"Because when I was a girl, and my parents fought, I used to wish for a different life."

"And that life involved rain? I have no idea what you mean." I can't remember when my dad was around very much, and I certainly can't remember both my parents being home at the same time long enough to fight in front of me.

"I remember watching a couple, and they were so much in love, and I remember thinking I wish my family was like that. And then the couple kissed. But it was the way he pulled her in, as if dancing, I just thought . . . I just thought that's what love is. It's dancing in the rain."

Without another word, I start to sway our bodies together.

Dancing with her in the rain.

Giving her that dream and hopefully one more wish from her dandelion.

∆

Time moves too fast, and before I know it, the next morning has risen.

I want to slow it down and be able to enjoy every moment of my time with her. Time is fleeting. Life is so very short. I know that more than most.

She is gone when I wake up again. This time, the first place I go looking is the small office, and when that comes up empty, I search the whole house, but she's nowhere to be found. That's when I see a flash of yellow blowing in the wind through the window.

Layla is lying outside on a deck chair.

Moving across the space, I make my way outside. She's curled up, reading.

The early morning waves crashing against the shore muffle the sound of my approach.

She doesn't notice I'm here, and I take advantage of that by watching her.

I could stare at her all day. Watching every breath she takes.

Her blond hair flowing with each pass of the wind reminds me of rays of sunshine beaming down and hitting the ocean.

She's ethereal.

As I observe her, my chest no longer feels tight. When I'm with her, I feel warm. Calm. Anything is possible.

What could possibly be going on with me? What does this shift in feelings mean?

Something has changed inside me. I feel different. Like anything is possible in this new world she's led me into.

I think this is what it feels like to fall in love. Unlike all the years since I tried to leave the pain behind, she gives me rest I've never experienced. Now, in my dreams, I can only see her face.

I must be falling in love.

My feet give out underneath me at the revelation. I stumble forward but am quick to catch myself.

"You're up." The sound I made must have alerted her to my presence. She's now sitting forward in the lounge chair, smiling at me. Her smile drops, and then she inclines her head. "What's wrong? What are you thinking about over there?"

"I bought the house," I blurt out.

"Um, what did you just say?"

"Today was supposed to be our last day, but I just couldn't let this go. So, I'm not going to."

"I don't understand. You didn't want to leave, so you *bought* the house?"

"Yes. Well, no. Actually, I bought it earlier. Those calls I've been making . . ."

"You were . . . buying *this* house?" She chews on her bottom lip. "Why would you do that?"

I step forward until I'm standing in front of her. Her eyes squint to look at me. The sun is behind me, beaming down on us. "The first day after seeing your reaction, I made the call to buy the beach house."

"But why?" she whispers.

"Because I'd give anything to see you smile like that. When you came into the house, the way you looked. I would do anything in my power to bring you that level of happiness."

"Why me? I-I don't under—"

"Because I'm falling in love with you," I admit.

It feels good to say the words. All the fears and anger from my past drain off me.

Like my fear has held me back.

Purging myself of it makes me feel anew.

"I think I'm in love with you, too." She stands and steps into my open arms, hers circling my waist. I tuck her into me and kiss the top of her head. "Where do we go from here?" she mutters into my chest.

"I'm going to be honest. I've never done this before. I'm not sure what the next steps are for us. But I'm willing to try an honest, true relationship. For you and only you, Layla."

She relaxes into my grasp.

This is what it feels like to be content. This is the moment for us.

I hope I'm making the right choice. I hope this isn't another bad one. I can be normal, right? Despite everything I've done, I can be happy.

Everyone deserves happiness. And I've already done everything necessary to guarantee our peace and that the past stays buried.

But can a monster have happiness?

Layla is the one thing I've ever cared about, and I'm terrified I'll ruin her. I won't. *You would never hurt her.*

You love her . . .

But will my love be her demise?

36

Layla

'm speechless.

He bought the house. He bought a house for *us*.

The *us* that, for the last two months since I met him, I didn't think was ever going to be a possibility.

Where's the logic in this move?

That's the part that has my tongue feeling heavy.

My mouth feels like it's been sewn shut, and I can't reason with myself to open up and ask these questions. He bought the house for me. He bought it because he saw me smile.

What does this all mean?

Cain has money, but to buy a house because someone is obsessed with it, well, that makes no sense.

Unless . . .

Maybe it's also a business thing. Maybe after my comment about the next project potentially being based on Cape May, he wants to be here to see if it will work.

Yeah, that's got to be it.

"It would be a great idea so you can see if a future development can be based on this town. Smart."

He pulls back and looks at me. "This has nothing to do with a new development." His hand reaches out, and his fingers land on my jaw, tilting my head up so that I can look into his eyes.

"This is about you. About us. I want to make you happy. I want a place for us to go. I've never had that, Layla. Not really. And I want to have this wish fulfilled with you."

"How will we make it work? I'm in the city, and you're currently in wherever the compound is being built and then off to another job so far away."

"We can make it work." He leans down and places a kiss on my mouth.

"But how?" I ask against his lips.

He pulls away from me and takes my hand in his, leading us to sit down together on the daybed.

"We come up with a plan together, that's how."

I turn my head to face him. His features are serious, and he's quiet. If I could see inside his head, I'm sure his analytical brain is doing mathematical equations of every outcome.

"Right now, I don't have a home."

"What?"

"I'm saying this all wrong as that's not important. What's important is, up until this point, I have moved from site to site, but I don't need to do that all the time. I can settle in one place."

"You don't?"

"No. I can reside in the city and take up a permanent residence there. Rent space to work, and when I need to travel to a site, I do."

"You would be willing to do that for me?"

He lifts my hand to his mouth and places a kiss on my knuckles. "For *us*."

Are we moving too fast?

I search his expression for anything to give him away.

That maybe he's not comfortable with the speed we are going.

But based on the smile on his face and, well, on my own, I think what he's suggesting is what I want, too. It makes the most sense.

"Layla, when you have lived your whole life with—" He stops himself.

"With what? What were you going to say?"

His lips part wider, but this time, it feels fake. "Forget it, it was nothing. Now that this is settled, what should we do today?"

I know what he's doing, but regardless, I don't press. We're on vacation, and I don't want to ruin the mood. "I'm not sure. What do you want to do?"

"How about we go for a swim?"

"Sure, I'll just throw on my bathing suit." I stand from the chair, and just as I'm about to walk inside the house, Cain picks me up and rushes to the pool.

"Stop. I'm not wearing a bathing suit." I playfully hit his back. "And neither are you."

He's wearing gray sweats and a T-shirt, and I'm in a sundress.

It doesn't seem to stop him because the next thing I know, we are doused with freezing cold water.

I kick and scream, and Cain laughs. *A full-body laugh.*

The sound is rare.

I have heard him laugh before, but never like this.

It's rich and soulful, and it makes me believe anything is possible. Because this man, who has always been closed off, has let his guard down and let me in.

Yep. Anything can happen with a few wishes and a whole lotta hope.

He places a kiss on my forehead and walks us out of the early morning, chilled water. When we get back up to the house, he sets me down on my feet.

"Grab what you need. We'll spend the day at the beach."

▲

We're going to be heading back to the city soon. Neither of us is ready for this fairy tale to end. Sure, we can come back now any time we want, but in this house, it feels like we are cocooned in a bubble, living in a fantasy world.

I'm not ready for the real world and the problems that arise in it to invade my happiness.

Together, we're having a picnic on the sand, watching the waves, and enjoying the sun.

He looks at me with such earnest interest. Sometimes, I don't know how to handle that look. No one has ever wanted to know me this much.

"You went through a lot with your parents. Tell me about it."

In almost a mumble, I say, "Why do I feel like I can tell you this and you won't judge me for it?"

"We all have our backstories."

"Yes. Well, mine is one giant lie. A truth even I don't like talking about."

He looks taken aback. How can it be possible for this man to randomly fall out of the sky and be perfect for me? Someone who may understand the hidden lives we lead.

"Go ahead. No judging," he says.

With a slight groan—because I don't tell this to everyone I meet, but this is Cain, *my* Cain—the words start to pour.

"The night of graduation, my cousin and his mom were at our house for a small after-party. Of course, my parents were fighting again, and I told my cousin how embarrassed I was by them. I said I wished I weren't related to my father as he was getting drunk and belligerent, which was my father's normal state when he wasn't working.

"My aunt heard us talking and piped up with a comment of how I didn't deserve her brother, who had sacrificed for me his whole life being married to my bitch of a mother. I had no clue what she was going on about, and when I asked, she said that now the truth could come out. I wasn't Glenn's kid.

"Irene was like a faucet that couldn't be turned off. She told me all about how my mother had cheated on my father early in their marriage and got pregnant with me. She wanted to get a divorce and put me up for adoption, but Glenn didn't think that was the right thing to do. He was in love with the idea of a family and told her she could quit her job, and he would take care of us both. My mother manipulated him, and over the years, he just got more upset and turned to drinking. They both were a nightmare to be around, even on their good days. But it doesn't matter because even the good days were all a deception. I packed up my stuff that night and walked out the door. I haven't talked to the family again since."

I finally look back up at Cain. I see my unshed tears reflected in his eyes.

Like he knows what it feels like when deep family lies are unearthed.

The destruction they cause.

"Thank you for telling me your story," he says, giving a squeeze to my hand that I didn't realize he was holding.

His smile has me sitting up straight. He gives me a strength I didn't know I needed.

Changing the subject from me, I look around the beach. "It's so beautiful. I remember always wanting to go to the ocean when I was a kid. Did you come to Cape May a lot as a kid?"

"Nah. Just a few times."

"Is it close to where you grew up? Where are you from again?"

"Enough talking. It's almost time to leave, and there's one more thing I want to do before we go." Cain picks me up, and together, we run into the water.

We splash around and have fun, but then something hits me as I look off into the distance and then back at the abandoned picnic blanket.

He did it again.

Deflected. His past left to the side to never be discussed.

He never wants to talk about anything from his past. I get it. I really do.

I hate to talk about my parents, who never cared for me either. Hell, the moment I graduated high school, after they told me what a failure I would be, I vowed to never speak of them again, so I can understand not wanting to talk about it, but if we are really going to try to make a go of this, I need to break down his walls.

Cain needs to let me in.

That's the only way we will have a future together.

He has to show me the skeletons in his closet.

And I have to learn to love those parts of him, too.

37

Layla

Days have passed since our weekend getaway. Now, I'm back in my apartment, alone, and back to camping out in my living room, missing Cain.

Since being back in the city, I haven't seen him; only phone calls and texts have kept us in contact with each other.

Working keeps me busy. But, if I thought that writing an amazing article for The Elysian would kick-start my career, I was wrong. Since the article has not been published yet, it's hard to leverage it for a promotion. It will be published next month, so hopefully, then I'll be able to take full advantage of the notoriety I'm hoping the piece gets. If all goes as planned, I can start applying for other jobs this fall. Or, at least, one can hope.

Unfortunately, that means that right now, I'm back home, working on the piece I didn't finish today at work.

I'm just not inspired in the office or by this boring as hell topic. How did I fall back into an article about freaking faucets? Now, I'm forced to work on it at home.

"The Best Faucets to Buy if You Love Retro" is my demise today.

I let out a sigh.

This blows.

I stare at the images of the faucets. Sure, they're cool . . . but they're also, you know, FAUCETS.

That's when I focus on the TV news program that has been on in the background. To this point, I haven't been paying attention, but now, the news anchor has updates on . . .

Another murder by The Compass Killer.

After the short commercial break, the female reporter is back on, front and center.

"Recent developments have indicated that there has been another body found. The ritualistic practices of the serial killer lead detectives to believe that The Compass Killer has returned and seems to be killing at an alarming rate."

She turns to her cohost. "What do you think that means for our residents, John? Why are the killings accelerating after so many years dormant? Is there any evidence that investigators have shared to explain this rash occurrence?"

"Well, Hailey, it's not good for our citizens, especially with the criminologists playing their cards so close to the vest. We need the police to be straightforward with the residents of our surrounding communities."

"John, do you think it is possible the states will enact a curfew as a result?"

"Well, let's analyze what we know of the original murders and compare them to the new ones. We have confirmed in all but one case, the victims were young women, early twenties, blond hair, blue eyes. All of this matches the original MO. of the serial killer that terrorized New York and New Jersey so many years ago.

"Victim Cynthia Richards did not match the age constraints, which explains why the police were not convinced it was The Compass Killer at first glance. Ms. Richards wasn't of the right age."

"But surely Ms. Richards must have had the same markers as the other victims."

"For our viewers back home, can you go over the evidence you think the detectives have, John?"

"Certainly, Hailey. Warning: The following material may be

sensitive to some of our audience members. The killer not only slices his victim's neck but would also paint a north-pointing compass arrow on their forehead with the victim's own finger. We believe he keeps the finger as a trophy and places their bodies pointing north before leaving the scene of the crime."

"This information is so very disturbing, John. Do investigators have any scenarios they are willing to share as to what set the murderer into the latest rash of killings? Maybe he was incarcerated for something else and released? Or maybe Ms. Richards was a copycat, and maybe her murder brought out the original . . ."

"Interesting spin. I guess only time will tell."

Their words spin in my head, and I think about the original cases and Cynthia's murder.

Cynthia, the woman who visited The Elysian and followed Cain.

I wonder what was different about her, or maybe the newscaster was right. She was murdered by someone else. Maybe that murder was made to look like The Compass Killer so that the killer could get away with it. Instead, it brought the original killer out of hiding.

There're so many questions that don't make sense in these reports. But I know I need to get to the bottom of this. I can't sit here writing about faucets when I could be doing something important.

I could help solve this crime. I could piece together The Compass Killer. I stand from where I'm sitting, a new resolve etching its way inside me. I start to pace the room.

Thinking of all the things I can do on my fourth pass over the small space, I stand in front of my computer and type in Cynthia's name. When the search engine loads, I look at a picture of her, and a shiver runs down my spine.

She's pretty.

Blond hair.

Blue eyes.

It's eerie, actually, because she sort of resembles me. Older. But the features are similar enough that it gives me the creeps.

When I see the name of the small town she's from, I jot it down. Then I open my email and fire off an email to my boss, letting him know I'll be working on my article at home and plan to be back in the office by the end of the week.

Next, I walk into my closet and start pulling out clothes. As I pack my bag, I pick up the phone and call Mara.

"How are the faucets? Still dripping?"

"They're on hold, but if boss man asks, I'm home, knee-deep in retro if you catch my drip."

She laughs at my bad joke. "What do you have going on instead?"

"I'm going away for a few days." The sound of the drawers opening grates against my nerves as I wait for her to ask the question I know she wants to ask. It takes her a few moments, but then she does.

"With lover boy?"

"Actually, no," I tell her, but I'm not dumb. Just because I'm not going away with Cain doesn't mean she won't continue with her pursuit of knowledge.

"Spill."

"I'm going to Somerset, New Jersey." Holding out two pairs of leggings, I pick the one that looks to be in better condition and then pack it. I'm not sure how long I'll be gone. Hopefully, only one day, but you never can tell where the truth will bring you, so I have learned to always be prepared.

"Why in the hell would you be going there?"

I stare at my half-packed suitcase for a second, wondering if I should tell her the truth. "Cynthia is from there," I mutter.

"Am I supposed to know who this Cynthia is?"

"The Compass Killer's first victim on his latest murder spree."

I can hear the familiar sound of a sharp inhale of breath escaping Mara's mouth. "What the hell are you up to, Layla?"

I don't need to be near her to know that Mara is probably seething. "You know I want more than this. You know I need a story to pitch in order to leave . . ."

"You can't possibly think it's a good idea to investigate a serial killer who happens to be targeting women who look like you."

"And that is exactly why I need to. Don't you see these women could be me? How can I sit back and not help? How can I sit back and not try to figure out who the killer is?"

"This is an absolutely horrible idea," she responds.

"Maybe, maybe not."

"And there's nothing I can do to change your mind? At least promise me you're not going alone."

"What kind of an idiot do you take me for?" A giant one because I am going alone. But instead of confessing, I bite down on my lip and stifle the lie.

"Be safe. Keep in contact with me. I love you, woman, and expect check-ins every day."

"Okay, Mom. I love you, too."

I end the call and head outside. My car is parked a few blocks over on the street. One of the reasons I keep a car in the city. Even though it's very annoying to change parking spots every day, multiple times a day, sometimes, when you're a journalist, it's necessary to have transportation. Case in point, today's idiotic adventure.

My phone rings as I walk; it's Cain. This is not going to be easy lying to him.

"Hi," I answer.

"I miss you." Hearing his voice makes my knees go weak on a good day; hearing him say these words, well, that turns me into a gooey puddle on the floor. "I miss you, too."

"I might be able to take off and see you—"

As much as it kills me not to see him, I can't, so I stop him before he can go on. I need to pursue this, and I can't let anything derail me from the story. "Actually, this week is crazy at work. Can it be over the weekend?" I lie again, a pattern I'm not liking, even though it's necessary.

"Of course."

"Thanks, you're amazing. See you Friday."

"See you Friday."

I feel awful, but I know I can't tell him the truth. He wouldn't be happy. He would tell me to back away, and I just feel that I need to pursue this. When I get in the car, I turn it on and start my trek to Jersey.

A little over an hour later, I'm pulling up toward the small town. The sun has already set.

I really didn't think this through.

It's dark. What can I possibly learn now with everything closed? Plus, I need to find a place to stay because, of course, I didn't think of that as I fled the city. I spot a Motel 8 that will have to do for tonight.

With any luck, in the light of a new day, I'll find something.

Hopefully, this isn't all a huge mistake.

38

Layla

At first, when I open my eyes, I forget where I am.

Then everything comes back to me. I'm in Somerset.

Still drowsy from sleep, I hear the sound of my phone going off.

Grabbing it from the side table, I see that I have several texts and a phone call from Cain. Seeing as I lied to him about where I am, and I don't want anyone to know I'm here, I don't answer.

I ignore every text and call. Probably not a good move, knowing how hot his temper can become.

The plan is to dress, grab a cup of coffee at a nearby shop, and then set out to find all the information I can on Cynthia. Once I'm done here, I'll head home. Easy peasy. No need to worry Cain with where I've run off to today.

Rising from the bed, I throw on some clothes and then brush my teeth.

Sitting on the bed, I grab the map I got at the rest stop on the way here.

With my red Sharpie, I start to map out where all the bodies were identified, starting with the initial victims from the old cases.

Once done, I look down at the completed markings.

Oh, my God. How can this be right?

I double-check everything because I don't trust this is a coincidence.

It's a pattern. *Holy fuck.*

The police never released this information to the public. *Unless they didn't put two and two together?*

The geological areas where the bodies were all found almost form a triangle.

Except for one.

Cynthia's body was found outside the proximity of the original crime scenes.

Instead of being part of the triangle, it lies outside of the path. This makes no sense. Why would The Compass Killer place her body away from the same path as the initial victims?

Cynthia's murder makes no sense, and it must have meaning to the case.

Why, after all these years, did he start killing again, and why does her homicide not fit the MO? She's the only one who falls out of the original age range.

Even the new victim is on the edge of the lines of the triangle. She fits the original age of the women murdered too.

What is special about Cynthia?

What does a triangle mean?

I open my computer and type in the definition of a triangle.

Meaning: A triangle represents manifestation, enlightenment, revelation, and a higher perspective. It is often used to mark the cycles of growth that lead to a higher state of being. Spiritually, it represents a path toward enlightenment or connection to an omnipresent being.

Hmm. Is that it? Is the killer looking for enlightenment?

No. That doesn't seem likely. With all the information I've gathered, nothing points to this motive. This whole pattern doesn't feel right.

Pulling out my notebook, I look over my comments.

That's when I want to groan and hit my hand against the table.

If I remove Cynthia—because she might be a copycat and doesn't fit the MO, the original pattern of murder locations changes shape slightly.

It forms the arrow of a compass facing north.

Okay, now this makes sense, but what does this mean?

After a little bit of online digging, I find that generally, this direction stands for hardships and discomfort. North represents the trials people must endure and the cleansing they must undergo.

This leads me to think this killer is likely very intelligent but also very broken. What could have made him so broken?

I jot down a list of things the killer might've experienced in his life. Terrible family. Abandonment. Sexual abuse. Then I put my pen down and look back at the map. The compass is pointing north.

What are you trying to tell me?

The biggest question keeps coming back to why is Cynthia different? Why is this victim important? If she doesn't fit the pattern, it has to be something else that brought her to the killer's notice.

It's on the tip of my tongue. I feel like I'm grasping for the connection.

Why would someone kill her and copy the pattern of a cold case? Maybe it's the killer, and she meant something to him, and her location is the key.

That could be it and would be a reason why the killer would come out of hiding.

Maybe her death was used to mark an anniversary? A special date, and he killed her to immortalize his talents for killing?

Okay, if her age is thirty-five, that would have made her eighteen when the killings took place. Maybe the reporter was right. Maybe he was incarcerated, and maybe she's the one who got away . . .

Okay, before I dig deeper into this, I need to see what else I can find. The local police might know something about this. Having a body show up right outside this town has to mean something.

Without thinking twice, I head out the door, hop into my car, and drive to the local police station to see what else I can get from the sheriff.

When I arrive, the sheriff looks like and sounds like everything I expect from a small-town sheriff. One where they don't like outsiders.

He's older. White hair and a pot belly.

His face weathered from years of service.

"Hi, Sheriff Michaels, I was wondering if I can speak to you about Cynthia Richards. I know she grew up—"

"Who are you?"

"My name is Layla Marks, a journalist from New York—"

"Stop right there, missy. This is a small, peaceful town. We don't want you city folk causing problems."

"I just wanted to ask you—"

"No. We don't talk to reporters. We already have the FBI breathing down our necks because the body was found only twenty miles from town. That, coupled with the fact that she grew up here. No. I won't speak to you. We don't need more reporters poking around. This town has been quiet for years. We don't need to stir the pot again." He moves to walk away and turns his back on me.

"Again? What do you mean again? Did something happen here?"

"No. I misspoke. Now, if you have nothing else, I have other things I need to do. I expect to hear you're gone when I come back."

A man like this will never listen to a woman, let alone an "outsider." I would have shown him my map, but something tells me he would have thought I was whacky.

I won't be getting any help from the sheriff, but there must be someone who can help me find out more about Cynthia. Someone who isn't too afraid to talk to a reporter.

I walk out of the station and look around the small town. I squint my eyes and look at the stone building across the street and down a block.

39

Cain

Something is wrong with Layla, and I need to know what.

When we hung up the other night, Layla seemed off. No one can slide a lie past me, especially her. My paranoia spiked this morning when she didn't answer my calls or texts.

When I still couldn't get in touch with her after I called the magazine, I decided to drive to the city.

Hours later, I'm here, standing outside her apartment, banging on the door.

But like before, she doesn't answer me. Where the fucking hell is she?

Sighing in frustration, I make my way down the three flights of stairs until I reach the basement. I head down the hallway, searching for the superintendent of the building to let me into her apartment.

I find the man in a small office, looking over some bills.

"Hello." I walk in. "I need your help."

He lifts his brow, but he doesn't seem to care, so I reach into my pocket and grab a stack of bills. Two hundred dollars should get this guy to move his ass.

"I need you to let me into Layla Marks's apartment. Apartment 204."

"I can't do that."

I pull out another hundred, and another, until I have one thousand dollars in my hand.

"Fine, but I didn't let you in."

I give him a nod. After I find Layla, I'll let her know it's time to change the lock, and then she needs to find another apartment and move. Maybe we can find one together.

Fuck.

What is wrong with me?

I'm already buying houses, relocating my office, and now . . . what? Moving in with her?

This isn't good. I'm wound tight, and this obsession can't be normal.

Or maybe it is? Maybe this is what normal people feel like when they fall in love.

I shake my head, pulling myself out of my inner rambling, and follow the super up the stairs.

When we are standing outside her doorway, he opens it and is quick to leave. Good news, I see nothing is out of place when I start to search.

When I head into her bedroom, there is still nothing wrong. I open drawers and the closet door, and that's when I have my first inkling that she's gone somewhere and didn't tell me. Her overnight bag she packed for Cape May is gone.

Now, how do I find out where she went?

Her friend. The only person like family.

Mara? Yeah, Mara.

She works with her, so that's where I'll go. To the magazine.

Twenty minutes later, my cab pulls up to the building. I head up to her office, thankful I know my way from the last time I was here.

I don't stop to ask if I can go in. I just swing the glass doors open and stride in like I own the place.

I'm about to head to her boss's office and demand he find Mara for me, when a woman I've never seen before steps in my way.

"What are you doing here?" she asks.

I raise my brow. "Do I know you?"

She places her hand on her hips, shooting off an attitude of *don't mess with her*. "No, but I know you."

"And you are?"

Her eyes narrow as she stares at me. "I'm Mara, Cain. But my question still stands. What are you doing here? I thought you were with Layla."

"Why would you think I'm with Layla?" I ask.

"She told me you guys were together." I lift my hand, signaling her to go on. "You guys were going to Somerset together."

The blood whooshes in my ears, and I swear the room starts to fucking spin.

What the hell is happening?

I grab Mara's arms, not hard, but enough to startle her. "Tell me everything," I grit through clenched teeth.

"I-I—" she mutters.

"Spit it out." My voice is harsh, but there is no time for this shit.

"She wanted to look into The Compass Killer. She decided to—"

"To what? Word for word. What did she say to you?" I cut her off. Why the hell would Layla go to Somerset? What is she hoping to find there?

"Layla went to find out more information on one of the victims. The one that started the cycle again. Cynthia Richards."

At her words, my chest tightens. Layla can't go there. She absolutely can't look into this case. "Why?"

"She thinks Cynthia's the key to the story."

"What story?" I know the answer, despite my question. But I need to hear Mara say it out loud.

"The story she's writing on the case."

"Son of a bitch." I storm off, grabbing my phone from my pocket and dialing.

"Cain, what's up? I'm in the middle of meeting with some people to—"

"Jim." Before he can say more, I cut him off. "I have to go to Somerset."

"Okay, what do you need?"

"I need you to locate a woman. She's twenty-five, blonde hair"—I take a breath—"blue eyes, fair skin." I hear the inhale of breath when I describe her.

"Is this about the murders?" he says quieter so whomever he's with cannot hear him as easily.

"Yes." I want to scream out more of what I know, but I can't find the air to speak.

"The police are saying it's not a copycat." I nod, even though he can't see me. My mind is reeling, and my chest feels tight.

It feels like I can't breathe, and I'm not sure what to do. How did we get this far where Layla is now investigating something I can't have her looking into?

"There is a woman there digging around. I have to stop her before she gets hurt."

"Jeez, Cain. Fuck. I don't want to get involved in cleaning up messes again."

"It's a little too late for that, don't you think?" And without another word, I hang up.

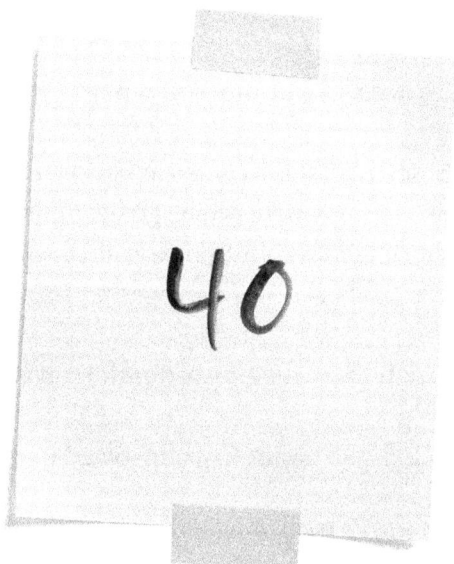

40

Layla

I decide to head down the road and stop in each store I find. It's a small town. Someone knows something, somewhere.

The first store looks like a craft store, and I decide to start there. Maybe Cynthia had a hobby. You never know.

I pretend to shop for a while before picking up a scrapbook.

Not one for this type of thing, but I'm not sure what else to buy. At least with this, I can use it as a journal or even jot notes in it one day.

When I step up to the register, an elderly lady with gray coiffed hair looks me up and down.

I'm preparing myself for another person like the sheriff, but after she observes me for a few seconds, she smiles. "You're not from here, are you?"

"Nope."

"What brings you to these parts? We don't get a lot of visitors. Well, not until recently."

This could be useful. "Ohhh, were they here about the girl?" I pry.

"Cynthia? Yes. But like I told them, I didn't know her. Will that be all for you?"

"It will." I hand her enough cash for the book. "Thank you so much."

248

"Mary at the shop next door might have some more answers. Be careful though, she can be a little mean spirited to outsiders at first." She winks at me.

And I can't help but chuckle. "Guess I stick out?"

"Yes, dear. You stick out. Mary likes to gossip more than be mad, so you may be in luck."

Laughing a bit, I turn and make my way outside, then head into the next store. This is a small furniture store. One that is light on the furniture and heavy on the knickknacks.

Lamps, vases, and candles are some of the things I see at first glance. Seeing the lamps, I feel guilty that I'm not writing the articles I should be for *Concept and Space*. But this feeling down in my gut that says there is a story here won't go away.

A woman who appears to be a bit younger than the last woman I spoke to smiles at me from behind an old desk that looks like it belongs in an elementary school from the fifties.

"Here about the girl?" She chuckles.

"Am I really that obvious?"

She looks me up and down and then frowns. "Yes. Plus, no one comes to this town."

My fingers trail against the surface of the wood in front of me, glancing around at the store before settling into my question. "Yes, I'm here about Cynthia Richards. Did you know her when she lived here?"

"She was a sweet girl, but that's all I know. She used to work part time at the diner four doors down when she was a senior in high school. I bet they know something."

"Thank you," I say before heading out. I don't bother buying anything, and I head straight to the diner.

When I get inside, it's pretty empty, save for a few waitresses on staff. Perfect.

I take a seat at the counter.

"How can I help you, dear?" a woman in her fifties says to me.

I pull the menu from where it sits next to the silver metal napkin holder and glance at it quickly before looking up. "I'll just have a coffee, cream and sugar, please."

"Sure thing." A few seconds later, she brings me my mug. "What brings you to town?"

"Just trying to get a bit of information on someone. I wonder if you can help me."

"You looking for information on Cynthia?"

I nod. They must never get visitors, or I stick out like a sore thumb.

"I'll tell you what I told the last reporter. She was a sweet girl. Worked here for a bit until she got caught up in a relationship with a troubled kid."

"What was the name of the kid?"

"I . . . I am not good with names, and that was a long time ago." She grabs a rag and starts to clean. Something tells me she does know, but she doesn't want to tell me.

"Oh, there's more to the story than that . . ." the other server says as she steps closer.

I incline my head.

"Tammy, hush your mouth," the other one warns.

"What? It's true. Or are you getting too old in the sack you really don't remember?"

The server gives the one I now know as Tammy a dirty look.

"What's the rest of the story?" I ask Tammy.

"Cynthia fell apart about the same time as the fire."

"What fire?" I ask, interested in getting more on this new piece of information.

"It was around the same time everything in New Jersey was blowing up with all those Compass killings. We had our own drama here in Somerset."

"It's hardly the same thing, comparing a fire to serial killers, don't you think?"

"Still drama to all of us. So, do you want to know or not?" she huffs.

"What happened?" It might not have anything to do with what I'm looking into, but something tells me if I get these women to talk, they might tell me something they wouldn't otherwise divulge.

"People don't like to talk about it around these parts, but during the same time as the women went missing, there was a fire, and two boys died."

"Did Cynthia know the boys?"

"Of course she did." The other woman shoots her another look.

"No one wants to remember those days." She scoffs at Tammy.

"And Cynthia, she showed up here after the fire crews had everything calmed down. She was completely distraught. Rightfully so. The one boy was her friend. She refused to say what happened. People thought she might be involved somehow by the way she was acting, but that girl couldn't hurt a fly."

I lean forward on the counter, placing my elbows down to get closer. "What happened?"

"Eventually, she started showing signs of PTSD. We don't have the people to help with that here, so they found a hospital over in New York that could help. Years went by, and she never came back to the town . . . until recently."

My mouth drops open, but I'm quick to rein in my shock. "She was here? In Somerset?"

"She was."

"When?"

She looks up to the ceiling as if she is trying to remember. "Hmm. Maybe about two months ago."

"What was she doing here?"

"She was digging for information about a boy she'd once had a relationship with. One of the boys from the fire." She whispers this as if talking about the boy will get her in trouble.

The phone rings, and the other server goes to answer it. Tammy slides closer, wiping the counter right in front of me. She leans in. "The troubled boy she was in a relationship with . . . his name was North Abbott."

"Thank you," I whisper. "Where can I find his family?"

"Oh, honey, it's the saddest story; they're all dead. Have been gone for years now, but that was before I was in town."

"Where did they live if you don't mind me asking? Where was their home?"

"End of Maple. It's the last house on the dead end. Abandoned, and behind it"—she shivers— "it's just woods. Creepy location, if you ask me. Now, it's just the family cemetery."

A chill runs up my spine, but my resolve is set. I'm going there.

I fire up the GPS on my phone as I walk back to my car. I have this niggling feeling in my brain that I just cracked open a huge clue about Cynthia. But I still don't know how she's associated with Cain. Why would she have been snooping and following the head of an architecture firm?

I head out to that area where Tammy said the Abbotts lived.

When I pull up, there is an old home. By the looks of the overgrown weeds and trees, no one has been here for years.

No one kept up this place.

No one came back to love it.

The realization makes me feel hollow.

The property was probably once beautiful. A place for a family to call home.

I don't go into the house. Instead, I peek in through a window. It looks as if it's been frozen in time. The grime and dust on the window obstruct my view, but I see enough to know that no one has been here since the boys died. A part of me wants to go inside, but technically, that's breaking and entering, and even though no one lives here, something tells me the sheriff would be more than happy to lock me up.

Instead, I continue to look around the outside, making my way closer to where Tammy said I could find the cemetery.

With each step I take, I can't shake off the foreboding feeling weaving its way through my body. That feeling when you're somewhere you shouldn't be, and eyes are watching you? That's how I feel now in this overgrown grass.

Each crunch through the landscape magnifies my fear. But I know it's just the anxiety. Misplaced fear having me question everything.

No one is here.

It's probably just nerves since, deep down, I know I shouldn't be here. This is an open investigation. That, coupled with the fact that I've lied to Cain, is the guilt that's making me nervous.

I take a few more steps, and then I see the old, broken arch of the cemetery.

I start to look around for where to walk, but this is worse than the path to get here.

Clearly, no one has touched these grounds in years, maybe even decades. Overgrown trees block out so much of the sunlight it has become dark and dank.

Using the flashlight on my phone, I peer down to read the names on the only tombstones visible. Both lying flat on the ground, an afterthought to the people laid to rest.

Like no one loved them or cared where they were buried. Covered with ivy, I reach and pull back the vines.

Here lies North Abbott
1987–2005

The boy Cynthia dated.

Beside it is another grave, this one is for Stone Abbott.

Why did she come back here after being gone for so many years?

With how dark it is getting here under the canopy, I know I should be heading home soon, but I will never be able to sleep if I don't uncover more details about this relationship between Cynthia and these Abbott boys.

Jumping back into my car, I head toward town. I'm not sure who to ask after striking out at the police department and the two other shops. What other institutions would have been around for a while that would know these kids from years ago?

As I drive into the main center of town, I squint my eyes and look at the stone building across the street and down a block. It looks old, like it's been here since probably the early 1900s.

If anyone knows the history of this town and its people, I bet I would find them in there.

The library probably has old archives of newspapers or local school information I can pick through.

If there was a fire in this town, it would have made the local papers. Maybe I can find the original story and track down the journalist who wrote it.

Once I'm in front of the building, I pull over and park, and then I grab my bag, notebook, and computer and head to the door.

The sound of the creak as the door opens is loud to my ears, and when I step inside, a woman, who looks to be in her seventies, greets me.

This could bode well for me. She could have been living and working here when everything happened.

"Hello, I'm Margret. I'm the librarian. Can I help you with, Miss?"

"Hi, Margret, I'm Layla. I was wondering if you could help me with something."

"Depends on what it is." She removes the glasses on her face and scrubs at her eyes.

"Have you been here in Somerset a long time?"

"Not only have I lived here my whole life, but I'm also a bit of a local historian." She winks at me. "Why don't you take a seat, and I'll see if I can help you."

Something tells me she's not used to guests and is excited to have someone to talk to.

I make my way over to the free seats, and she takes the one across from me.

"What were you interested in hearing about?"

I lean forward, placing my elbows on the table. "I was wondering if you had any information you could tell me about the fire that took place in this town," I ask.

"You're going to have to be a little more specific than that. I've been working here for decades."

"Did you know the Abbott boys?"

She draws in a deep breath. "I did."

"Can you tell me about the family?"

Her jaw tightens at my question. "It's a pretty sad story. Are you sure you want to talk about this?"

I nod.

"The Abbott family." She exhales. "They had lived in Somerset for years. Generations, actually, like me. They were lifers. Unfortunately for them, their lives weren't as long. I remember the Abbott boys from their youngest days. I'm closer in age with North's grandparents. But they also died young. That family is cursed if you ask me."

"What makes you say that?"

"The grandparents died in a tragic accident, and then their father—" She stops herself from going on.

"What?" I ask.

"Stone and North were left with their mom a lot. She wasn't from here. He met her when he was in college." Her hands start to shake. "Depressing story really."

"Why?"

"She was a—" She shakes her head, and I give her a small smile.

"Please go on."

"She was bad. Not a good mom. Always drunk. Drugs. They almost lost the boys a couple of times through CPS because of her."

"Where was the dad?"

"He worked out of town. I don't remember what he did, but he traveled a lot. One time, CPS did take the younger boy, North. It was when he was away, but then the father came home. Then he was gone again, jail this time. The state did the boys a big disservice by leaving them with her."

"Why was he sent to jail?"

She shakes her head. "It was a sad time, as I said. I don't want to gossip . . ."

I know she's not comfortable telling me, so rather than have her close up, I switch topics.

"The mother. Is she still around?" I know that Stone and North are dead, but there was no tombstone for a woman.

"The mother up and disappeared one day. Nobody has seen or heard from her since." She leans in conspiratorially. "If you ask me, she was the first victim of The Compass Killer."

"Where is the evidence for that?"

"The police aren't talking about it because they don't want to cause hysteria, but all the women fit a very similar profile. They all look like Gloria Abbott." The woman shakes her head. "The whole situation is so sad. That poor, sweet, broken boy, North. He never stood a chance."

"Does anyone know what happened that night?"

"The family cabin burned down in the middle of the night. Both the Abbott boys were in it. The bodies"—she trembles— "the bodies aren't actually at the cemetery because they were burned in the fire. Only a few bones are buried."

"That's horrible."

"I know, and there was no money. The town collected funds for the gravestones."

She raises her hand and points at the corner of the room. There is a small, old computer. Probably has been here for decades.

"That computer has the archives from old articles. That's where you can see more about the fire."

Sitting down in front of the computer, I turn it on.

It takes a long time to power up.

Once the home screen opens, I see files on the main page.

They are dated by year.

"What year was the fire?" I ask her, my voice probably too loud for the room.

"It was 2005," I believe.

I click on the folder, and then when the articles pop up, I start to thumb through them. They are all PDFs of scans from the original newspapers. When I reach the one titled "Tragic Fire Kills Brothers," I click on it and enlarge the article.

The story talks about how both were at their cabin. That a phone call was made from the house at 9:30 p.m. A little after 1:00 a.m., a fire sparked. It started with a faulty wire, and both brothers died in their beds.

I keep reading.

There's a picture of the Abbott boys.

Stone and North Abbott.

I enlarge and stare.

My eyes lock on a young man with long, unruly hair. The brown locks cover half of his face and eyes. It's hard to see him. He's very skinny and looks frail. Malnourished.

I zoom in more. He looks familiar. But I can't place it.

It's the eyes.

I squint my eyes, hovering in front of the screen. Who does he remind me of?

And then it hits me.

Cain.

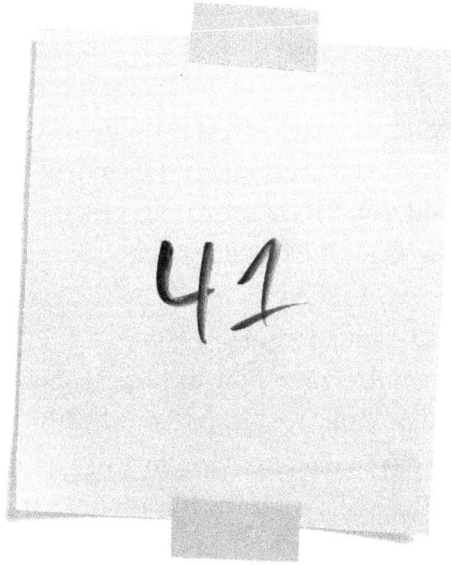

41

Layla

These eyes.

They look so similar. Yet . . . Different. This boy gives a hollow stare back at me from the newspaper photo.

Sad.

Insecure.

Lost.

This can't be Cain. My Cain is not the boy in this picture from years ago. It's just a coincidence.

Or . . .

I stand from the computer and make my way back to the librarian. She's sorting through a stack of books in front of her. When I'm standing in front of her, she glances up, her nose wrinkling behind her glasses that are now back on her face.

"One more question." I give her a small smile. I'm sure my endless questions are annoying her at this point, but I really don't care.

I need to know.

With a small sigh, she closes the book. "Go ahead, ask your question."

"Did the Abbotts have any more family in town? Say . . . a cousin?"

"Not that I know of." Her lips form a straight line, and her eyes lift, trying to access a memory maybe. "Nope. I don't remember any family. But then again, they were closed off. A strange bunch." She goes back to the stack of books and whatever she was doing when I interrupted her.

Cain must be related to this boy. He has to be a cousin. Because although they look alike and have the same eyes, it cannot be Cain. The Cain Archer I know and have fallen for is a successful business owner.

He's not this boy who died years ago.

The whole idea is ridiculous. How would one even—no. There's no way a teenage boy would know how to fake his own death. That's not something he could pull off. Yet, despite myself, I wonder.

Why would he have faked his own death?

I laugh, drawing a stare from the librarian. I need to calm down. I don't need to get into hysterics in the middle of this library. Here I am, losing my cool, and that's the last thing I need in the middle of investigating this story. And there is no reason to come up with crazy conspiracy theories about how he could do it.

It can't be him.

It. Is. Not. Him.

Yet it feels like I just stumbled onto the truth.

I look around the old stone library. The smell of first edition books permeates the room. This building has probably been here for hundreds of years. The stone on the outside is weathered and—

My stomach bottoms out.

Our conversation on the way to Cape May comes back to me. His words ringing out the truth I so desperately want to deny.

"When I was young, my house was really bad. I used to leave but had nowhere to go, so I went to the library. Old stone building with a secret room. That's where I first read Huxley's Brave New World. *That's where I first dreamed of a paradise. One where I could be protected."*

The blood starts to pound in my veins, my heart beating fast as I gaze around the old room.

I feel dizzy.

My footsteps wobbly.

I head back toward the librarian. "Yes, dear?"

"I-I was wondering. Can you look up the reading history of patrons? Can you see the books checked out by North Abbott?"

It feels like there is a jackhammer pounding in my chest as I wait.

Her fingers hit the keyboard on the computer in front of her. "You're lucky we updated the system a few years back."

"What do you mean?"

"If you had come here a few years ago, I would have made you rummage through the old boxes in the attic." She starts to scan the database. "Today is your lucky day."

"You found him?"

"I did, and it seems the younger Abbott boy tended to check out the same book, over and over again."

My ears hum with the blood rushing through them. "What book is that?"

"It seems he checked out Huxley's *Brave New World* several times."

The room begins to spin. I can feel bile crawling up my throat.

"Are you all right, dear? You look a little pale."

I take a deep breath, willing myself to calm down. It feels like rocks are in my throat as I try to find my words to ask my next question. "Are there any secret alcoves in the library?"

She shakes her head. "No, not that I'm aware of, but—now that you mention it, Somerset was built around the time of the Revolutionary War. They say before the war broke out, this library was used for meetings. Can you imagine? You may be standing in a place where a rebellion meeting happened." Now she's smiling coyly at me. "You're welcome to explore."

"I might just do that. Thank you." Moving back away from the desk, I start to walk around, searching for anything that could be useful.

After fifteen minutes of examining every row of shelves in the library, I'm about to give up and leave when I see what looks like a knob behind a stack of books in the corner. The books aren't on a rack. They are amassed on the floor as if someone is still organizing them. I move closer, and that's when I see a very small door, similar to a priest's hole, hidden behind the books on the floor.

With tentative hands, I squat low and open it.

The door swings open inward, and it's dark at first. I make the crack bigger, and now with the light, I can see inside.

It's a small room.

I push the door some more until I can fit inside. My knees give out under my body when I scan the room. It's the room that he spent his happy moments in as a child.

Cain *is* North.

Cain Archer is North Abbott.

And that means everything is a lie. Everything he said is a lie. No. No. No. I can't believe he would lie to me because that would mean everything he said—

Oh my God.

All the different personality traits. The warning from Barbara. The comments from Mara hearing things about him. His strangeness with other people.

The path of his career without much publicity. The subtle hints to his past with the little nooks and crannies he built into The Elysian.

The Elysian itself is a clue.

It's been right in front of my face the entire time.

A house of mirrors.

Homes built to look like their surroundings.

To blend and not be seen. Pretending to be what they're not . . .

It's all a lie.

How did I not see it?

I think back to the night he was staring at the television in a trance. The way he grabbed my wrists. So much pain in him channeled against me as I just stood by his side.

Cain is North.

And North is The Compass Killer.

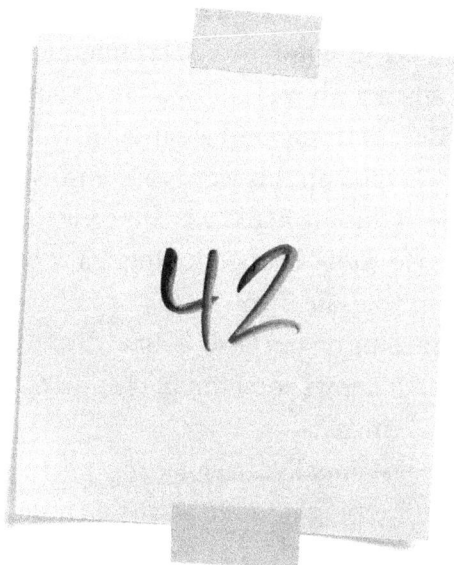

42

Layla

The air is too heavy here.

I need to breathe.

My heart hammers in my chest. It beats so hard that I think it will explode. Around me the world spins, and my ears ring as I weave in and out of the stacks to claw my way back out of what I just found in this library.

My limbs are heavy, like I'm trekking through quicksand, making each step nearly impossible. If I don't get out of here, I will pass out for certain.

Stumbling through the door, I swallow in a giant gulp as soon as the warm summer air hits my face. Shutting my eyes as I try to regulate my breathing and calm down.

My foot slipping on the old stairs, I lose my balance, and when I fall forward, I collide with a firm chest.

My lids fly open, and I crane my neck back to see who I ran into.

I'm met with the light eyes of a gentleman who's older than me. He looks to be in his fifties, but he's let his hair go white, reminding me of Richard Gere. His white hair is a stark contrast to the blue of his eyes, which appear soft and kind. "I'm sorry. I didn't mean to run into you," he says, and I step back and move to go around him.

As I do, he grabs my elbow, not hard but enough to stop me.

He moves closer; that way only I can hear what he speaks to me. His voice is a low whisper, but his words are unmistakable.

"You aren't safe in this town; there is someone that will do you harm for digging where you shouldn't be looking. Pack your bags and head out now. I can't keep you safe if you stay."

This man stopped me on purpose. That's why he grabbed my elbow, too. This son of a bitch knows something. He thinks he's trying to scare me, but instead, I'm enraged.

The fear and uncertainty I've been feeling are quickly replaced with absolute anger. His bumping into me wasn't an accident, and now I'm getting threats.

Still standing close to each other so no one else can hear, I hiss out, "What do you want? Why did you stop me? And don't tell me it's that warning. There's more. You know more. Tell me now!" I roar.

"I know why you're here. I know the answers you're looking for, but you need to stop digging."

I grit my teeth. "And . . . ?"

"I've warned you. Some stones are better left unturned."

"I don't believe that one bit. You just don't want your precious town to be touched. No stone is better left unturned when innocent women died for this secret."

Stepping back, I place my hands on my hips, no longer caring how loud I get. "Justice needs to happen for those girls, and their families deserve closure."

"Look at you. You can't possibly think you're safe." His stare is pointed, and then he lifts his hand and touches a lock of hair that rests on my shoulder.

"Don't touch me. I'm safe."

"No." He shakes his head with a slight chuckle. "You look just like them. You're not safe. Plus, you've been spending time with the wrong person. You have a target on your head now." His words give me pause. How does he know this?

"Why? What do you know? Do you know North Abbott?" He doesn't answer. "How about Cain Archer?"

His pupils widen. "You're playing a dangerous game, lady," he warns.

I pull back my shoulders and stand taller. I won't have him or anyone else intimidating me.

"I'm not doing anything wrong. There's a story here, and I'm just investigating it. I won't be scared off. I could be the only person who can finally stop the killer, and I'm following through."

He laughs humorlessly at my words. "You have no clue what you're doing, and it's going to get you killed."

I can't hear any more of this. I'm done. I start to walk away again.

"Wait." He huffs. "Damn it. Here." He thrusts a file that I didn't even notice he was holding. "If you won't walk away, read this, and maybe you'll piece it all together."

I take the file and head straight to my car.

When I get into the seat, I let out a deep breath. I pull down the mirror and look at myself.

My hair is disheveled, and my face looks extra pale from lack of sleep and water.

Maybe that guy was right. Perhaps I am in over my head with this story, and I don't know what I'm doing. I'm not trained for going toe to toe with a serial killer and should probably leave this to the professionals.

I need to turn over everything I have found to the police.

Not the local ones around here. It's obvious they want to bury everything under the rug, but maybe I can go to the FBI who's looking into The Compass Killer.

The idea of going to the police about Cain doesn't sit well in my heart. There's just this ache to make sure I'm right before I make a report. Not just for Cain, but what kind of journalist will I be if I don't check my sources?

Turing the car on, I'm ready to drive back home when I remember the folder I set in the passenger seat. With the car still running but parked, I open the folder. My eyes try to understand what I'm seeing.

Holy shit.

Is this for fucking real?

How can I trust this?

Better question, can I trust a man I don't know to give me accurate information? Who was the man on the steps, and how does he even have this detailed information?

At the top of all the sheets is letterhead reading "Pemberton Psychiatric Hospital".

That's where I need to go, and they will have answers for me.

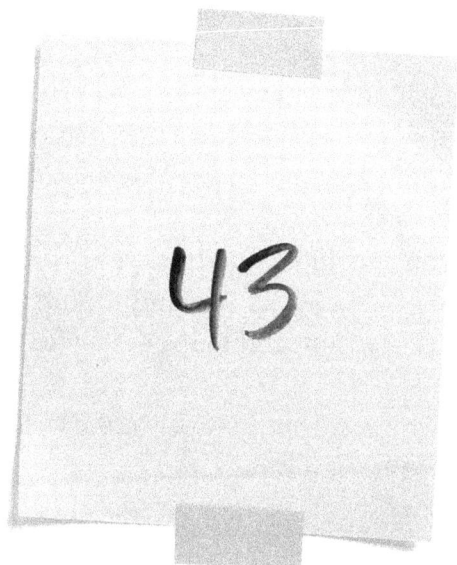

43

Layla

Driving to the hospital, I feel out of sorts like I'm having déjà vu. It reminds me a little of The Elysian, set out in the woods in the middle of nowhere.

I'm close to Kittatinny Mountain. It's not that it's that far from Somerset, only about an hour, but still, it feels like I'm in the middle of no man's land.

If the location weren't eerie enough, the building does me in. Straight out of a horror story. Looming in the distance, large, weathered red brick with a limestone entrance, covered with overgrown shrubs.

I have to shake off the feeling I'm being watched as I enter the building. The whole place creeps me out to the point I'm breaking out in goose bumps. This place is right out of a TV show where ghosts roam the hallways.

I'm certain they do.

My imagination couldn't have come up with a scarier version of this place. Yellowed walls and stained linoleum floors. I'm surprised this place still exists. Most old hospitals like this were shut down by the state years ago.

Good news is it's still here and maybe will help me close my investigation. Hopefully, the staff will be helpful . . . and not be creepy like the building.

Entering the main room, there are few chairs set up, none that look comfortable, and a woman sits behind a plexiglass window.

Stepping up to the window, I ask, "May I speak with the superintendent of the hospital?"

"Do you have an appointment, Ms. . . . ?"

"Ms. Marks. And no. But it's very important. A confidential file has come into my possession, and I'm sure they will want to speak to me on the matter."

"Very well. Have a seat." She gestures to the waiting area.

Walking over to one of the metal chairs, I sit down. It's as uncomfortable as I knew it would be. Something tells me this place doesn't get many guests. Or if they do, they won't want to come back ever again after sitting here.

Not long after I sit, the door on the right of the receptionist's desk opens.

A woman who looks to be in her early seventies walks out with her hair pulled up into a tight bun, and the few gray hairs are a striking contrast to the majority of her jet-black hair.

"Ms. Marks, follow me, please."

Falling into step with her, we make our way through the door and into the hallway. The bright fluorescent lights flicker above, making my eyes blink in irritation.

"I'm Ms. Turnery. I was told you wished to speak with me." She opens a door on the left and enters, and I'm quick to follow suit.

"I'm here to ask you a few questions about a former patient of yours—"

"I'm sorry you've wasted your time coming to our facility, but I will not disclose any information about a current or past patient with you. I'm sure you must understand confidentiality rules we must follow at this hospital."

"As much as I respect that, I need your help with something that came into my possession." I pull the file from my bag and slide it across the desk.

Ms. Turnery's eyes go wide at what I assume is a familiar folder. "How did you get this?"

"I obtained it from a family member."

She narrows her eyes, raising the folder to look at the label. "That's impossible because there were no living relatives for this patient."

I shrug. "The man who gave it to me claimed to be an uncle." Leaning forward, I rest my elbow on the desk. "Listen, I can respect your policy, but I'm not asking for any additional information, just whether the documents are, in fact, authentic."

"What do you intend to do with them?"

"Honestly," I shrug, "at this point, I'm not certain what I need to do. But obviously, if they aren't genuine, there's nothing for me to do."

The stern woman in front of me crinkles her forehead before she swivels her chair to face the computer on her desk. Using her keyboard, she's typing something when her eyes squint and she leans forward. She picks through the documents in the folder, and then moves away from the monitor, handing me the file.

"They appear authentic, but that's all I can help you with. Now, what do you plan on doing, Ms. Marks?"

"Thank you. As I said, I'm not certain what my next steps will be, but I do appreciate your assistance."

With this research trip complete, I make my leave from her office, heading back out of the scary hospital and to my car.

It will be dark soon; this whole trip is taking much longer than I expected. Truth is, I won't be able to go back to the city tonight. I have too much to do here still, so back to the Motel 8 on the side of the road where I crashed last night.

In the room, filled with energy based on my findings, I fire up my computer and pull up everything I can find on Cain. It's time to solve the puzzle of who he is and how or if he has committed all these murders.

I'm not sure how much time goes by. My eyes are stinging from looking at the computer. My hands hurt from the notes I jotted down in my notebook and then taped up on the wall beside me, making my own version of an evidence board. Lifting my hand to my face, I scrub at it. It's going to be a long night. I should grab a coffee and food.

I fire up the app for food delivery and see the local diner does deliver. I hit the screen, ordering breakfast for dinner and a large espresso. That should help, and then I look back at my computer and continue my search.

A knock makes me jump.

My food. Better yet . . . mmm. Coffee.

"Coming," I call out, shutting the computer lid and making my way to the door. I remove the lock, sliding the metal out of place, and swing the door open wide.

A gasp escapes my mouth. "You."

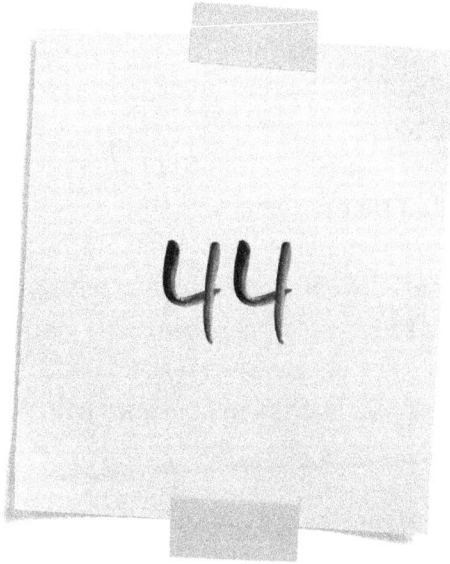

44

Layla

God, my head hurts.

Did I drink too much? I don't even remember what I had or where I went.

Wait.

I shake my head, trying to wake myself up. My eyelids are heavy, and I can't seem to open them. From the position I'm sitting in, I move to lift my hand, but nothing happens.

What the hell?

I shake my head back and forth, blinking my lids rapidly until my vision comes into focus.

That's when I see where I am.

A ramshackle shed or cabin. Walls made of wood planks, and it's dark, only a single candle lighting the space. The air feels wet, muggy. Tilting my head down, I see the reason I couldn't rub my eyes. My hands are tied to the chair I'm in.

My heart starts to thump heavily in my chest.

"Hello. Is anyone there?" I shout.

When no one answers, I try again, this time, my panic bubbling up like a geyser. "Help. Can anyone hear me? Help me!"

I scream again and again. I scream until my voice gets dry, and my throat hurts.

I'm alone, probably in the middle of nowhere, tied to a chair.

How did I get here?

He took me.

The deliveryman that came to my motel room. No, wait a minute. That wasn't a deliveryman.

This is all because I went to the hospital with that file folder.

The guy on the steps was right. The case is getting me in trouble.

But how could I not go to Somerset and confirm the information about Cynthia after seeing her so many times with Cain?

And then there was the paperwork . . .

The folder.

After their mother disappeared, the state had both Abbott boys see a psychiatrist for counseling. There was no information on North aside from the notes with his doctor, but his brother, Stone, was committed for a short time based on his mood swings. They suspected him of having a breakdown, or so the file stated. He was sent away for two weeks.

But he was immediately released when his two weeks were up.

None of this material makes any sense.

For the weeks he was away, North was sent to a foster home. Since his brother was declared okay, they suspected Stone of having an addictive disorder, schizoid personality disorder, borderline personality disorder, and bipolar disorder. But in the end, Stone was sent home.

What happened then—I found out from my research back at the motel—was a very young North moved back into his family home and was raised by his older brother, Stone.

As I'm processing all the memories of what I read and found in my search, I hear a sound.

I whirl my head around and see that the door is open.

A man I don't know enters the room and strides over to where I am until he is standing before me. He leans down so we're face-to-face.

His head cocks to the side as he studies me. The moment he does, a gasp leaves my mouth. The puckered skin on his neck from a fire makes me draw back in fear.

"What about you does my brother find so interesting?" he taunts me.

Stone.

This is Stone.

He's not dead.

A sick feeling weaves its way through me as I realize just what I've done.

How could I have ever doubted Cain?

How could I have ever believed Cain capable of gruesome murders?

Staring into his eyes is like looking into a dark and deep abyss. Endless and deadly.

He's what nightmares are made of.

My body begins to shake, and Stone laughs right in my face. A strange laugh that makes chills run down my spine.

His hand reaches out, a pointer finger trailing across my throat. "So weak. So frail."

He pulls back swiftly, removing his finger from my skin. I suck in a shuddering breath, lift my gaze, and look at him once again. That's when I notice that his other hand is holding something.

In his grasp, he's rolled up the file I had at the motel.

He uncurls it, removes the contents from within and discards the folder to the floor. He starts to pace in front of me. Skimming over the papers, he pays specific attention to my handwritten notes.

I can't stop the way my body trembles.

He's flipping through everything. The sound of crinkling paper fills the small space between our ragged breaths.

"Did this psychobabble bullshit keep you entertained?" he spits out. "None of that's true." He throws the diagnosis paper on the floor and steps on it. "And when I convinced them that I was perfectly fine, I was sent home."

"Y-You murdered those women."

"I was simply keeping my brother safe. He's all I have."

"How can you say that? They didn't even know your brother. None of those women. You're the very monster the doctors thought you were."

"You know nothing. They were all like *her*. I had to kill them. I killed every last one of them to protect North."

"Cain would have never wanted that."

"That's not his name," he bellows. The sound of his loud voice bounces off the wooden walls of the shed. "You don't know North. You don't know what he wants. What he needs. He's my brother. He's MINE." When he turns to face me, something about his face is different from when he first entered the room.

His face has somehow become distorted. His features hardened. His eyes are dark. He looks deadly, and the scary part . . . He looks just like Cain did that day. The day he stormed out of The Elysian restaurant.

He's spiraling. But with Cain, I never felt scared.

Stone terrifies me.

And as he creeps toward me, the moonlight shines in from a small window, and something gleams on the table behind him. A knife.

"Now, we're going to have some fun."

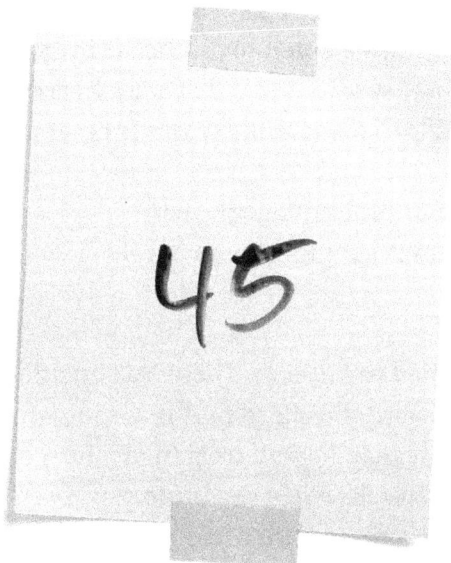

45

Cain

Answer your phone. *Answer your damn phone, Jim.*

He doesn't. Just like he didn't the last time or the time before that.

I'm hauling ass, trying to get to Somerset, but I need Jim to answer the phone and tell me what the fuck is going on.

Layla hasn't been answering my calls all day, and now this.

Fuck! Something's not right.

Driving as fast as I can on the freeway, I pray I'm not too late.

Coming to Somerset is a risky move. It can ruin everything I've built since I left that life behind.

Left behind everything that happened. Tried to bury the monster I found deep inside me. Hoping and praying that if I could get out, they died in the fire.

But now, I'm going to a town where I should be dead.

I haven't been there in seventeen years. Not since I was a teen. Not since that fateful night.

The night I died, yet I didn't. The night where I came out of a fire a new man.

All I wanted was to survive, to start over. I wanted to leave that fucked-up life behind and move away from all the damage found in that hellhole of a town. I also wanted to disappear from Cynthia. She didn't need to see me, and I sure as hell didn't want to see her again.

Before I head into town, I make one stop at a cottage on the far outskirts.

I haven't been to Jim's cottage in years.

Not since I came that night. I ran a mile to get here. Blood on my hands.

I had to do it.

To save her, I had to kill him. There was no other choice.

After . . . Afterward, I went to find Jim.

Jim was the only man I could trust in my life. Local firefighter who fostered me for two weeks when my brother was sent away to the hospital. Mother had disappeared. She had left us all alone. Or so I thought at the time.

I was young, so very fucking young, and I had no idea where she went, just that my older brother was gone, too. Jim took me in until Stone could come back.

The door looks exactly the same as it had all those years ago. I can still see my bloody handprint that had stained the wood. Staring at the door, I notice it's open. Slightly ajar.

Shit.

I push it open, transported in my mind to that night. The night I told him what I did. The night he came up with a plan.

A plan we would both have to live with.

A fire.

I told Jim what I found at the cabin. My father's old cabin by the lake near our house. The only thing our father left us after he was sent to jail for killing the man he caught in bed with our mother.

After he went to prison, my mother boarded up the cabin.

The last good memories I had of the place were when I was a small boy. No point of going back since my mom became a drunk and stopped bringing us to the lake.

It wasn't until that night that I returned and found *him*.

After I killed him, I panicked. I didn't know what to do. He was dead on the cabin floor.

I ran all the way here and woke Jim. He came to the cottage with me and saw what I had done. I made a call and followed the instructions he gave me to the letter.

Where to start the fire. How to accelerate it. Then I left.

Jim took care of everything. He was the firefighter who was called to the scene first.

He was the one who planted the burned bones. The one who made sure the report was filed. I don't know how he did it all.

I was able to walk away, and he was able to help me start a new life. Now, here I am, seventeen years later, and the past has finally come back to haunt me.

I move through the house, and my footsteps halt.

There is Jim. Lying on the floor in a pool of his own blood.

I start to run to him, but the blood is everywhere. If I get too close, I'll leave evidence that I was here, so I step back from Jim's mangled body and look around the room.

That's when I see it on the wall. Written in blood. A postcard addressed to me.

North.

Beneath my name is the symbol he always used to mark his victims.

The Compass Killer is back.

My brother is alive.

Fuck.

I need to stop him. I am the only one who can make all this madness stop once and for all. I thought I did what was necessary years ago, but he's been lurking in the shadows this entire time.

I pull down the postcard taped to the wall and see that it's an image of Cape May. *He's been following me.*

There, written on the image are three words:

She will die.

Flipping it over, I see more written on the back. A clue . . .

You'll find her where it all began.

I have to return home.

46

Layla

I come to again, my head shaking away the confusion of what must have happened.

Either I passed out, or he knocked me out, but it doesn't matter because both had the same outcome. And now, I'm no longer in the chair. I'm laid out on the floor.

My heart pounds as I take in my situation. Arms pulled taut above my head, hands tied together with rope. I am tethered to the beam behind me.

I try to kick, but that's when I realize this time, my legs are restrained, too. My ankles are tied.

Oh, shit. Is this how he killed them? A chill runs up my spine.

He has me placed so that the shape of my body makes my arms point in a specific direction. North. I'm lying here tied down and pointed north.

I'm the next victim of The Compass Killer.

My limbs shake as I try to pull my arms free. The rope burns at my wrists, chafing the delicate skin.

"Oh, I see you've decided to wake up and join me for *fun time*."

Stone crosses the space, and then gets down on his knees, crawling over my body.

I try to buck my hips to move him off me, but it's no use. I can't get enough force behind my movements to do anything.

"There, there. It will all be over soon. Just shush and be a good girl," he coos, lifting his hand and letting me see the knife he's holding.

He looks unhinged as he stares at me. His gaze doesn't meet mine. Instead, he looks through me in a far-off zone.

His arm moves quickly, and the blade is pressed against my throat.

It's not cutting, though, just resting, but if I were to move, it would slice through my skin.

"Tell . . . tell me about N-N-North," I quietly stutter out. I need him out of this trance. When he looks at me, it's as though he can imagine my body drained of blood.

If I can get him to talk about his brother, maybe I can buy myself more time to come up with a plan.

His eyes go wide at my question, and he pulls the knife from where it rests.

I almost let out a sigh of relief, but I don't dare move.

It could tip him that I'm trying to buy time, and I can't have that.

When I can no longer see the blade, my body starts to relax. I'm still scared, but when I look into Stone's eyes, they are no longer hollow and lost. He's present with me now, and although this version of him still petrifies me, I know for the time being, I'll be alive.

"North . . ." he says to himself, and then he lifts off where he's crouched over my body and moves to a standing position.

My chest heaves when he turns around and moves toward the chair against the wall.

When he slumps into the seat, I do exhale.

"North has always been my responsibility," he starts, then tilts his head up and closes his eyes. "North didn't have the childhood I did. I'm older than him."

"You raised him?"

His eyes open and meet mine. "I did." He leans forward, placing his elbows on his thighs. The hilt of the blade is still in his hand, but it's not raised. Instead, it rests on his leg.

"How?"

"I'm much older than him. Ten years. North wasn't planned. And the truth of it . . . he wasn't wanted, either. Our mother resented him being here and ruining her perfect life. From the minute he was born, she hated him."

My chest tightens, knowing full well what it felt like to be the unwanted child.

"She was terribly unhappy—"

"Where was your dad?" I interrupt. I know a little about this, his job kept him away, but I need to hear this from him to understand more than the town gossip.

"He traveled for work. He was a builder." He nods. "The apple didn't fall far from the tree. We all are . . ." His words trail off. He shakes his head. It's like he's pulling himself back to the present. "She would cheat on dad when he was away. She became an alcoholic, a drug addict. Even before they both were gone, I was the one who cared for North. He was mine."

"What happened to your dad?"

"Dear old Dad . . ." He smirks. "He got smart and came home early one day. Found Mom's lover in bed with her." His smile widens. "So much power in dad's hands that when he grabbed her lover's throat, it didn't take long to strangle him. A crime of passion they called it. But unfortunately, a crime, nonetheless. Went to jail and then died there, too."

"And your mother?"

"What my mother put North through, now that was a crime. He was so small when Dad went away. And I wasn't old enough yet to take care of him. If I were, I would have killed her sooner."

My mouth drops open. I knew his mother disappeared. I knew she was probably dead, but to hear him admit it . . .

My jaw chatters as I shake.

"She starved him, and there wasn't anything I could do. Calling anyone would have gotten him shipped off. We would have been separated. She beat him when he cried. Hated him for destroying her life. Did you know she made money sleeping with men? Sometimes, she'd bring them back to the house. They would look at him . . ." He closes his eyes, his jaw tightening, the grip on the knife turning his knuckles white. "It was only a matter of time before she let them have a turn with him, too."

The rage in his voice has me shivering, but despite the fear he inflicts in me, my heart lurches in my chest for the Abbott boys. A frightened child raising another frightened child forced to grow up too soon. Forced to watch the person you love most in the world tortured and abused by the mother who should've loved him the most.

Despite the fact that he's absolutely mentally unstable, I can't help but wonder if he was always like this or if she made him this way.

"What happened next?" I whisper, my voice laced with sadness.

Stone gets a far-off look and walks back over to me. "The time came. I heard her with one of her men. She was going to let them hurt North."

"What did you do?"

"I did what I had to. Gloria was my first. I stopped her and saved my brother. I held her down, and when she lay beneath me struggling, kicking, begging; I sliced her neck. To save North. Always for North."

Stone kneels down by my hands, and I feel the pressure from the knife, slowly cutting through my palm. I can't scream out.

It's all too much.

Everything is going fuzzy in my sight. I see him bring his blood-covered fingers up to my forehead. Wetness creeps over my skin.

Bile coats my mouth at the tone of his voice. "Everything for North."

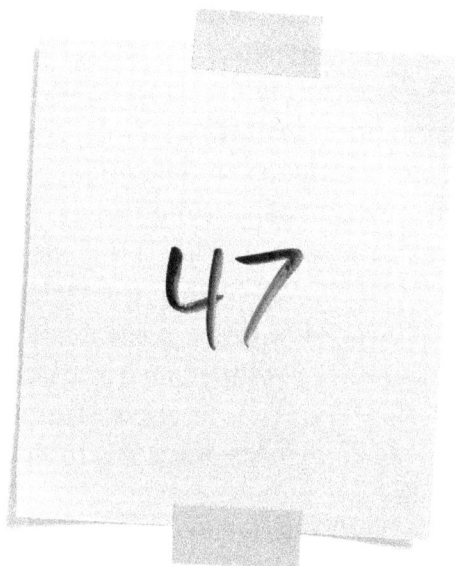

47

Cain

The car weaves all over the street, swerving left and right as I try to make it in time to Layla. It's not much farther. I just need to go faster.

I make the turn, and then I'm on a back road. I can't drive too fast on this gravel, or I'll crash. I won't make it to her. But I need to get there.

I might already be too late.

Stone doesn't need much time to do his crazy fucking shit. The only saving grace is that he's left me a clue. He wants me there. He wants me to watch him kill her.

That's what he does. He wants me to know, wants me to see how he behaves.

Like that day all those years ago. The day my life changed.

The day I was forced to become Cain.

"Please. You can't kill me."

Stone is hunched over Cynthia. His face close to hers. I move forward to watch. To see what he's doing.

"You should be honored." Stone scoffs. "I don't pick just anyone."

"But—"

His free hand reaches out, silencing her.

"Shh," he coos, and I watch as he trails the blade across her throat. "Be a good girl."

Cynthia shakes beneath him, and that's when he runs the blade across her throat. A bright red crimson line spreads in its wake. It's not deep. Not enough to kill.

I need to do something. Say something. But I'm transfixed.

Stuck in place, watching the blood. I'm so enthralled that I don't notice Stone looking toward me.

"North."

I shake myself out of the trance and look at my brother.

"It's time."

I stare at him, not understanding. "Time for what?"

"Time to be the man I know you can be. Everything I have done, I've done for you."

He stands, leaving a sobbing Cynthia on the floor.

"Please help me, North," she cries. I don't look at her. Instead, I watch my brother as he comes closer.

He stands in front of me, reaches out his hand, and takes mine in his.

"This is for you. She is for you."

"Why?" I ask.

"Everything I have ever done is to protect you, North . . ." He places the hilt of the blade in my hand. "Now it's your time."

The knife gleams in my hand. The blade beckons me to use it. It taunts me. My reflection staring back.

It would be so easy.

I move toward Cynthia. Stone is behind me.

"Straddle her stomach," he says, and I follow his order. Stone steps up behind me. He's guiding me with his words. "Place the knife on her neck."

I do.

"Now cut, North. Slice her neck."

"Please, North. Don't," Cynthia cries.

"Shut up, Cynthia!" Stone bellows, his voice ringing in my ear. He's too close. I can't breathe.

"I did everything for you. I killed them all for you. All for North. Everything for North." He's talking to himself, not to me. His voice is in my ear, yet so far away.

The whooshing sound in my ear has me shaking my head back and forth, clearing my mind from this fog.

"All for North." He moves from behind me. His hand swipes at the blood on her throat. He coats her forehead, a triangle. No . . . an arrow.

The arrow he paints on all his victims.

The arrow that points north.

I watch as he paints. This is different. This time he uses his finger, not the hilt of the knife, like he did with Mom.

Mom.

The first.

Cynthia . . .

How many has it been?

He pulls back. "Do it, North."

And I do. I tighten my grasp, and then I stab.

But I don't stab her.

I turn and stab him.

I know Stone intends for me to finish what he started with Layla. It's the only thing that allows me to breathe. Stone will wait until I'm there. He needs me to finish the job I never did the first time. For now, she's safe.

Finally, I have reached the deserted road. It leads to the property where my father's cabin used to sit before Jim and I burned it down. I park the car. There's no access for my vehicle.

I swing open the door and then take off, sprinting toward the location where this all began. I need to keep her safe, no matter what I must do.

48

Layla

Stone looms over me, his warm breath fanning my cheek. "My brother should be here soon. Let's play a game." He reaches the knife up, and I shudder, but then my hands are cut loose. "I'm going to let you go. Let's see how far you can run . . ." He moves down my body and unties my ankles. "Ready or not . . ." He chuckles as he pulls me up to my feet, and I start my escape.

Once outside the shed, darkness surrounds me. My arms pump through the air.

I run as hard and as fast as I can. But my strides are shallow and slower than I want.

I'm not fast enough, even though I don't know where I am going. I need to run harder. But I can't. My strength is all but gone. The last of my energy is being depleted as I move. My calf muscles strain with every move I make.

The dehydration is kicking in as my mouth becomes parched and dry. My chest heaves as I try to find my bearings, but I don't know which way will lead me to safety.

A feeling of being stabbed penetrates my body.

Wetness coats my skin. I'm hurt. With the adrenaline coursing through me, I almost forgot that my hands are bleeding.

I should stop, but I can't. I need to get as far away as possible.

Pushing through the pain, I dash through the trees. I need to get through these woods and back to safety. As far from the shed as I can possibly get.

Running becomes harder because my clothes catch on branches, the smaller twigs whipping against my face.

One branch snags my arm, cutting me and causing me to stumble forward.

Shit.

Warm liquid burns.

I need to stop the bleeding.

Pain ricochets throughout my body as I drop to the ground. Ripping at my shirt, tearing the piece that was cut by the branch. I need to staunch the blood flow. As I wrap my arm, I hear a rustling ahead.

Panic kicks in.

The pounding of my heart sounds so loud against the quiet of the night. I hold my breath. Willing myself to be completely silent and praying Stone doesn't find me.

But it's Cain who bursts through the tree line.

I cry out, running toward him on shaky legs. But to my horror, Stone steps out from behind a tree with a cruel smile plastered on his face. His hand lifts, and then I'm screaming, trying to warn him, but it's too late. Stone's hand comes down, hitting Cain over the head with a branch.

I scream again and again. My loud, piercing shrieks echo through the night.

Cain falls hard to the ground, and then Stone bends over his brother, ensuring he's out cold before stalking in my direction.

I should run.

I know I should, but my feet are stuck in place, eyes glued to Cain. He can't be dead. I need him. Need to tell him I love him, and we'll get out of this together.

When Stone reaches me, he thrusts his shoulder into my belly, lifting me up and dragging me back to the shed. I cry out a sob as the new position causes pain to lacerate through my body.

He's going to tie me up again. I can't fucking let him do this to me. I expect him to lay me on the floor, but he's placing me in the chair again. Moving to tie me up.

What am I going to do?

I can't let him go through with this.

But then, as I struggle, a piece of research I read once filters through my brain. If he ties me to the chair, I can get out. It's my best shot.

The research I read said that you need to make your body bigger by pulling your shoulders back, expanding your chest, straightening your arms, and pushing to flex against the rope. Once your captors leave you alone and you collapse your body back in, you'll find yourself with more slack in the rope, making it easier to escape.

I do just that, hoping and praying that Stone doesn't notice.

He doesn't. He has no clue what I did.

"I'm going to get my brother. And then, dear, sweet, stupid Layla, I'm going to slit your neck. Better yet, North will do the deed. It's time he does what he needs to do. And he will start with you."

Without another word, he's gone.

The moment he's out the door, I collapse my body, and the ropes do just as I read. It worked. The ropes are loosened. With them no longer strangling my limbs, I can try to escape again.

I take a deep breath and start to move. Now is the time to execute a plan. I hold my breath, praying I have enough time to get free before he returns.

I'm almost climbing out of my bindings when the door swings open.

I expect Stone to walk in, but instead, Cain appears in the entrance.

Stone strides in behind him with an arm wrapped around Cain.

And a giant knife at his throat.

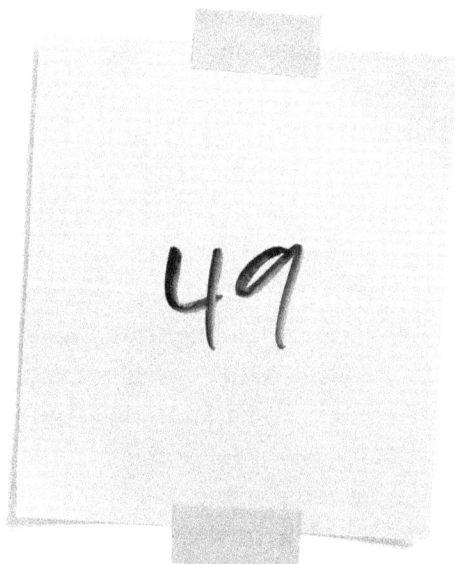

49

Layla

"Don't do this."

"Too late, baby brother." Stone laughs. "It's already done. Just like the one before. And the one before that. I've been killing the women trying to harm you since Mom. I have always been the one to protect you."

"Those women . . . They're not mom. Their only sin was looking like her—"

"Shut up!" Stone bellows, cutting off Cains's words and the *truth*.

The truth, that none of the women he murdered, had done *anything* wrong. They just unfortunately looked like the woman who had hurt his little brother.

"You have to stop, Stone. I know why you did it. I know what my life has cost you, but it's done. It's enough."

"It's not enough. Everything was fine. You were fine. Then you had to find her, fuck her and now everything I've done for you is fucked up. You owe me, baby brother. You owe me her blood."

I watch from where I'm strapped down, biding my time. I need a clear plan, a way for both Cain and me to survive this.

I watch as Cain tries to talk sense into his brother. But Stone ignores

286

him. "You weren't strong enough then. But you will be strong enough now."

They're talking about Cynthia. What happened seventeen years ago.

"You thought I was so easy to kill. You left me for dead. But you weren't smart enough. You never checked if I was breathing. You never checked my pulse. You were a pussy then, and you're a pussy now. But I will make a man out of you."

"How did you survive the—?"

"How did I live past what you tried to do to me? You failed, that's how. Twice in one night. You and Jim thought I was dead, but I wasn't. I slipped out the back window while the fire raged, and you both left me to burn. Then I ran into the woods and hid in a hollowed-out tree until you were gone, and I could escape without being seen. You guys couldn't stop me. And now . . ." Stone's eyes meet mine. Hollow. Dark. Dead eyes. "There's more blood to be spilled. More stones to be turned."

"It's done, Brother." Cain says, his chest rising and falling with his words. "It's over. Everybody who could have hurt us, are gone. You no longer have to fear Cynthia."

"I never would have had to fear her if it weren't for you." he breathes out. "Her death is on you. You couldn't live in the shadows. You brought the compass killer back to life. I had no choice but to rise from the dead. It's your fault I'm back. I had to fix your problems."

"I—"

"Don't get me wrong, I'm proud of you—"

"I never wanted your approval."

"And here it would seem I haunted you all these years. Your name is fitting . . . Cain. I guess that would make me Abel. The brother you killed. You should be thanking me. I did it all for you. I killed them all for you."

"It wasn't your responsibility. What happened to me wasn't your fault."

"Our mother deserved it. She was going to sell you." Stone starts coming completely unhinged. His eyes frantic and crazed. "She deserved it," he parrots while he grabs Cain's hair. The knife nicks Cain's neck, and blood trickles.

"Just do what your brother wants, Cain," I plead.

"No. I won't sacrifice you, too, Layla."

He has to listen to me, damn it. I watch the blood that bubbles up from where Stone grazed him.

I need to figure out a way to get the knife away from his throat.

I need to get his attention, and I know just the way. I start to wiggle free. My eyes never leaving Cain as I do.

He implores without words for me to stop. Mouthing the words. Pleading silently.

But I pay him no mind. Instead, I make a loud groaning sound to make Stone aware I'm still here and struggling to get out.

It works.

Stone pushes Cain out of the way and takes a step toward me. He charges, but I've given Cain the distraction he needed. One minute, Stone is moving toward me. I brace for impact, but nothing happens.

Instead, Cain has grabbed him and is pulling his body away from me. Throwing his body onto Stone's until they are tumbling out the door into the night. I can hear the sounds, but it's too dark out there; I can't see.

Moving fast, I pull free, throwing the ropes off me as I stand and follow.

When I step out into the dark night, the moon showcases a showdown. The brothers are scrambling against each other. The knife flying. Both jumping. Hands reaching out. Punches being thrown. I watch them struggle. They're both fighting for possession of the knife. Blood splatters with each throw of an arm.

I try to charge, to pull Stone off Cain. But as I try to climb onto his back, Stone pushes me off him. My body plunging hard onto the ground. As I try to stand, my head is woozy, and I stumble as I watch the fight continue.

Another swipe of an arm.

Another kick.

And then Cain is on top.

The gleam of the blade in his hand. Cain leans down, the blade now held to his brother's neck.

Stone laughs. "Do it." Cain doesn't move. "Fucking do it, I said. End it once and for all. You know this is the way it was always meant to be."

I take in the picture before me. The way Stone's body lies on the ground. The way he's moved his arms to point north. He's in the exact position I was held in. The same location Cynthia was in when North betrayed Stone by letting her go.

I can see the struggle on Cain's face.

He doesn't want to do this. He doesn't want to kill the brother who always put him first, who protected him. Who showed him the only love he ever knew.

"Brother, you have once chance. If you don't kill me this time, I will kill her."

Without another word, the knife slashes across Stone's neck, ending things once and for all.

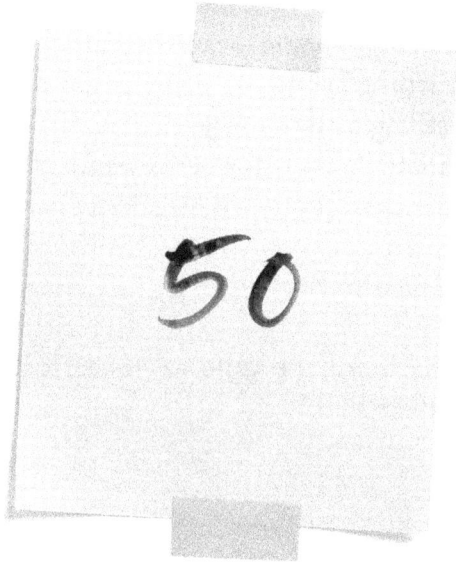

50

Layla

From where I'm perched, I see Cain fall back onto his knees, dropping the knife.

I hurt to move.

Hurt to think.

Chances are I have a concussion.

It takes me a minute to move, my chest heaving as I try to find purchase from where I was thrown to the ground. I push myself up to stand. My first step is wobbly as I move toward Cain. The air around me is thick with death as I trudge through the muddy terrain from the earlier rain. When I make it over to him, his head is hanging low, his body melted forward over his brother.

Cain is weeping.

The sound causes my heart to lurch.

"Cain," I say, and a strange sound emanates from his mouth when I do. A laugh. A cry. I'm not sure.

His head turning over his shoulder, eyes dark, he spits out, "Fitting. I'm no better than him. Stone was always right. I am no better. I finally did it. I finally earned my name. Only took me seventeen years."

To him, he is Cain. The man who murdered his brother. The man who was granted a new life. In a new place. He is still the one who killed his own kin.

His face is now downcast and staring at the lifeless body of the life he took.

I step closer. Slow and steady. He reminds me of a raging caged animal; one I don't dare spook.

"I took his life, but I'm no better. I'm a killer—"

"Stop. What you did tonight doesn't make you a killer."

"You don't know what you are saying." His crazed eyes find me again.

"Yes. I do. You are no killer. This wasn't murder. This was self-defense." I tentatively place my hand on his shoulder and squeeze slightly. Beneath my touch, I feel the hard lines of his stiff muscles. "You're nothing like your brother. You're nothing like him at all. Despite what you did, you are a good man. A man I love no matter who you are. North or Cain. They are both a part of you, and I love both parts."

"Then you love a fucking monster," he chides.

"Not a monster, a hero. You saved me. You saved Cynthia once."

A choked cough escapes his mouth. "I'm nobody's hero, especially Cynthia's."

"You are. You don't see it now, but you did save lives. And now it's over. It's time to find the peace you deserve. It's time to go home."

"I can't. I have seen too much. Done too much. I have no home."

I wrap my arms around him and feel as he melts into my embrace. Allowing my words to soak in, allowing himself the reprieve from his thoughts. "Let's go. We have to go to the police and let them know this was self-defense. You were saving me."

"I'll go to jail for not turning Stone in all those years ago and then again now."

"No, you won't."

He turns in my arms and looks at me. His eyes are narrowed and confused.

"We aren't going to tell them about your mom. Or Cynthia. We aren't going to tell them about North. As far as we know, North died that day."

"But—"

"No buts. I fit the MO, and I was the one investigating The Compass Killer. As far as I am concerned, you saved me. It was self-defense. I owe you my life, and this is how I am going to pay that debt."

"You are too amazing. I can't believe you would still want to be with me after everything that has happened."

"Of course, I do. I see you. The real you. Both sides of the mask is the man I've fallen for. I love you."

"I love you, too. There's nothing I wouldn't do for you," he says before crashing his lips against mine. His kiss is hungry and desperate. Emotions flow through him that are primal and a bit scary. But I'm not afraid. As I told him, I love both sides of this complicated man.

His kisses become gentle until we eventually pull away completely.

"What do we do now?" he asks.

We both look down at the body and then at the shed. "Burn it," I say. "This place signifies evil, but the final drop of blood was shed, ending The Compass Killer's reign of terror."

Cain nods. "There shouldn't have been anything left here after the last time."

Together, we go into the shed, and this time, Cain uses his flashlight to look around. With the threat dead, the structure isn't as intimidating. The monster has been slain.

Cain grabs a jug of what must be oil and starts to douse the structure. Once he's satisfied, he leads me back, and then he lights it on fire.

As he watches the flames eat up the last remaining part of his father's property, his head hangs down.

I walk up to him, stepping close to take his hand in mine.

"I'm sorry."

He answers, but I can't hear him. A mumble, as if he's talking to himself. Maybe coming to terms with what he did.

"I would do it all over again," he says. "I'd do anything to protect you, Layla. Anything."

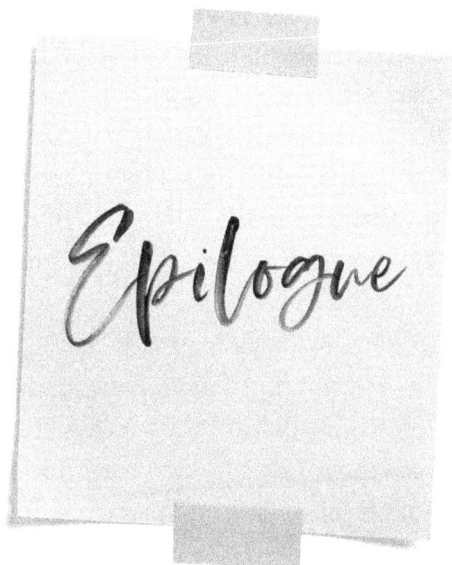

Epilogue

Cain
Sixteen months later.

I watch Layla from where I'm sitting. She's frantically running around the house, cleaning. As if there is anything left to clean in this place. There's not a speck of dust, nor any items out of place. I know what this is. Layla is nervous. Despite her attempts to pretend today isn't a big deal, it is.

Today, her first book releases.

A year ago, after we went to the police, told them the story we came up with, and gave them the body of Stone, Layla decided to write down her experience. After all, she was the final victim of The Compass Killer.

The difference is she's the one who lived.

Layla asked for my blessing, and of course, I gave it to her. How could I say no to something so personal for her, but just what she needed to feel whole with her career?

Since that day, Layla wrote the story of The Compass Killer, offering exclusive details of the murders of the girls that Stone revealed to her during her time in captivity.

The article she wrote was huge, gracing every newsstand across the country. Front-page material. She was offered a book deal and a job working as an investigative journalist.

Today is the release day of said book.

I can tell she doesn't want to make a big deal about it. The nerves of what she omitted in the story, the facts only we know, still sit heavy for both of us, but this was the only way. I live now in plain sight.

As Cain Archer. North burned in the fire so many years ago. All the remnants of him are ash now.

Today, instead of resting, Layla is already back in front of her computer, investigating a series of murders in New Hampshire.

The next murderer she will hunt for and hopefully find.

I walk farther into the room, but she hasn't noticed me. I'm carrying a bottle of champagne and flowers. I place the flowers down on the side table in her office.

We live at The Elysian now. About six months after the ordeal, she left her small rental apartment in NYC and moved to Upstate New York with me.

I'm here for another three years because I talked the investors into buying more land that'll make the entire exclusive community over twenty square miles. They're building various town centers that are all unique. I designed each and every one of the additional areas and will oversee the entire building project.

"What are you doing here?" she says, looking at me. "Don't you have work to do?" Her nose scrunches.

"I'm here to do what you won't."

"And what, pray tell, is that?"

"Celebrate your book being published." I move closer and grab a clean coffee mug that's on the desk. I pour her a taste of champagne.

"My mug? Really?"

"It seemed fitting. You're drinking from it and always working, after all."

She throws her head back and laughs, and that's when I drop to one knee. Her eyes go wide seeing the movement, her mouth now hanging open.

"What are you doing?" she gasps out. The mug starts to rattle as her hands begin to tremble. Reaching out, I take the mug from her fingers and place it on her desk.

"I love you, Layla, and want to spend the rest of my life with you. Will you marry me?" I say as I present the box I had in my pocket. Tears fill her eyes as I slip the large, brilliant-cut diamond on her left ring finger.

"Yes! Of course, I will marry you," she answers before leaning down and kissing me.

I move from my kneeling position and stand, pulling her into my arms. We stay entwined for a moment, our mouths touching, our tongues entangled.

When I pull away, I say, "Enough of this love stuff. You have more work to do, Miss Newly Published Author."

Layla sits back at the desk with a laugh and lifts the mug with champagne to her mouth. Her smile is warm as she looks at me and then back at the ring on her hand. I truly am filled with a feeling of peace at seeing her happy with my jewelry on her hand.

She takes a few sips of champagne before turning back and frowning at whatever she has on the computer monitor.

"What's wrong, Layla?"

"I'm just thinking about this case."

"What about it?" I move to stand closer to her desk, hands on her shoulders, looking down at her.

"It's just—everything is so airtight in this new caseload I'm looking at."

"What do you mean?"

"The killer. The Saturday Butcher . . ." She points at the computer. "It's all so perfect. The MO, it never deviates. It just got me thinking."

"What about?"

"He never deviates. He never alters his pattern."

"Okay . . . I'm not following you."

"Maybe it's release day jitters." She sighs.

"Maybe what's release day jitters?"

She pivots her chair, her body facing me, her head tilted up.

"What if the book doesn't do well? What if someone . . . ?" I know what she's about to say. What if someone finds out I'm North? What if it all comes crumbling down?

But she surprises me by saying nothing along those lines. "It's just that I left things out. There are loose ends. And not just the glaring ones you and I know. But looking at the Saturday Butcher, I see the other details more clearly now. One thing just doesn't make sense."

I don't answer.

"It's peculiar." She lifts her left hand and scrubs at her head as if she's trying to remember. The afternoon sunlight reflects off the diamond that sits newly upon it. "After everything. After all that he said and did, Stone never did tell me why he killed Cynthia. It just—"

"It just what?"

"It doesn't fit. Not like the rest. Her age. The location. The pattern . . ." She stares off across the room. I follow her gaze to where the *New York Times* headline article she wrote is framed on the wall. Beside that is the corkboard she used for research, the articles about the murder staring back at her. She stares a bit longer, her gaze focused on the one about Cynthia, the original article. The title that read, "The Compass Killer or A Copycat?" She lifts her mug and takes another sip before putting it down and facing me. "I guess . . . it was to protect you?" She lifts her eyebrow as she poses that question.

I shrug before speaking Jim's catch phrase. "Some stones are best left unturned."

"I just can't help but wonder why . . ."

"You should let that one go, Layla." I reach my hand out and trace my fingers over the frame that sits on her desk. The dried dandelion on display. The one that symbolizes her wishes. The wishes that I will do *anything* to give her. "You're safe." I drop my hand and grab hers. "The whys of the case no longer matter."

I lift and kiss the knuckle right below her new ring.

"For the rest of our lives, now and until forever, know I will do anything to make sure you stay that way. I will always protect you, protect us. I've made sure we were safe before. No one will ever try to come between us again . . ."

Acknowledgments

I want to thank my entire family. I love you all so much.

Eric, Blake, and Lexi you are my heart.

Thank you to the amazing professionals that helped with Here Lies North:

Emily Lawrence

Suzi Vanderham

Jenny Sims

Marla Esposito

Jaime Ryter

Champagne Formats

Hang Le

Jill Glass

Kelly Allenby

Danielle Sanchez

Lulu Dumonceaux

Julie Linart

Thank you to my fabulous agent Kimberly Whalen.

Thank you to Sebastian York, Ava Erickson, Kim Gilmour and Lyric for bringing Here Lies North to life on audio.

Thank you to my AMAZING ARC TEAM! You guys rock!

Thank you to my beta/test team.

Mia: Thanks for being my blurb fairy.

Parker: Thank you for always talking plots with me and helping me find the sprinkle.

Leigh: Thanks for always alpha reading, and the red ink. 163 times in 11 chapters . . .

Melissa: Thank you for organizing my thoughts and plot with me. I couldn't have done it without you.

Vanessa: Thank you for always taking the time to let me vent. You're the best.

I want to thank ALL my friends for putting up with me while I wrote this book. Thank you!

To the ladies in the Ava Harrison Support Group, I couldn't have done this without your support!

Please consider joining my Facebook reader group Ava Harrison Support Group

Thanks to all the bloggers! Thanks for your excitement and love of books!

Last but certainly not least...

Thank you to the readers!

Thank you so much for taking this journey with me.

CPSIA information can be obtained
at www.ICGtesting.com
Printed in the USA
BVHW042302030822
643781BV00011B/26/J

9 798985 786330